SHORTY IS IN *Love* WITH A REAL *One* 3

A NOVEL BY

SHVONNE LATRICE

$19.99
ISBN 978-1-966375-19-7

CHAPTER ONE

Oden: *Hungry?*

Me: *Always hungry. Want some Raising Canes or Sonics?*

Oden: *Raising sounds good. I will bring it soon okay?*

Me: *Okay. I love yoooooou.*

Oden: *No you don't.*

Me: *Yes I do, so much.*

Oden: *I love you too pretty.*

$\mathscr{I}$ smiled down at my phone before setting it on my desk. I walked over to the sink and started to do my nightly skincare routine, because I knew after I ate I was gonna be tired as fuck. Not to mention the fact that I was gonna be getting dicked down afterwards too, so there would be no time to clean my skin.

After finishing up with my face, I changed into my nightshirt and some fuzzy socks to get comfortable. Tasmine was spending the night with Anton, so Oden and I would be here all alone tonight.

I couldn't wait to just chill with him. I always looked forward to the time we spent together. And even though we'd hit more than a few snags, I felt like our relationship had become stronger. I was closer to him now, and felt like I could tell him anything. I was already comfortable with him before, but these days my comfort level was so much higher.

As I cleared my computer and books off my bed, and set up the backrests for us, someone knocked on my room door. I had no idea who it could be because Bella was still in Arizona, and I knew Tasmine was probably getting sexed by now. *Lord, please don't let it be Perry trying to come over here and eat me out.*

"Huelo?" I opened the door smiling. "What's up?"

"I was wondering if you got the notes from yesterday's class? I wrote that shit down in my phone and it got deleted."

"Oh wow, that was a bad idea. It's always best to have a hard copy. But umm, yeah, I have it. One second."

I walked away, expecting him to wait outside, but he came in, looking around a little bit. He then closed the heavy door, and started to come in further.

"Where is Tasmine?"

"Oh she stepped out for a second," I replied. "Okay, here they… are." When I turned around, he was all up on me, on my side of the room. "Huelo."

"Come on, Khyle. I already know how you get down." He grabbed my face to try and kiss me but I moved away.

"What are you talking about?"

"Don't play that innocent role with me, baby. I know you like to fuck."

"Huelo, move. I don't know what the fuck you're talking about!" I shouted, as he shoved me down onto my bed. "Stop!"

"I like it rough, too," he gritted, as he pinned me to the bed and began to kiss on my neck. "You smell so good, Khyle. Fuck, I've been waiting forever for this."

"Please, Huelo," I begged.

"Don't beg, that's making my dick harder." He ran his hand up my nightshirt, clutching the waistband of my panties before trying to rip them.

"Please, Huelo, stop!!!"

CHAPTER ONE

Oden Bishop

Five minutes earlier...

Grabbing the food from my car, I hopped out and hit the alarm. Luckily, someone was coming out of Khyle's dorm hall, so I was able to slip in without having to call her. As I rode the elevator up, I leaned my head back on the wall to rest my eyes for a second. I'd been busy all fucking day and couldn't wait to end the night with my girl. That was the shit I looked forward to. It made me work harder knowing I would be able to finish my night off with my shorty.

"Hey Oden," some girl waved, and I nodded to say what's up. I felt bad sometimes that people knew me and I had no fucking idea who they were.

As I neared Khyle's door, I could hear faint screaming, like someone was arguing with their roommate. When I made it closer, I realized it was coming from her room.

"Please, Huelo! Stop!!" Khyle screeched.

The fuck? I asked myself, immediately becoming angry.

I saw her door was cracked, because either her or Tasmine's heel had gotten caught in the door, preventing it from closing good. With the quickness, I dropped the food and burst in there to see this big ass nigga pinning my girl down as she squirmed and fought. He was so into what he was doing, that he had no idea I'd shown up. I made my way over to them, trying to contain my anger while on the premises of this school. I had to be calm about this bullshit.

"Get the fuck up," I stated, my voice steady, with my .45 pressed deeply into the back of his head.

Huelo's hands shot up in mock surrender as he lifted his body off of Khyle. She scooted to the corner of her bed, sobbing violently, while fixing her clothes. I wanted to kill this nigga so bad, and the only thing saving him was the location we were in. I didn't want to traumatize Khyle by blowing his head open, and also, I knew I'd be caught in less than a day if I murked him on school grounds. It all seemed worth it though, as visions of him forcing himself on my girl kept replaying in my mind.

"I'm sorry man she— she wanted—"

"Shut the fuck up while you're ahead my nigga," I gritted.

"Ple-Please—" he started to whimper.

"God was looking out for you tonight, boy. Go enjoy your life." I shoved him repeatedly until we reached the door.

"Enjoy my li—"

"Yeah, finish your bucket list." I gave him a grin and then closed the door in his face. I was killing that nigga within the next 24 hours so he'd better live it up.

"Oden!" Khyle rushed to me and I picked her up, hugging her tightly.

"Are you okay?" I sat down on her bed while she still had her legs wrapped around my waist. "Relax, baby, I got you."

"What if you hadn't have been coming over tonight?" She pulled away to look into my eyes.

"But I was, so don't think like that."

I knew what she was saying though, and I was happy as fuck that I came over tonight too. I was already mad that this nigga attempted to rape my baby, but I could only imagine how angry I would have been had he succeeded.

I thumbed her tears away and pecked her lips a few times. She hugged my neck and pressed her body into mine, making it seem like we were damn near one. I hated seeing her this afraid.

"I have to get rid of him, Khyle," I whispered. She just nodded and then kissed the side of my face gently. "Get some stuff, we're gonna move tonight's plans to my spot."

"K," she replied and climbed off of my lap.

I helped her gather some things that she would need, and once she was done, we picked the food up from the hallway so we could trash it. Instead of stopping somewhere, she decided to just cook me something simple at my crib; angel hair pasta with shrimp to be exact.

We sat at the table in silence for a little bit, just eating and thinking.

I knew she was still a little freaked out by that nigga trying to rape her, and that bothered me. I hated that another dude could have her shaken up like that. It pissed me off. Not to mention the fact that I had to let his bitch ass go free instead of pushing his wig back.

"You like it?" she half smiled, referring to the pasta.

"Of course. You know I love your food… and you."

"I love you too, Oden." She ate some more of her pasta and then looked at me. "No more breaking up."

"That's a given, Khyle. We've dealt with the rough shit already, so there won't be anything strong enough to pull us apart."

"Yeah, we've proved that already, huh?" she flashed her beautiful smile.

"We did." I bit down on my lip and pulled her chair closer to me. Wrapping my arm around her shoulders, I said, "You are so beautiful."

"You're so handsome," she chuckled lowly before our lips met.

Our tongues came in contact, making our kiss become heavier and more sensual. I began groping her sexy frame, and once I realized that this couldn't be stopped, I picked her up and carried her to the bedroom.

***

The next night…

I'd just gotten out of the shower, so I was getting dressed in all black. I had some shit to take care of, and I couldn't sleep until the job was done. The one thing I hated above all else was people disrespecting me or the ones I loved, especially my girl.

"Where are you going?" Khyle sat up in my bed, covering her perfectly round breasts with the sheet and comforter.

"To handle something," I replied, opening my burner phone to check my text messages.

Roone: *Ready. Meet you at the spot.*

"For how long?" she questioned.

"Not too long at all. I will be back before you even wake up, pretty."

I made my way over to her and leaned down to kiss her lips, remembering I had some things to talk about with her. School would be over next week, and I wanted to know what she planned to do for the summer. There was no way I could let her go to California for a long period of time.

"What?" she half smiled.

"Gotta talk to you about something, but I will see you in a little bit."

And with that, I left out, locking up and getting into my whip to head over to the warehouse.

When I got there, I saw Lloyd's car parked out back, so I knew he and Roone were here already. I smiled to myself, as I locked my gun into my waist and grabbed my silencer from the glove compartment.

"What's good?" I grinned, walking into the little room Roone told me they would be in. Huelo's glazed eyes widened at the sight of me. "You don't look too happy to see me," I frowned as if I were actually confused by his reaction.

"Please, man," he cried, dropping his head and shaking it. The three of us stayed quiet as he sobbed like a little bitch. "Please."

Grabbing a chair, I placed it in front of him and stared for a few moments. It was crazy to me that he thought he still had a chance to live after I walked in on him trying to rape my girl.

"Are you familiar with me, Huelo?"

He picked his head up to look me in the eyes before asking, "Huh?" He sniffled. "I— yes, I— well, I've heard of you and seen you, but familiar? Like friends? No."

"Why the fuck would I be asking you if we're friends my nigga?" I turned my lip up at his stupidity. "I asked you if you were familiar with me, meaning do you know shit about me? Have you heard anything through the grapevine?"

"Yeah I—"

"Then why would you think that you could get out of dying tonight?" I rose to my feet.

"I'm only 19, man! She gave me the wrong signals! She said I could come in her room, and then she laid down and told me to get on top of her," he sniffled again, face drenched with tears.

"Aww shit," Roone sighed when he saw me cheesing down at Huelo while twisting the silencer onto my gun.

"What is that?" Huelo shrieked.

"So she asked you to come over and fuck, but then started screaming? I'm confused." I stroked my chin hairs, looking down at his ass. Little did he know, he'd just taken his suffering level a little bit higher.

"I think when she saw you come in, she tried to play me. She's trying to play us both! When y'all got back together, she'd just come from a date with me! We had sex that night, O."

PHEW!

"Arrgghhhh!" he groaned in pain after I shot him in the stomach, prompting Roone and Lloyd to move back from him a little. "Ahhhh!" he hollered and cried while clutching his middle area.

Seeing how much pain he was in brought a calmness over me as I watched him with a subtle smile.

"Now, Huelo, can you explain to me again what happened?"

PHEW!

"Ahhh!" he shouted through tears as the bullet ripped through his shoulder.

"Tell me you lied!" I barked, sending another through his other shoulder. "Tell me!" I walked up on him.

"I lied, ahhh sh—it ma—n. I-I'm so—rry!" he wept, while still groaning in pain. Blood was getting everywhere.

"I know you did, nigga. I've seen you play football, bro… you could have actually been something. Too bad you tried to test the wrong pussy. You disrespected me, Huelo, by touching my girl." I began laughing before saying, "I honestly don't know what you were thinking."

"Pl-please c—all an… an ambu—lance," he mumbled as blood continued to seep from his mouth. He was drenched in his own blood, making me smile.

"Nah, I got you."

PHEW!

I sent a bullet through his head, making it fall back.

"Burn him down?" Lloyd asked, and I nodded before leaving.

I needed to prepare myself for the possible consequences of what I'd just done. I knew shit could go bad, but I refused to allow a nigga to do what he'd done to my shorty. I was Khyle's man, and therefore, I needed to make sure she was safe, happy, and comfortable at all times. Whatever comes to me because of this will be well worth it. I would do whatever to protect mine, and since I had no family, Khyle was like a precious gem to me.

CHAPTER ONE

Shayne Luke

Letting the water run down over me, I smiled to myself. I loved staying here with Lloyd in his beautiful townhouse. Not only was his place really nice, with expensive furniture and appliances, but Lloyd was for real *that* nigga. The way he treated me, and the way he fucked me was something I'd been missing from Pierce.

I was hesitant about never going home to Pierce, but I think Lloyd and I needed this time together. I got to experience what it's like being his girlfriend, and now I've realized he was who I wanted… for sure.

"Are you asleep or what?" I heard Lloyd's deep voice coming from behind me.

"No, just thinking." I turned to him and let the water get to my hair.

"About what?" He dropped his head down a little to plant soft kisses on my collarbone, while letting his hands run all over my body.

"Us. I like being here with you, but Pierce has been calling me—"

He kissed me on the lips, and then lifted me up to bring me down onto his dick. Hugging his neck tightly, I ran my fingers through his short curly hair, moaning loudly every time I hit the base of him.

This was the shit I was talking about; the sex was phenomenal and way better than I'd had with any other man, including Oden. Maybe because Lloyd had feelings for me, he treated my body better. I wasn't sure, but what I did know was that he needed an award for his sex game.

"Shit," I whimpered when he pressed me up against the shower wall and began to pummel into me.

He took my nipple into his mouth and started to suck hungrily while winding his hips. I just pressed my head back into the wall to enjoy all of the pleasure he was delivering to my body. Picking his head up from attacking my nipples, he gripped my ass and began pounding my center feverishly as I reached for an imaginary handlebar to grasp.

"Fuck, Shayne," he grumbled before kissing me nastily.

We cried out together once we both released, and sat there tonguing it up and hugging for a little bit before he let me down. After helping one another bathe, we got out and got dressed, since we always brushed our teeth before showering.

"What are you doing after work?" Lloyd asked as he dropped his chain over his head.

"Nothing. I thought maybe I could cook some food for you tonight. What do you have a taste for?" I sauntered over to him, and wrapped my arms around his torso. He looked and smelled so good like always, even though he was dressed fairly simple.

"I won't be home until late, like 11pm. Oden called a late meeting, and then he has some other shit he wants us to do.”

“So you’re not gonna have dinner with me because of Oden? Does Oden suck your dick for you? Does he have you crying out like a little bitch because of how good his pussy is?”

“Not even, shawty,” Lloyd chuckled, tucking his full lips in while eyeing my frame. “Aight. I will come straight here after the meeting so we can eat.”

“Thank you, baby.” I giggled like I always did when I got my way.

Lloyd leaned down to kiss my lips gently but deeply, and then grabbed his phone before leaving out of the townhouse.

I rushed to the window to watch him pull out in his fly ass Mercedes, and then I darted to the bedroom to get my purse. Once I had everything I needed for rehearsal, I left out to get into the rental Lloyd had gotten me until my new Range Rover he purchased me came in; we had to have it shipped since it was heavily customized. I cheesed widely as I thought about the life I was currently living.

Pulling from my parking space, I sped out of the lot and headed straight to my old spot that I used to share with Pierce. I’d only been away for about four days, but that was a lot of time to go without communication with your significant other. However, I was only coming over right now because I knew Pierce was at work. I wasn’t ready to face him just yet.

When I walked into my old apartment, my heart dropped at the sight of Pierce sitting on the couch. I didn’t even see his car outside, so I was a bit caught off guard at the fact that he was here. I was not prepared for this, and was hoping I could convince him that I’d been gone somewhere working or doing anything but playing house with another man.

"Baby, what the fuck?" he shot up off of the couch.

He was shirtless, showing off his beautiful chocolate skin and hard abs. I loved chocolate, but Lloyd was my new chocolate love. I smiled subtly just thinking about him.

"I'm sorry, baby—"

He hugged me so tightly it almost knocked the damn wind out of me.

"Are you okay? What happened? Where is your ring? I've been calling yo' ass for days, Shayne!" He stared deeply down into my eyes, wearing a sexy scowl.

"I was working…"

I stopped talking and just decided to tell him the truth. There was no way Lloyd would let me stay here with Pierce tonight, and there was no way Pierce was gonna allow me to be gone for a couple more days, nor would he let me pack clothes in front of him.

"Working? What the fuck are you—"

"Pierce, sit down and let me talk to you."

We both sat on the couch, and I took his big hand into mine, then started to caress it. I kept my eyes on his hand, because I needed to gather my thoughts so that this wouldn't come out so harshly. Pierce loved me a lot, and it showed in his actions; however, I didn't feel the same. Yes, I cared for him and loved him as a person, but did I want to be with him? No.

"What's up, Shayne?"

Gaining eye contact with him again, I said, "Pierce, for a long time now, I haven't been happy. Just let me finish speaking. I haven't been happy with you and our relationship. I tried to stick it out, but that's just not working for me anymore, honey." I rubbed the side of his face as he looked at me sadly. This was so hard. "I've met someone else, Pierce, and I want to try and see how things with him and I go."

Pierce began laughing, and then stood up to pace the area in front of me. I watched him as he scratched his head while nibbling on his lip. My stomach began to knot up, and suddenly I wanted to take back everything I'd said. Not because I didn't mean it, because I did, but because I saw the hurt in his face even though he was frowning.

"So you haven't been happy, and now you're moving on? To who? Oden?"

"Oden? What? Where did you get that from? You know he's practically married to my little sister, Pierce."

"So you've never fucked him? I saw the way he looked at your body at that pool party that night, Shayne. That smug expression on his face was of a nigga who had seen what was under your clothes before."

"Oden is just like that, Pierce. That nigga has never even seen my pussy, let alone gotten some of it. Stop being paranoid."

"Who is the nigga? It doesn't matter." He dropped down to his knees in front of me. "Shayne, just tell me what I've done wrong to make you unhappy and I will fix it."

"No, Pierce, it's too late. I told you I've met somebody already."

"And you love him? So soon?"

I hadn't realized that I'd fallen in love with Lloyd until now. I'd never felt this way about any man, so it was very obvious. Lloyd made me happy just from me being in his presence. The way he talked, how he was about his money and making sure he got it by any means necessary, and how safe I felt when we went out places. Lloyd was a man you married and had children with, while Pierce was just boyfriend material. My father used to tell me that not every man was husband material, and now I understood him.

"Yes. He and I have been involved for some time now, Pierce. So yes, I love him. I'm in love with him and he's in love with me."

"Did he tell you that?"

"Not yet, but I know—"

"You don't know shit! You don't even know when you have a good nigga sitting in fucking front of you! I have busted my ass to keep you happy but that shit doesn't matter, huh? You don' met some other nigga and now it's fuck Pierce I see."

"Yes, you are a great guy, but just not for me! I need a man who is going to do what he has to do to make sure his money isn't funny, and if it is, I shouldn't be stressing about it. Lloyd is just different from you! He's a man's man, and you're a… you're a little boy, Pierce."

"A little boy? Wow. Well get your shit and get the fuck out of my crib then since I'm a little ass boy, bitch."

"Only reason I'm gonna let that slide is because I know how hurt and angry you are, and I can't blame you."

I stood up and walked back to our old bedroom and he followed me. He sat there on the bed, silent, as I packed as much clothes and shit that I could, leaving the engagement ring on the dresser. Lloyd said he would have a moving truck come if I needed it, so I was gonna leave the big stuff for them.

As I was zipping my huge ass Louis Vuitton suitcase up, I heard light sniffles. See what I meant? He was a straight up bitch.

"Pierce, really?" I looked over my shoulder to see his head dropped into his hands.

"Fuck you, Shayne," he mumbled, not picking his head up.

"Pierce."

I sat next to him on the bed and hugged him. After a few moments, he wrapped his arms around me and kissed my neck. He then trailed the kisses onto my cheek, and when I tried to move away, he pinned me to the bed.

"I love you, Shayne," he whispered as he tried to pull down my tights.

"No, Pierce." He didn't listen, he just kept kissing my stomach and trying to get my pants off. "Pierce, I said to stop!" I shouted when he pressed my hands to the bed and got in between my legs.

"Relax, Shayne." He put his hand down into my tights to touch between my legs, while his other hand held my wrists.

"Really, Pierce? You're gonna rape me?" I asked him, not even turned on a little bit by him playing with my clit.

He kissed my lips again and then fell to the side of me, sighing as he covered his face.

"Just get the fuck out."

I promptly sat up, before standing to get my things. Without even saying goodbye, I left the apartment and headed off to work. I knew this was the right decision, but I still felt like shit. Lloyd would fix that tonight though.

CHAPTER ONE

$\mathcal{I}$'d been thinking about what Huelo tried to do to me ever since the night of the incident. I wasn't sure where he and I went wrong, but he was a completely different person that night. The Huelo I knew was sweet, and a little bit shy, but that night he was a monster.

I'd never been so scared in my life, and just the thought of Oden not coming in bothered me. I wasn't sure why the thought of that scared me when I was in fact saved, but it did. Huelo would have straight up raped me had my boyfriend not been bringing me food. I shuddered as I sat down in my seat, ready to hand in my Women's Studies final paper. When I did sit, I looked at the seat next to me for a few moments, since that was where he always sat.

"Okay class, I know I usually never take roll, but since this is the last day, I decided to. When I call your name, please come bring your paper and then you may leave," my professor spoke loudly over the class.

The class responded and nodded simultaneously in response. She began reading the names, and once she got to Huelo, I cringed a little bit. I knew Oden had done something to him, even though he hadn't come out and said it. That night he left out wearing all black was probably when it happened.

"Has anybody seen, Huelo?" the professor frowned, scanning the class. The class shook their heads 'no' in response. "Hmm, okay."

She moved on and finally when she made it to me, I handed off my paper. I turned to leave out but she stopped me.

"Yes?" I adjusted my purse strap.

"Have you seen Huelo today?" she quizzed.

"Why are you asking me? Why would I know where he is?"

"Well, because I know you guys are good friends, well at least in class. I see you guys talk all the time, and sometimes leave class together."

"Oh, well our conversations stop once we leave the building. And I haven't seen him today, this is my first class."

"Okay, thanks, Ms. Luke. Have a great summer," she smiled.

I quickly left her classroom, and headed towards my dorm. I had a little time before my history class started since Women's Studies only lasted a few minutes. As I got near my dorm, someone grabbed me from behind, prompting me to scream loudly as fuck.

"Baby, calm down, it's just me," Oden turned me to face him. I watched as people walked by us, looking at me like I was crazy.

"Why would you do that!" I shoved him twice, and he just pulled me into a hug and kissed my forehead gently.

"I'm sorry, I wasn't trying to scare you. I wanted to surprise you."

He leaned my head back to kiss me deeply, before our lips parted and our tongues began to dance.

I pulled away and wiped my lip-gloss off of him while smiling.

"Sorry I shoved you."

"It's okay. I got you something." He flashed his sexy grin, while biting on his bottom lip as he reached down into his pocket.

"Oh Lord, what is it?"

"Here." He pressed a resident parking pass into my hand, prompting me to stare up at him in confusion.

"Oden, thanks, baby, but I don't have a car."

"You don't?" he frowned, cocking his head while wearing a smile.

"No, I don't."

"Then what's that?" he pointed behind the dorm building, chuckling.

I looked at him and then darted around back with him right on my heels. I froze when I spotted a navy blue BMW 6 Series Sedan with a big red bow on the front. I glanced back at his fine ass, before feasting my eyes on the beautiful car once again.

"Baby, you listened to me when I said I wanted this car," I began crying as I ran to it. He followed me and handed the sexy keys to me. Yes I said these damn keys were sexy; no other way to describe it.

"I listen to everything you tell me, Khyle. Wait, let me get a kiss before you get inside." He grabbed my waist and pulled me towards him, kissing me so hard my head leaned back.

When he let me go, I unlocked the vehicle and slid into it. He got in on the passenger side, and just laughed here and there as I cooed and shrieked over the details. The leather was red, and it had wood grain all throughout the dash, just like I wanted.

"Is this really mine?" I asked, hands on the wheel.

"Yeah, it's yours, baby. Even if we break up, it's yours."

"We won't break up, Oden."

"Trust me, I know. I just want you to understand that this is your car no matter what happens. Even the days when I'm mad at you."

"So that means I can have my other nigga in it?" I grinned.

"You got another nigga?" he asked in that low sexy tone he used sometimes. I just nodded, biting my lip at the feeling of him caressing my inner thigh. "Damn, that sucks." He grumbled against my neck before kissing it, as his hand traveled up my skirt and pushed my panties to the side. I gasped once I felt him push two fingers inside of me. "Fuck, Khyle."

"Not on my new leather," I whined, pushing his hand from between my legs.

"Then take me to the club."

"The club? We can just go to your house."

"Nah, Palace is closer, baby. I'm about to damn near nut in my fucking jeans, so please let's go to the club."

"I guess that could be fun," I laughed, cranking my car up and pulling out.

We made it to Palace in less than 10 minutes, and Oden carried me through the back and up to his office. I'd never been in his office before, and I hadn't realized it until now. Before I could get a good look at the room, he was kissing my neck and pulling my dress up. As soon as he threw it off to the side, our lips met. Using one hand, he unsnapped my bra, and then pushed my panties down before sitting me on the couch.

"Your body is like art, Khyle."

I just smiled a little as he kissed from my lips down to my stomach. Caressing his hair, I let my head fall back when I felt the warmth of his breath near my center. He hadn't even put his mouth on it yet and I was already going crazy.

Putting one of my legs onto his shoulder, he pecked my lower lips repeatedly, before swiping his tongue between the folds. My chest heaved up and down rapidly, and all he was doing was kissing my pussy lightly, and letting his tongue travel in between every now and again.

"Oden, you're killing me," I whimpered.

Chuckling, he lifted my other leg onto his shoulder and began sucking my clit. My body seemed to relax now that he was actually doing what it had anticipated. Closing my eyes, I bit down on my lip as he feasted on me. Looking down at him, it turned me on to see how into it he was. I could tell this was his favorite thing, and that shit was a big turn on as well. That's why he was so fucking good at it.

"I'm about to cum, Oden, fuck," I cried, voice shaking as if I were cold.

He ignored me, speeding up his tongue flicks and going harder with the sucking of my button. I was crawling up the couch, but he gripped my ass to pull my pussy back into his mouth. Scraping my nails across the leather of the love seat, my moans became high pitched as he took me over the edge, allowing the orgasm to tear through my body. I panted heavily, and just sat there as he licked me clean and pecked down below.

"I ain't never heard you scream like that," he rose to his feet with a smirk.

"Fuck you," I laughed as I began to unbuckle his jeans. He removed his shirt to expose his chiseled abs and chest while he watched me.

When he was finally naked, I saw his dick was already hard. We always got turned on just from giving head to one another. Wrapping my lips around his tip, I began to suck on it gently just the way he liked. When I felt his hand on the back of my head, I knew that was my cue to move down on him. Easing my wet mouth further onto his dick, I began moving up and down, letting his head sit in the back of my throat for a few seconds whenever they came in contact.

"Khyle, you get better every time, babe."

He humped my face slowly, and unlike the last few times, it was easy to take the thrusts. I just kept sucking him up, matching his pumps, which caused him to moan a little louder than usual. After giving him all I had, allowing my saliva to completely cover my chin, he came. I'd learned a trick from giving him head, so when he released, I made sure it went straight down, missing my tongue. The taste wasn't bad, just the texture was strange and I didn't like it.

"Come here."

I loved when he said that.

Pulling me to my feet, he kissed me hungrily and deeply. The kiss was so hard that our faces were about to damn near become one.

Placing me on all fours, he got behind me and wiggled his way inside of me. I pressed the side of my face into the couch pillow as he pumped me at a medium pace. I could feel my second orgasm arising already, so I bit down on my lip and spread my legs a little.

"Perfect… I get to see the pussy as I'm beating it up," Oden commented in between subtle moans.

"Ahhh, ahh, ahh!" I began to cry out when his thrusts became harder.

He was slamming into my spot while rubbing his big hands up and down my back. Holding onto the pillow that I was lying on, I sniveled lightly as I exploded on his rod. He kept going, beating it up with precision, which prompted my body to spill its juices in record time.

"Fuck!" he hollered out, still pummeling me from the back while gripping my waist. "This lil' pussy is lethal," he grumbled.

"Odeennn," I whimpered feeling him deep inside of me and yanking another orgasm out.

"I'm about to cum, can I cum inside you?"

"Ye-yes!"

A few more hard pumps and loud moans from us took placc, before we both released. We stayed in position, panting for a little bit, before he finally pulled out of me. He made me sit upright on the couch, and then dropped down, spreading my legs to eat my pussy again.

"Oden, I have my history final," I moaned, as he began to suck on my button gently. Shit it felt good.

He pressed one of my legs into my stomach and went ham, so I just let my head fall back to enjoy the pleasure.

CHAPTER TWO

Tasmine Randall

"So Huelo is like for real… gone?" I questioned Khyle, as she, Bella, and I looked around Victoria's Secret. We wanted to spend some time together since we would all be going to our hometowns in a couple of days for summer break. Perry didn't want to come out today, and truthfully, I didn't really mind. It was the same whether she came or not because she never talked.

"Yeah, I mean, I didn't ask Oden out right, but the night it all went down, he told me he had to get rid of him."

"Damn, bitch, but I don't blame him. Huelo should have known who he was fucking with. Oden is not some playground thug," Bella shook her head as I nodded in agreement.

I admit I was feeling a bit weird being so close to a murder and the murderer. I knew Oden, Anton, and Truman were the real deal, but because I hadn't actually witnessed anything, it was easy to push it to the back of my mind. But knowing both the victim in a sense, and its killer, had me feeling strange. But I guess I needed to get used to this shit since I had no plans on breaking up with Anton.

Honestly, it was still crazy to me that I'd actually gotten the guy that I used to fantasize about. I came to Vegas with the intention of meeting him, but I had no idea that I would actually get as far with him as I had. Even better was that he was a great guy and I was just as happy with him as I'd assumed I'd be.

"Well, he deserved it for coming at you like that. I just thank God that Oden was coming to see you. I would have wanted to get at him myself had he succeeded," I said, sighing. Huelo had gone from being a nice cool guy, to a fucking thirsty ass psychopath in a matter of hours.

The three of us got in line to check out with the little sexy underwear we'd gotten, and a couple of bras. They were usually pretty expensive, but today they were having a nice sale. That's the only damn reason we came. Yes, Anton gave me money, but I didn't feel right spending it. The money he gave me literally just sat in my account; well, my savings since I moved it. I did like the idea of having such a hefty backup though, just in case something happened.

"Excuse me," some girl cut through the line to get past me and look at the perfume rollers.

When I looked over, I realized it was Selinda's ass. I chuckled because I couldn't help it. She was so fucking stupid, and knowing that she'd done all that extra shit when Anton wasn't even her child's father made her look even dumber.

"Is there something funny?" she turned to me, eyebrow raised. I admit she was dressed nicely, and her hair and makeup looked flawless. She still didn't have my nigga though.

"Yeah, you," I half smiled, prompting Khyle and Bella to look back and forth between Selinda and I. They'd never seen her ass before, but they'd heard about her.

"Is there a problem?" Khyle questioned.

"No, this is just one of Anton's fake ass baby mamas right here, Selinda."

Khyle and Bella both looked to Selinda for a few moments before bursting into laughter. I'd told them everything I knew, which was everything Anton told me, so they had plenty to laugh at. Just thinking about it, in combination with seeing them chuckle, caused me to join in with them.

"And you think I'm the only one who's claiming Anton as their baby daddy?" Selinda turned to face me, and moved up with me in the line.

"No, but it shouldn't matter because your baby ain't his, chica," Bella answered for me.

"It's cool, Bella." I glanced at her before turning my attention back to Selinda. "No, I know about the others and just like you, they lied. Tell me how you can you get pregnant with a condom in place?" I cocked my head.

"Look, I don't know who Anton paid to have the results fucked with, but Antonio is his son and I will prove it! And I'll be getting money from the both of your asses."

"Good luck with that, Selinda. But you should focus on finding the real father and making him pay, instead of wasting time trying to pin a baby on another man just because you want more than a wet ass from him."

By the time I said that, I had reached the counter of Victoria's Secret, so I placed my things on it to be rung up. I could feel the heat radiating off of Selinda as she stared a hole through the side of my face. I acted just like she wasn't there, and eventually she sauntered off mumbling some shit I didn't care to hear.

After the three of us checked out, we stopped to get something to eat at Sonic's. It was dope riding around in Khyle's brand new car. It was so beautiful and even the inside smelled expensive. She was so lucky to have this shit, and by the smile she wore, I knew she felt the same.

"Are you scared to leave Anton here while you go to Louisville for two and a half months?" Bella asked as we sat in the car, waiting for the Sonic's employee to bring our food out.

"No. He's gonna visit me, and I'm gonna come back at the end of July to stay with him until school starts back up."

"Damn, your parents are okay with that?" Khyle quizzed. She knew my parents were on the stricter side, and always had stipulations that needed to be met before I did anything.

"Yes, but only if they like him after they meet him. So in two weeks, he's coming to Kentucky to stay for three weeks straight to get to know them." I nodded and smiled at the thought.

"Damn, he's putting in work, chica. Luckily for me, Santino and I live in the same state. He does have to come back a month early in July to start football training, but I trust him." Bella pushed her hair behind her ears.

"You should, he loves you," Khyle nodded.

"What about you?" I inquired, sitting up between the two front seats where she and Bella sat.

"Oden is gonna come visit me in a couple weeks, but he's staying until the middle of July, and only going to Vegas a few times here and there for business. He said Truman is gonna run shit for the time he's gone. Then August 1, I'm gonna come to Vegas and stay until school starts, like you, Tasmine."

"Damn, I guess it all worked out for us, huh?" Bella grinned, and we just laughed as we nodded in agreement.

Once we got our food, we decided to sit outside of Sonic's and just eat it there. After that, Khyle dropped Bella off at her dorm to be with Santino, and then she took me to Anton's before going to see Oden.

"Damn, I thought you were never coming back." Anton walked into his living room, wearing only a towel wrapped around his waist. He made it over to me, and leaned down to kiss my lips.

"I would never leave you hanging," I smirked, as he turned around to head to the back.

"Yeah, aight," he called over his shoulder.

I was flipping through TV channels when he returned, wearing sweats, socks, and a t-shirt. When he plopped down next to me, I got a good whiff of his cologne. He wrapped his arm around my shoulders, and then craned his neck to peck my lips a few times.

"Guess who I saw today?" I smiled just before he kissed me again.

"Who?"

"Selinda."

"Oh Lord."

"Yeah, she seemed to be pretty upset still. She still thinks you're the father of her child."

"I'm not surprised. She harassed me for the longest. I'm sure she thinks I paid the DNA lab off or something."

Laughing, I said, "She does! She tried to make me believe you had more women claiming you as their child's father outside of her, Kai, and Violet."

"She's crazy."

"You never told me how Violet felt about you not being her baby's father." I rubbed my hand up under his shirt to caress his abs.

"She was cool about it I guess… she umm, she didn't trip."

"Really?" I sat up.

"Yeah. I don't really want to talk about them when they don't matter to me, baby. You're leaving in a couple days, so I really want to focus on you."

"Okay," I cheesed, feeling all warm inside.

He hooked my chin with his pointing finger, and slipped his tongue into my mouth. He was right. I wanted to enjoy the next couple of days with him, and that didn't include discussing lying ass Selinda, Kai, and Violet.

CHAPTER TWO

Bella Bacigalupi

Back in Arizona... Two weeks later...

$\mathcal{I}$ walked out of the large parking structure, and hit the corner to enter the restaurant Olive and Ivy. I wanted to make this visit quick because I had to be somewhere later, and I didn't want any suspicions to arise, due to me being late. I had one hour to spare, and I didn't even want to use all of it. Hopefully I wouldn't have to, or there may be another brawl upon me.

"Hey," I walked up to the table and pulled the dark brown chair out before sitting down. "I don't have much time."

"That's why I wanted to see you when you had a free day, Bella," Dean pleaded, eyes looking sadder than those puppies on the ASPCA commercials.

"I don't have much time between my family and Santino."

"Santino," he shook his head and looked off for some seconds. "Bella, I know I wasn't that great to you, but it was because I was dealing with some shit."

"Like what?"

"Would you like something to drink?" a waitress approached the table.

"No, no thank you." I looked up at her and she nodded before asking if we wanted food. Dean ordered some and I declined. "Now what were you dealing with?"

I knew I shouldn't have been here, but I felt bad for the guy. Santino really did a number on him, and seeing him have to walk home dazed and confused with a bloody face, tugged at my heartstrings. I knew Dean was no saint, but that didn't stop me from feeling sympathy for him.

"Football. You know I planned to make it to the NFL, but I don't think that's gonna happen. I'm playing less in the games, and the scouts aren't really looking."

"Hey, maybe this semester will be better, Dean," I touched his hand.

"This is junior year for me, Bella. Niggas that are gonna make it do not go past sophomore, year and you know that."

"You may be different."

"I don't want to be different. All this proves is that I'm not as good as some other people. Anyway, that shit has had me on edge for the longest. I took it out on you when I shouldn't have."

"Why are you telling me this?" I took my hand from his.

"Because I miss you, and I'm still in love with you. I know if you take me back, things will be different this time. I'm thinking of quitting football, and just getting a degree in business or something. We can get married once you graduate."

"Dean, I thought you understood me," I squinted my eyes, while searching his.

"Huh?"

"I explained to you that I was in love with Santino, and that I wanted to be with him, and marry him."

"Yeah, but that was because of the way I had acted during our relationship, Bella. That wasn't the real me. The real me is the guy that helped you come from under that dark cloud, after the man you so called love ditched you."

"He ditched me because he had to, and he was only 15 years old, Dean. Stop bringing that up. He made a mistake, but he was a kid. He's made up for it!" I yelled loudly, but quickly lowered my tone out of embarrassment.

"And when I came to your rescue, Bella, I was only 16 and a half. I was young too, but I still stepped up and was there for you, just like he could have been."

"No he couldn't! His parents wouldn't let him!"

"So! People's parents forbid shit all the fucking time, and what do kids do? They agree to it but renege once they get to school. By saying that, he could have still kept up you guys' relationship while at school, then went home and acted like he hadn't been with you."

I sat there speechless because I for really had nothing to say. He was right but I didn't want him to be. Santino could have very well been with me during school hours, but he chose to cut me off completely. My stomach started to knot up, because I was feeling stupid and very upset. I wanted to cry, but I couldn't in front of Dean.

"No, Dean. He couldn't," I finally said.

"Bella, I am the one who really loves you. I was tripping and shit before but I'm good now. I've accepted that I won't make it to play professional football, and that's calmed me down a lot."

"I don't want you, Dean, I want him."

"So you'd rather be with a man that would leave you when you're going through something, versus one who would stick by you and help you through it."

"He wouldn't leave me again," my eyes watered and my voice trembled.

"Yeah? How can you be so sure, Bella?" He sat back in his chair so the waitress could set his plate down in front of him.

"I have to go." I got up abruptly, and rushed out of the restaurant.

I made it to my car inside of the parking structure, and then sped out, headed straight to Santino's. His parents were out of town again, in the UK, so he had the house to himself for a month and a half. My parents were warming up to our relationship, so they did allow me to stay with him overnight a few times, if my dad was in a good mood.

"Hey, beautiful. The food is almost ready, so follow me to the kitchen," Santino answered the door and helped me out of my jacket. He'd always been a good cook, ever since I'd known him.

I said nothing as he grabbed my face in his hands to kiss me deeply. My knees got weak, and hawks, not butterflies, consumed my stomach as we sucked one another's lips and let our tongues entangle. Finally, he pulled away, smiled, and then led me to the kitchen where a wonderful smell filled my nose.

I stayed quiet as we washed our hands and sat down at the bar with our plates of lasagna. Because we were both partially Italian, we bonded over our love for Italian cuisine.

"Like it?" he asked, kissing my cheek.

"Of course, it's great."

"Aye, what's wrong with you? You're usually always so upbeat, mami."

"Why didn't you just be my boyfriend while we were in school, and then pretend like you were following your parents' rules?" I asked lowly, and the sound of his fork dropping came soon after.

"What are you talking about, Bella?"

"When you got me pregnant, you said your parents forbade you from being with me. But you could have still been with me while we were at school, and then acted like you weren't with me when you went home for the day."

"Where is this coming from? I thought we talked about getting over that shit and moving on, Bella?"

"Why does it matter where it's coming from? Just answer the question."

"It matters because after a while, I'm gonna get tired of rehashing this same shit. I understand I hurt you, baby, and I am sorry! I don't know what or how I can prove to you that I was a kid, and I panicked. My parents were throwing threats out at me like it was nothing, and then I had you pregnant when I was in no place to take care of you and a kid!"

"So you just leave me, even though you could have talked to me while at school?"

"Why, so the people who worked at the school could tell on my ass?" he barked.

"Why would they tell on you, Santino? They don't give a fuck about what one kid is doing, out of all the kids that were at that school." I sucked my teeth at his fake ass.

"Oh, they do when your parents threaten to stop helping them fund certain festivities, or threaten to pull the funding from the library they were having built. Mami, my parents were heavily involved in our school, funding a lot of shit there. And in return, certain staff were told to keep an eye on me. Believe me, I'd thought about being with you only at school until I graduated, but when the principal made it clear that he was watching me, I knew I couldn't."

"You never told me that," I softened my tone, feeling like a fool for allowing Dean to get into my head.

"I didn't tell you because I thought I'd explained myself enough, and that you had forgiven me. Bella, I love you, but if you can't push forward with me, then I don't know if I can do this."

"No, no, I can get over it. I *am* over it. I just had a little slip up, Sanz. But I promise I won't bring it up anymore, okay?" I cupped his face and stared into his beautiful hazel eyes.

"I hope so, because I wanna make you my wife, Bella."

I smiled hearing him say that, before pulling his face towards mine for a kiss. We sat there kissing for a little while longer before returning to eat our food.

That was the last time I let that situation from high school fuck with me, and the last time I gave Dean's ass any of my time.

CHAPTER TWO

Truman Morrison

"Ahh, Truuu," Chiina whimpered as I sucked on her clit like a piece of candy.

Her juices were running down, and I was lapping up as much as I could. Sadly, I loved eating her pussy way more than Pilar's. I didn't know what it was exactly, but I craved eating Chiina's pussy.

"Mmm," I moaned as if I were enjoying my favorite meal.

"Uhhh, baby," she sniveled in her sweet voice as she exploded.

After licking her clean and savoring the taste, I trailed my lips up her flat stomach, until I made it to her mouth. Kissing her for a little bit, I dropped my head down to suck on her neck.

I stayed leaving small hickeys on her because I wanted niggas to know she wasn't available. It was shady, considering that I was chasing Pilar while fucking with her, but I had feelings for Chiina. I couldn't quite let her go like I was supposed to.

"Truman, I have to talk to you," she whined as I made my way to her nipples.

"About what, baby?"

"Do you love me?" she inquired, prompting me to stop teasing her body with my tongue.

I came back up and stared down into her soft pretty face while in the push-up position. Her smooth caramel complexion seemed to be glowing, and the fullness of her lips along with her pretty slanted eyes made her so fucking alluring. After taking in her beauty and thinking about the time we'd spent together, I realized I had an answer to her question.

"Yeah, baby, I love you," I nodded, and smiled once I saw her do so. "Why did you ask me that?" I grabbed her hand and kissed the palm of it, still hovering over her.

"Because something happened." Her eyes darted from mine, and off to the side, signaling that she was nervous.

"What happened?" I turned her head so that she was looking up into my eyes again. "You know you can tell me anything."

"I'm pregnant."

"What?" I jumped from in between her legs and off of the bed, dick swinging and everything. She'd just blown my mind right now.

Sitting up with a confused expression, she repeated herself.

"I'm pregnant."

"How? I use protection and every fucking thing!"

"You haven't been strapping up for the past two months, Truman! I told you I wasn't on birth control and you said you would just pull out," she reminded me as I paced my spacious bedroom.

"Yo, I have to go. I will talk to you later or something." I walked briskly out of the bedroom, headed to the bathroom so I could shower and leave.

"It's 8 o'clock at night, Tru!"

"So!"

"Truman!" I heard Chiina call my name just before I slammed the bathroom door and locked it.

"Fuck!" I shouted once I cut the shower water on.

How could I have done some dumb shit like get her pregnant? Yeah, I did love her, but I also loved Pilar. I wasn't trying to be stuck with either one of them permanently until I knew for sure who I wanted to be with. But Chiina having my baby would fuck up everything. I would have to deal with her for forever basically, and Pilar wouldn't stick around for that shit.

Why couldn't this have waited until after I chose? It wasn't as easy as it sounded. Pilar and I had history, but she had her moments where she was boring as fuck. On the flip side, I loved talking to her, and the fact that she had her own shit and didn't need me. Not to mention she was beautiful. It was just some days I wished she were more exciting and not so blah.

Chiina on the other hand, was fun and sexy, and always down to try some new shit, whether it was in the bedroom or a simple food item. The only thing I didn't like about her was her age. She was young, and sometimes she didn't understand shit that I was going through. However, I loved the way she lifted me up and made me seem like the greatest nigga in the world. I just didn't know who I wanted more.

I heard Chiina knocking on the bathroom door as I entered the shower. I just ignored her and proceeded with my routine. Once I was clean, I got out to brush, floss, and rinse my mouth with mouthwash, before coming out of the bathroom. As I neared my bedroom, I could hear Chiina crying faintly. I entered the room and saw her small frame jerking subtly under the covers as she sniffled. I wasn't in the mood to deal with this shit at all.

"You're really leaving?" she asked once she heard me moving around the room to get dressed.

"Yes, I'm leaving."

"I'm sorry, Truman, it just happened," she cried.

I declined to respond and just continued to get dressed. After checking myself out in the mirror, I grabbed my baseball cap and pulled it down. I was looking good, smelling good, and I was hoping a new shorty could make me feel that way too.

"Don't wait up," I told Chiina as I hit the lights in the bedroom. I felt bad for the way I was treating her but I wasn't ready to face that baby shit.

I made it to the Cosmopolitan hotel, and parked my car with valet. It was around 10:05pm, and I planned to have a good ass time at Marquee. Marquee nightclub stayed crowded, and it was hard to get into for muthafuckas that weren't me.

"What's up, Tru?" my homeboy Foster dapped me up.

He worked the entrance of the club, so he already knew to hook me up. My boys and I were cool with the manager, so he always moved shit around for us if needed.

"What's up, you have a table for me?"

"Of course, but it's just you tonight?"

I glanced to the right side of me to see three pretty ass black girls, smiling and shit. I checked out their bodies, and squinted my eyes to see what their body language was telling me. They were definitely ready and willing to get some shit started, so they were cool with me.

"Nah, them too." I pointed to the three girls, who giddily ran to my side.

"Cool, follow me." Foster waved the four of us in and we followed.

As soon as we made it to the table, a hostess was bringing in a bucket of ice with champagne sitting in it. I made sure to let her know to bring another bottle, along with some bourbon and Patrón since the ladies wanted tequila and I wanted something dark. And once the hostess brought the drinks back, the four of us started to turn up.

"So what's your name?" I looked at the prettiest one. She was light skinned, had hair down to her butt, which was nice and round might I add, and a body comparable to a Coke bottle. I couldn't wait to be fucking her tonight.

"It's Courtney, and this is Hannah and Geraldine."

"Geraldine? Damn," I chuckled. "You look good though," I said, softening the blow after coming for her name. She was destined to be somebody's mama and grandma, but she looked like my favorite porn star. "I'm Truman."

"Truman," they all sang in unison.

"Yeah… so what you doing up in here all alone?" Courtney asked, licking her lips.

"So I can be with y'all," I grinned and so did she. "Come here and let me talk to you alone for a second, Courtney." I scooted to the far end of the couch and she followed. "Why don't you help me relieve some tension," I whispered in her ear before kissing it.

"How?"

"Talk into the mic."

"Talk into the mic?" she frowned, but when I gestured towards my crotch she understood immediately. "Ohhh." She looked over her shoulder at her friends, before getting down on her knees.

I unzipped my jeans and pulled my dick out, allowing her lips to wrap around it. Some song by Ty Dolla $ign blasted over the club as I watched Courtney's sexy ass suck me up like she was a professional.

"Damn, girl," I furrowed my brows. This was definitely one of the top five blowjobs I'd ever gotten. "Shit."

I gripped her hair tightly in my hands just as I let loose into her mouth. Biting down on my lip, I allowed her to clean me up before I put my dick away. Just as I was about to ask her to come home with me, my phone buzzed. I looked down at it to see I had messages from Pilar.

Pilar: Heyyy, I know it's late but I just got off work. Wanna come over?

Pilar: Please, I miss you.

Me: Of course, baby. Anything for you.

"Ready to go?" Courtney pulled me back to the situation at hand.

"Umm, nah, something came up. But put your number in, baby,

and I will hit you tomorrow."

"Okay."

After I got her number, as well as her friends', I dipped out of the club, letting the ladies continue to enjoy my VIP. I made it to Pilar's in no time it seemed, and after texting her that I was outside, she came to the door fairly quickly.

"You look nice. Where are you coming from?" she hugged me around my torso as I walked in.

"Handling business with O and Tony," I replied before kissing her lips a couple of times.

"So I was thinking about what you said the other day."

We sat down on the couch, and I turned to face her. She was grinning widely, which in turn made me smile. Pilar was so beautiful and I loved the fuck out of her. But Chiina… never mind.

"Oh yeah?" I cleared my throat.

"Yes, and I know you've been working hard to get me back. I want you to know I appreciate it all, and I think I'm ready to be back in a relationship with you."

"You are?" I bucked my eyes. I'd only been working her over for a couple of weeks, but true enough, I'd been doing the most.

"Yes. I miss you, and I can tell that you're serious this time."

"I am baby, very."

I watched her crawl to me and then straddle my lap. She started to kiss on my neck while rubbing up my shirt, and while she got me in the mood my phone buzzed.

Chiina: You still love me? If not I think I'm gonna leave your house tonight.

Me: I still love you baby girl. Don't leave. I will be back in the morning. I love you okay?

"You okay?" Pilar sat up, prompting me to hide my phone.

"Yeah, why you stop?"

She giggled and then resumed kissing my neck and caressing me with her soft hands.

Chiina: Okay.

Me: Say it back, and promise me you will stay put.

Chiina: I love you too, and I won't leave. I promise.

Me: Working late, but will see you soon.

I slipped my phone into my pocket and then laid Pilar on her back so I could take control of this make-up sex.

CHAPTER TWO

Anton Nickerson

Oden and I were sitting in the car, smoking our own blunts with the windows up. The only time we did this was when we were in a car that wasn't shit to us. There was no way we'd be hot boxing in something we cared about.

"What time are we supposed to meet Bernie again?" I looked over at Oden as he tilted his head back to blow out a thick cloud of smoke.

"Quarter 'til 11pm."

Bernie was Billz' close homeboy, and they basically 'ran' Las Vegas together. Bernie was more behind the scenes with shit though, so Billz got all the notoriety in a sense.

At the moment, Bernie had agreed to meet with Oden and I, in order to discuss and dead the problem we had with Billz. We'd caused them to lose a lot of money by intercepting their shipments and burning down trap houses. Billz was too bitch-made to confront us himself, or to retaliate, so Bernie reached out. Little did he know, Oden and I had no plans on squashing shit. Billz knew he wasn't ready to deal with a war from us, which is why his ass should have never started anything.

"We gon' let him talk or what?"

"Yeah, I want him to be relaxed before we ice him. The only thing is, once Billz finds out his homie is gone, that nigga may leave the state. I wanna catch his ass."

"Maybe we can get Bernie to tell us something, like a location before we kill him."

"That would be perfect, but Bernie isn't a bitch like Billz, so he may stand his ground and take this bullet like a man."

"You ain't lying about that."

We finished our blunts, and a few minutes after that, Bernie was calling Oden's burner phone. He chopped it up with him for a little bit, and then we exited the car, guns locked in our waists. We entered the small home that was far off and in the middle of pure dirt and rocks. I know Nevada is full of that shit, but this was some for real desert life over here. Not a bush or tree in sight.

"Welcome," Bernie grinned, gold slugs shining just like Truman's.

"What's up?" Oden and I said almost in unison as we dapped him up.

The three of us sat down at the cheap black table sitting in the middle of the living room, and just stared at one another, waiting for someone to talk.

"My nigga, you're the one who called this fucking meeting, so what do you have to say?" Oden hissed, adjusting the hood that was pulled over his head.

"Right. I mean it's simple. I just want to know how we can fix this little problem we have. We both wanna get money, and our businesses are totally separate so it's possible," Bernie grinned.

"Your boy had my shit shot up and tried to burn it down," Oden replied.

"Yeah, but you know that shit didn't even really do anything. So what a couple windows were broken, everything else was good, right?"

"It's more about the principle my nigga," I chimed in, ready to pop his ass.

"Look, Billz is sorry, trust me. He has a new wife and everything, and he's not trying to have beef with anybody, especially y'all."

"Then why did he start this shit?" I asked.

"He didn't, technically. Oden did when he had y'alls team burglarize two cars from a function we threw, and then killed Smitty."

"Where is Billz?" Oden inquired, prompting Bernie to laugh nervously.

"Look, you don't need to see Billz, you just need to talk to me. I'm the brains of this shit anyway, he's the face of it. Look, what do y'all want? Money? Anything, we can work something out."

"Money? Muthafucka, do you know who I am?" Oden rose to his feet, brows dipped in the middle. "What you pay for your mortgage I smoke in my blunts, nigga. Don't you ever disrespect me by offering me some fucking money."

"Wait, hold up!" Bernie jumped back a little when Oden retrieved his gun. "My bad, man, I was just trying to figure out how you wanted to do this shit." Bernie's hands were up in mock surrender.

"Tell us where Billz is," I stood up.

"I can't do that," Bernie shook his head.

"Well then, this should be a message that he'll receive."

PHEW! PHEW!

Oden sent two bullets through Bernie's head, and then we left out. I was sure Billz would hear about that shit in less than 24 hours. Hopefully, then his ass would come out of fucking hiding to at least avenge his boy's death.

"That was fun," I said as Oden pulled out onto the street.

"Right," he chuckled. "We have a meeting tomorrow morning, may have access to a fleet of cars."

"I can't tomorrow."

"Why?" he glanced at me and then back at the road.

"Gonna see Violet and my son."

"Damn, and you still ain't told Tasmine the deal?" he scoffed, shaking his head. "You let her go home to Louisville thinking you ain't got no kids?"

"Yeah, I mean, I didn't know how to fucking tell her. When I went to see her, she had bought me a cupcake and shit, with a balloon. She was so happy thinking the baby wasn't mine that I just lied."

The look on Tasmine's face made it hard for me to come clean. Not only that, I was still in disbelief myself. And I highly doubt she would still be with me if it were my baby. I couldn't risk losing her again, so I just didn't come out and tell the truth. I wasn't sure how long

I'd be able to hide it, but her being gone to Kentucky helped greatly at the moment.

"You know this shit is gonna blow up in your face, right?"

"Yeah, I do man, I do."

***

The next morning…

I stood at Violet's door with all the shit she'd asked me to get from Target. I'd spent over three hundred dollars, but that wasn't shit to me, especially when it came to my… son.

"Thank you, Tony." Violet answered the door wearing a short tight dress. Her body had snapped back, not completely, but almost. She was looking good, but that still didn't change the fact that her son being mine was mind-blowing.

"You're welcome."

I walked in and stared at my son, sleeping on the couch with some circular pillow surrounding him. He was small as hell, with chubby round cheeks. He didn't really look like anything yet, but Violet said that was because he still needed time to cook. Whatever that meant.

"You hungry? I was gonna make myself an omelet." She looked up from what she was doing in the kitchen to make eye contact with me.

"Uh, yeah, I am kind of hungry." I sat down on the couch next to Athen.

Why was it so hard for me to accept this? I saw the damn DNA test yet it was still so difficult for me to believe. I guess because I always thought the woman that bore my son would be somebody I loved and cared for like Tasmine. Speaking of Tasmine, how was I gonna tell her this shit?

"You wanna hold him?" Violet walked over wearing her pretty smile, before picking up Athen and handing him to me.

He seemed so fragile, as he moved a little bit in my arms. I smiled when he made a sound, and moved his small fingers. His eyes seemed to stay closed 24/7.

"Cute," I chuckled lightly as Violet sat next to me and touched his nose.

"Tell daddy he should spend the day with us," Violet cooed as she took him from me and lifted her shirt. "It's okay," she grinned at me when I was about to get up, so I just sat there frozen as she breastfed him.

"Wow," I mumbled, running my hands down my face.

"Well, are you gonna stay here with us?"

"I guess I could do that."

Regardless of what I wanted, this was my son and I needed to be a father to him. He needed to come first before everything, including Tasmine. I know she wouldn't want me here with Violet and Athen all day, but I could no longer worry about what she wanted and didn't want when it came to him. I was determined to be a better father to Athen than mine was to me. And so far, I could tell Violet was gonna be a better mother than mine for sure.

CHAPTER THREE

Oden

That same morning…

"Cecil," I smiled, approaching the older black man dressed to the nines. I, too, was dressed up in my full-on Armani suit.

"Oden Bishop, how are you?"

"I'm good, but I will be better if I see what you have here."

"I know, follow me."

I did as he asked and trailed him into his big warehouse. We got onto a shabby elevator, and took it down some floors before it finally stopped. When it opened, I swear it felt like I was at a damn luxury car dealership.

"You like what you see, huh?" Cecil laughed as we stepped off of the elevator.

There were all kinds of fucking expensive cars; Wraiths, Maseratis, Lamborghinis, Teslas, shit, the list goes on. There were about seven fucking cars of each, some in different colors. I was salivating and fantasizing, just thinking about all the damn money I was gonna make from shipping these cars overseas.

"Where the fuck did you get this shit?" I questioned.

"If I told you I would have to kill you," he smirked. "But just know they can all be yours my friend."

"In exchange for what?"

"Nothing big. I just need you to go to a meeting for me over in Modena. I can't make it, because I have something else to tend to, but it's a big deal and it's gonna make me a lot of fucking money."

"Italy? Cecil, man, I don't know. I mean you're cool and all, but I don't know you well enough to be handling your affairs."

I met Cecil a long ass time ago when I'd just started out in this car theft business. He was higher than me, but not on Akachi's level, my boss at the time. For some reason, he and Akachi stopped working with one another, and I hadn't seen him in years. We'd only gotten back in contact a couple weeks ago, and he claimed he had something I wanted. This shit was too suspicious for me though.

"You may not know me, Oden, but I know you. This deal that I'm trying to close in Modena could help the both of us."

That piqued my interest.

"How so?"

"Let's just say I've built a relationship with someone very high up in Maserati. He's willing to supply me with as many cars as I want for a low fee. You wouldn't have to go around stealing anymore, Oden."

"He's making the deal with you, not me. And I'm not about to be answering to anybody, no offense, Cecil."

"I know you're not. You've worked too hard to get where you are to demote your position," he sighed and ran his finger across the trunk of the Lamborghini. "He has connections with Lamborghini too, Oden."

"You ain't saying shit, Cecil. You're repeating yourself and since I'm tired of doing the same, I'm gonna go. But it was nice seeing you."

"Oden!" he called after me, stopping me in my tracks. "I will admit that I'm not getting cars out like you. My business isn't what it used to be, and it probably never was if I'm being honest with myself. I broke away from Akachi because I thought that I was ready to do my own thing but I wasn't. I need you in on this deal because Giovanni wouldn't make the deal with me until I promised him he could work with you too," he finally admitted.

"Wait," I chuckled, scratching my eyebrow with my lids lowered. "You made a deal that included me, without even speaking with me? And then you call me down here on some fake shit, when really you wanted to convince me to go along with your lie? Why you didn't just say that shit in the beginning, instead of trying to ship my ass off not knowing anything."

"You're right, Oden—"

"And that's why you've never gotten to Akachi's level! You don't know how to handle your fucking business. What you should have done was come to me like a fucking adult and tell me the deal!" I barked, leaving him silent and pinching the bridge of his nose.

"I apologize is all I can say. But Oden, understand that we can make a lot of fucking money if we do this shit. He's willing to give us these fucking cars for cheap, and we wouldn't have to deal with time frames and all that other bullshit in order not to get caught from stealing."

I admit that what he was saying to me sounded good, but I didn't like the fact that he'd been so presumptuous. For him to just assume that I would be down for this shit pissed me off. He had no idea what the fuck I had going on, yet he threw my name out there like he owned me or some shit. And since he did that, the only way I would agree to meeting with the nigga in Modena, was if Cecil agreed to my terms.

"I will go, but we will not be partners of any kind, meaning we won't work together. You will have a deal separately from him."

We stood there staring at one another as I waited to see if he would agree. It wouldn't make a difference to me. Yeah, getting cars without having to burglarize them sounded great, but I was perfectly fine with how I was currently running shit. So all of this was really on him. I was not about to work with Cecil, because I was sure he would be hard to control, and I would end up killing his ass. I'd hate to do that, which is why him being on his own needed to be a part of the deal.

"Fine," he mumbled so lowly that it was almost hard to make out.

"Excuse me?" I questioned even though I'd heard him. I hated when grown ass men spoke like they were scared or afraid. Use that muthafucking bass in your voice.

"I said that's fine. Just get us the deal, and make it clear to him that—"

"Nah, you make it clear before I get there. I don't want to have to explain shit on your behalf. When I get there, I plan to discuss my deal, and maybe get some information on your part as a small favor because we go way back."

I didn't like being this way with Cecil, but he had pissed me off assuming I would fucking fall in line. And to make matters worse, through the course of this conversation I'd realized that he thought I was either gonna be working under him or with him like we were the fucking Parker Brothers or something. I had my own fucking team that included Anton and Truman, not his average ass.

"Okay, okay. The flight is departing in two days, I can have your ticket sent."

"I have a jet, thanks."

I'd recently acquired a jet because I wanted that shit, and I was sure it would come in handy. First class was nice, but sometimes a nigga wanted to be alone, drink bottomless champagne, listen to music, or shit, fuck his girl right then and there. I couldn't really do that on a damn Delta Airlines' flight.

"Oh nice, how much did it run you for?" Cecil smiled as we stepped back onto the elevator. "Mine was a solid 10 million."

"Wow, I see you low balled it," I chuckled, feeling him stare at the side of my face.

I wasn't even trying to insult him; I was just being honest. The cheaper private jets were ten million and under. I wasn't fucking with that, which is why I waited until my chips were stacked so high that I could no longer see the top of it before I got a jet.

"Damn, I guess so. How much was yours?"

"A little over 35 million." I looked over at him to see his mouth on the floor.

I had way more money than he thought I had but that was because I made my money work for me. I didn't just export cars overseas and be done, I invested my shit and then opened a club and liquor line. My club was being featured in all types of local newspapers, and I was even being contacted to have it relocated and put in one of the hotels on the strip. As far as my liquor line, it was gonna be coming out as a menu item in a few restaurants, and I must say, I didn't know such a thing paid so well.

Still though, I wasn't the flossy type. I had a few nice cars, a jet, and expensive clothes, but I lived in my cool ass townhouse. A mansion just didn't appease me, and I didn't feel like I needed it.

Although my money had gotten longer than it used to be, I didn't increase my expenses because that was how niggas went broke. The point in making more money is to provide cushion, not to hit another fucking wall. You'll stay broke doing that bullshit.

"You have a good one, Cecil. Send me Giovanni's information, please." I stepped off the elevator. I guess my jet price still had him stunned because he hadn't said a thing since.

I slid into my Porsche Panamera once I left out of Cecil's warehouse, and peeled off. I was gonna pick Khyle up so we could go to dinner tonight. She was leaving in a week, and even though I was coming to California shortly after, I was gonna miss my shorty. I was gonna miss sleeping next to her, feeling her soft skin, smelling her hair, and even listening to her insults which only told me she loved me. And now that I was going to Italy this weekend, I planned to take her away before she left.

As I parked my car next to my Lexus truck, I saw a familiar figure standing by my townhouse. She was walking in a small circle, staring at her feet with her arms folded across her DD cups. Her body was looking good as fuck, I'm talking thicker than oatmeal, and my dick immediately turned brick hard. She picked her head up to move her golden locks from her face, and when she spotted me getting out of my car, a smile formed on her full lips.

"Naomi," I sighed as I neared her. Damn!

"Oden!" she squealed, jumping into my arms. Hugging her soft body felt so good that I temporarily closed my eyes. Once I realized what I was doing, I stepped back from her. "I missed you!"

"Yeah, umm, I thought you moved to Colorado?" I frowned, cocking my head.

"I did, but things have changed in my life so now I'm back."

Naomi was my girlfriend some years back; the first girl I'd ever given that title too. Our relationship was the shit, like I thought I was gonna marry her, but then it went left. Every time I looked up, she was accusing me of cheating on her, and going off about me being around other women. It was to the point where if we were out in public I would be hesitant to even speak to someone I knew if it were a female. Eventually, I couldn't take that shit anymore, so I told her to kick rocks.

She fought me on it at first, but finally gave up. About four months later, she ran off and married some nigga, then moved to Colorado. I felt some type of way about it initially, but after like a week I was over it. She was a headache to me, and I was overjoyed that she would no longer provide me that pain.

"Right, so you're back for good?" I asked as I slipped my key into the door. When I walked in, I saw some of Khyle's things that she'd left here.

"Yeah, I am. Since when do you have candles, Oden Bishop?" Naomi lifted one of the lavender candles that Khyle kept in my living room. It was for decoration and scent she said.

"I don't. My girlfriend likes what it adds to the living room, and the scent is nice too," I shrugged, hanging my keys up.

"Girlfriend? I had no idea you had a girlfriend." Naomi sat down on my couch with a confused expression, almost like she was perplexed.

"Yeah, I do. I have for a while now, actually. Her name is Khyle."

I picked up a picture I had framed of Khyle. She'd taken it on the beach one day in California. Her long hair was blowing, her smooth skin was being beamed on by the sun, and her sexy ass body looked perfect in the bathing suit. The way the sand stuck to her supple skin had me fantasizing about fucking her on the beach every time I looked at it. The picture was so beautiful to me, that I had it blown up and framed for myself.

"She looks like a model," Naomi giggled. "This actually looks like a Victoria's Secret swimsuit ad." Naomi continued to stare at the photo. "She's cute though," she shrugged, making me laugh as I put the picture back.

"She's beautiful and you know it." I sat down next to her.

"Yeah she is, but I expected that. You've always had good taste in women."

"What can I say?"

"So would your girlfriend mind if we had lunch or something? I'm not trying to get with you or anything, I just haven't seen you in a long time."

"I would definitely have to run it by her. But Naomi, I actually have to go get her for dinner tonight, so…"

"Oh, so I guess that's my cue to go, huh?"

We stood up together.

"Not to be like that, but yeah, I have to get ready."

"Let me get your number then," she smiled, taking her phone from her purse.

I inhaled sharply because I was hesitant, but then I just read it off. I knew Naomi, and she wasn't the type to chase a man who was involved. If she just wanted to be friends, then I was cool with that. I just hoped Khyle was too.

CHAPTER THREE

Shayne

Tonight, my job was having a party so we could kind of mingle and get to know some of the other performers, managers, huge fans, and just a whole slew of people. I didn't want to go alone, and since Lloyd was busy, I asked my little sister to come. She was super excited which made me feel good, because I hated dragging people along when they didn't really wanna go somewhere. And I was lucky because she was leaving the country tomorrow, so the party was happening just in time.

"Damn, look at my shawty," Lloyd came up behind me, running his tongue across his bottom lip as he hugged my body.

"I'm guessing you like what you see?" I giggled as I placed my hands on top of his.

I loved when he held me; I felt so safe and secure. Leaving Pierce for Lloyd was definitely the right choice.

"Very much, but you knew that already. That's why I had to take you from your nigga."

He turned me to face him, and backed me into the nearby wall. Placing his big hand between my legs, he nibbled on my ear, which got me super wet.

"Lloyd, I have to go," I chuckled, prying his hands from my body.

"I will see you tonight. Make sure when I come home you're in the bed naked. I don't want to have to take anything off."

"K," I giggled like a schoolgirl yet again. He always made me do that.

After Lloyd left, I finished getting ready and then hopped into my new Range Rover so I could get my sister. I texted her once I was approaching UNLV, so by the time I pulled up in front of her dorm, she was coming outside. She looked cute in her all white tube dress with matching white stilettos. She wore a little bit of jewelry, mainly her ring and necklace from Oden. Her hair was hanging down her back like mine, and her makeup was simple and beautiful.

"You look nice," I told her as we kissed using the sides of our mouths. "I like the all white."

"You too," she sized me up.

I was wearing a red number with a plunged neckline, and an opening around the rib area. It was tight, short, and sexy; just what I wanted. I had on red pumps to match, with silver jewelry to complement it.

"Thank you."

"So where is this party being held?"

"Inside of the Harrah's Hotel. It's this big ass room with chandeliers hanging down and everything. I haven't seen the setup, but I've seen the room before."

"Will there be free drinks?"

"Yes, but have you forgotten that you're only 18?" I chuckled as I pulled onto Las Vegas Boulevard.

"Excuse me, I'm 18 and a half," she corrected me as we laughed.

I parked my car with valet, and then the two of us headed inside of the hotel, walking until we made it to the big room. We couldn't miss it because there was a big ass sign with my co-workers and I all dressed up on it, and balloons nearby.

"You look so cute on here." Khyle touched the photo as I showed the doorman my work ID and Khyle's ticket to come with me.

"Thank you," I replied to her.

The party was actually not really what I would call a party. It was more of a social, with people standing around talking, drinking champagne, and eating little snack foods. After introducing Khyle to my boss and a couple of other higher ups, we found a seat at a table after getting a few hors d'oeuvres.

"I'm proud of you, Shayne. You really made this shit happen."

"Thank you, baby girl. And yeah, I was worried for a second that I was gonna fail like Pierce, but I'm happy I pulled it off. Seems like it took forever though."

"Not really. Speaking of Pierce, how is that going?" Khyle inquired as we both accepted the flutes of apple cider from the young Asian girl.

"I finally did it. I can't believe I forgot to tell you. I finally told him that it was over and that I was in love with Lloyd."

"Did he cry?" she joked.

"Yeah, he did, actually. He was sobbing lightly. It was such a turn off and just solidified the reason why I no longer wanted to be with him."

"Dang, so now can I meet Lloyd?"

"Yes, he's coming to Los Angeles when you get there, so all of us are gonna have dinner with mom and dad. I think you will like him."

"Me too. I usually like Oden's friends, and I'm sure he's no different. Tasmine met him. She said he was nice and sexy."

"Where did she meet him?" my brows furrowed. I didn't like other girls being around him when I wasn't there.

"Some party Oden had thrown with his friends. "

"I see," I sipped my cider. "Was he with any girls?"

"I don't know, she didn't tell me all of that. All she said was that he was there at the party, and that he was a fine piece of chocolate."

I simply nodded in response.

My co-worker, Blair walked over to the table, so of course the subject was immediately changed. We began talking about different things, and after a while, I was ready to go.

Saying bye to all the people I knew, and recently met, Khyle and I headed out so I could get my car from valet. On the ride home, it was quiet until Khyle broke the silence.

"Don't get mad at Lloyd, Shayne. It sounds like he's really into you."

"Who said I was mad?" I chuckled breathily.

"I'm your sister, I know you. You're definitely upset right now."

"I'm fine, Khyle." I patted her thigh as I pulled up to her dorm.

We hugged one another tightly, said 'I love you', and then she got out of the car. I stayed there watching her until she had made it inside of the building safely, and then I peeled out, ready to confront Lloyd. When I got home, he of course wasn't there, so I took a hot bubble bath, put on a facemask, and then changed into my pajamas. By the time I was rinsing that gunky shit off of my face, I heard the front door.

"Do you love me?" I asked Lloyd once he entered the bathroom and hugged my body tightly from behind.

"I care for you. I love you, but if you're asking me if I'm in love, I don't quite know yet, shawty."

"Oh."

He turned me to face him, and then sat me up on the sink before getting in between my legs.

"Why?" he moved my hair from my face.

"I just wanted to see how you felt about me that's all." I toyed with the sink while looking down at it, because I was too nervous to make eye contact with him.

"Listen, I like yo' ass and a lot. I like you enough to let you live with me, which I have never done. I like you enough to still call you my girl and brag about you even though I know the homie hit. I wanna be with you, and I ain't worried about no other girl, Shayne. I barely look when other bitches cross my path."

"Really?" I whined, poking my bottom lip out, which prompted him to laugh.

"Yes, really. I'm sure I will fall in love with you, baby. We're definitely headed there. Shit, I may already be but I don't know. What I do know is that Shayne Luke is the only girl I'm checking for."

Draping my arms over his shoulders, I kissed him gently. He hugged my torso tightly in his muscular arms, as our kiss became more passionate.

Every day he was proving why I'd made the right choice.

CHAPTER THREE

Oden and I had just gotten back from spending time together in Italy. We originally stayed in Modena, but that was only for a night. We left there and went to Rome and Florence, which was so much more romantic. I'd never even been out of the country, nor on a private jet until I met Oden. I guess that was the life you lived when you had a nigga like him.

"I never wanted to leave!" I shrieked, falling back onto his big bed fully clothed.

"It was nice. I've been there before, but it was because my grandpa had some shit to take care of. It was a long ass time ago though." He got onto the bed too.

"I guess we both needed it." I turned to face him, and we just looked at one another in the semi dark bedroom. "I love you." I pecked him softly.

"I love you too."

Caressing his hair, I hugged his neck and began to kiss his full lips before sucking on the bottom one. I loved his lips. I enjoyed kissing them and the way they felt against my pussy… my whole body.

"What are you thinking about?" I questioned him because his mind seemed to be elsewhere. Usually whenever I even touched him he would be groping me by now and damn near tearing my clothes off.

"I wanna ask you something. And just give me an honest answer, aight? I'm not gonna get mad."

My stomach tightened as I began to rack my brain, trying to recall if I had done anything and hid it from him. The last time he'd said something like that was when he'd found out about the abortion and dumped me. I knew I hadn't done anything so horrible since, but I was still worried nonetheless.

"Okay, ask me."

"So remember the girl Naomi that I told you about?" he kissed my hand and I nodded. "She has moved back to Las Vegas and she wants to know if we can have lunch sometime before I go to California to see you."

"Why does she wanna have lunch?"

"Just to catch up. I haven't seen her in a long time, and vice versa, so she just wants to have a friendly lunch."

"Why did you guys break up?"

I remembered him telling me, but I had forgotten because I didn't give a fuck about the bitch. I don't remember it being anything too crazy, but I didn't like the fact that she was someone he chose to be his first girlfriend. She had to have made one hell of an impression on

Oden for him to choose her as such.

"Because she started being very insecure. She didn't want me around other women, or speaking to other women at all. The only female I was allowed to chop it up with was Anton's mom, which I rarely even do."

"Do you think she still loves you?"

"No," he answered quickly. "She had a husband, so if anything, she probably still loves him and shit, you know?"

"Yeah," I nodded. "Well, I guess a simple lunch won't hurt. It's not like it's dinner or anything, so I'm fine."

Honestly, I wanted to say no, but after hearing him explain why he and Naomi ended their relationship, I didn't want to sound like her. I mean, could you blame her? Oden was a very handsome man, standing at 6'4, with wild beautiful hair, trimmed facial hair, sexy lips, not too muscular but you knew he worked out, and he had enough money to live a couple different lives and his own at the same time. In a sense, he was every woman's dream, so knowing he was around them was a bit unsettling for a woman in a relationship with him.

"For real?" he scanned my eyes.

"Yes, it's fine. If she just wants to catch up at a friendly lunch then okay. And I trust that you love me and won't do anything."

It wasn't fine. It absolutely wasn't fine. But the part about me trusting him was somewhat true. I knew Oden would never step out on me with some random bitch, but someone he once wanted to be in a relationship with? I wasn't so sure.

"See, that's why I love you, Khyle."

He crushed his lips against mine, and tongued me down as he got in between my legs. I rubbed up and down his muscular arms, as his big strong hands grabbed at my frame. When he moved to my neck, my throat jumped, signaling that I had to throw the fuck up.

"Wait, Oden," I nudged him off.

"What, baby? Khyle!" he called after me as I darted out of the bedroom.

As soon as I got in the bathroom, I lifted the toilet top and puked my guts out. I was panting heavily in between vomiting, and my eyes started to water. I didn't know what the hell was wrong with my ass, but I didn't like this shit one bit.

"Let me get you some water," Oden rubbed my back gently before leaving the bathroom.

While he was gone, I tried to remember what I had eaten while away in Europe. In the middle of thinking, I threw up some more, feeling like I was two damn seconds away from fucking dying. When Oden came back with the water, it suddenly hit me that this was exactly how I felt when I found out I was pregnant the last time.

Standing up to flush the toilet, I then rinsed my mouth as best as I could before downing the water. Once I finished, I brushed, flossed, and rinsed while Oden sat on the closed toilet top watching me.

"You okay now?" he inquired, bringing me into him, grasping my waistline.

"I think I'm pregnant," I whispered, rubbing his wild hair as his hands rested on the small of my back.

Tilting his head back he replied, "You do? Wanna go buy a test from the store?"

"Yeah."

We hurried out of the house and went to the nearest pharmacy for a couple of pregnancy tests. We got three of each of the brands they had, which turned out to be really expensive, and then rushed home. I was afraid because I pretty much knew what they would read, but a part of me was hopeful that I was wrong and just sick. As much raw sex as Oden and I had been having though, God would have to really be on my side for me not be pregnant.

"You have enough pee for all these?" Oden chuckled.

"I don't know, but get me something to drink, baby, just to make sure."

When he left, I peed on the first one, and by the time he returned I had enough urine for another. We stayed in the bathroom until I peed on all the tests I had, and when I was done, I decided to check the very first one I did.

"What does it say?"

"It says I'm pregnant, but let's wait for the others."

He nodded in response, and we just sat there in the bathroom, not saying a word. Time passed on, and I checked each and every one, and they all said the same thing. I knew I was, and now I felt like I was gonna pass out.

"What do you wanna do?" Oden brought me into his chest.

"I can't get another abortion, Oden, I just can't do that. I'm gonna keep it," I whispered the last part, but he still heard me because he pulled away.

"Like I told you before, whatever you want to do I'm with you. I wouldn't want a baby with anyone else, anyway," he grinned. He was so handsome.

He bent my head back a little to kiss me. My eyes closed out of reflex, as our tongues came in contact. He picked me up and carried me out of the bathroom, taking me to his bedroom where he undressed me.

As he trailed kisses down my stomach, and propped my legs up onto his shoulders, a question arose that I'd been dying to know the answer to.

"Oden, how did you know I'd had an abortion?"

Pausing, he replied, "That girl told me."

"What girl?" His answer prompted me to sit up on my elbows.

"The one you used to live next to. She has some long ass curly hair, and them bugged out eyes. Uh, Rachel."

"Raquel?"

"Same shit."

"But how would she know about the abortion?"

"Said she overheard y'all talking about it or something like that. But I need you to focus on what's going on right now. My dick is hard and I wanna eat some pussy."

Smiling, I spread my legs wider for him, just the way he liked, and then threw my head back once his mouth connected with my center.

How the hell was I gonna explain to my parents that I was having a baby? But more importantly, how did that bitch Raquel know I'd had an abortion?

CHAPTER THREE

Santino

$\mathscr{I}$ woke up in my bed feeling hella good. I didn't want to get used to this bomb ass mattress, knowing I was gonna be back on that dorm shit in no time.

Wiping my eyes, my mind drifted to my homie, Huelo. That nigga had been missing in action since the last two weeks of school. I wasn't sure what the hell happened to that nigga, but I knew it couldn't be good if his parents called me looking.

Huelo wasn't the type of dude to just dip and not tell anybody. I was sure something terrible had happened to him, but my only question was why? He was a good guy, and all he did was play football. He didn't even go anywhere but school affiliated parties. The last time I saw him, he told me he was hitting a party up, and the nigga never came back. Now there were posters all over the school and shit. The simple thought made my stomach ache.

"Do you always sit covering your eyes like that for this long?" I heard a voice say, making me jump back. I looked to see it was Leena, lying on top of my comforter, propping her head up with her hand.

"How the fuck you get in my shit!" I shouted, getting out of the bed.

"Your parents let me in. You know they love me and don't approve of that little bitch, Bella," she snickered, turning onto her back.

I know what y'all are thinking and hell nah, I didn't introduce this bitch to my people. She saw my parents and I out to dinner one night, and took it upon herself to let them know who she was, which was nobody at all. Because she was pretty and appeared to have her shit together, my parents approved of her. They thought she was my girlfriend, and always referred to her as such, no matter how many times I'd corrected them. They really wanted her and I to be together, but that was *never* gonna happen.

"Leena, what did you tell them?"

"Nothing, calm your ass down. I could have squealed on you and let them know you tried to kick me to the curb to be with that bitch, but I decided against it."

"Watch your mouth. And I didn't *try* to do anything; I did do it. Look, you have to go so I can get ready and shit, Leena."

"No, you see, because I did you a favor, you need to be nice to me. You know if I tell your parents that you've hooked back up with Bella, they're gonna kick your ass out of this house and you'll have nowhere to go this summer."

When would these bitches learn that I couldn't be blackmailed?

"And that's fine with me. I can sleep on the streets until school starts back up, which I will then get drafted from to the NFL. I can manage, so do what you have to do, but get the fuck out."

Leena looked into my eyes with that same sad expression she always gave me when she didn't get her way. I guess she really thought that she'd be able to hold my little secret over my head, but that wasn't gonna work. I loved Bella, and I would sacrifice anything to be with her, including a place to lay my head. No longer would I throw my baby to the side because of what other people thought and/or wanted. Bella was gonna be my wife and the mother of my children, regardless of who had a problem with that shit.

"Why do you love her so much!" Leena shouted, standing to her feet. Her fists were balled up, and her chest rose and fell rapidly like a bear or some shit.

"I just do. She's perfect to me, and that's who I wanna be with. I've never wanted to be with you like that, Leena. If I had, I would have made you my girl but I didn't."

"So what am I supposed to do, Sanz? Just forget about you and move on? Forget all the time we spent together, and just erase you from my heart?" Tears began streaming her face, and I honestly didn't know what the fuck to say.

"I don't really know how to answer that. I did my best to keep you from falling deep into this shit. I explained to you time and time again that this union wasn't going anywhere. I mean, what the fuck? Ain't like I led you on."

"What if I agree to be low-key?"

"Like my side bitch?" I had to laugh at that one as I started towards the bathroom within my room. I pulled my toothpaste down, and began using my electric toothbrush to clean my teeth.

"Yeah, but you ain't have to say it like that. I could be like your mistress. A mistress is better than a side bitch because she gets treated well. And I promise when Bella comes around I won't say anything to her."

I rinsed my mouth with warm water before flossing and then using Listerine. When I was done, I quickly washed my face with some soap, and then cut the shower on. While the water heated up, I walked to the doorway of my bathroom and towered over Leena.

"No," was all I said before closing the door in her face.

I cleaned my body in the shower, and then grabbed a towel to wrap around my bottom half. Before opening the door, I silently prayed that this bitch was gone. Sadly she was still there, stretched across my chaise.

"I need to get dressed," I stated calmly as I sifted through my drawer for some boxers.

"Will you text me later? Or maybe we can go get some ice cream and talk about my offer."

"Leena, no. I don't want you as a side chick, a mistress, a fuck buddy, a girlfriend number two, nothing, mami. I'm not interested. You're a cool girl, so you can find another nigga in no time. But please, leave me be." My hands were in the prayer position.

She glared at me for a couple moments, and then snatched my bedroom door open before storming out.

"Good riddance," I mumbled to myself.

I got dressed and went downstairs to see if my parents were there.

I saw my dad reading a newspaper, and my mom sipping a margarita. She swore she didn't have a drinking problem, but who drinks margaritas at 10am, when they're not on vacation? Whatever.

"I'm gonna step out for a little bit," I peeked my head in.

"Where to? With Leena?" my mother smiled, pushing her long dark hair back. Her deep chocolate skin was always something I'd admired. It had always been so smooth and vibrant.

"No, just out."

"Alone?"

"Nah, with some friends," I lied. I hated that I couldn't tell them I was going with Bella. Now just wasn't the time. I needed to stay here until summer break was up for me.

"Oh, well then… have fun." My mom scanned me from head to toe, as my father continued to pay me no mind.

Declining to respond, I left out of the house.

I made it to Bella's house about 10 minutes later, and swooped into a park right in front. I always loved coming here, before her parents hated me, because it felt good to be around a family that actually loved one another.

"Hi baby," Bella beamed, looking pretty as ever. She had on a short yellow dress that showed her sexy soft golden legs, and her hair was in a braid on the side.

"Aye, wait." I pulled her back outside of the house and kissed her nastily. I knew I couldn't do that in front of her parents, so I had to get it out of the way now. "I wanna fuck you so hard right now," I grumbled against her lips.

"We can, my parents left to go see a movie."

Before she even finished her sentence, I scooped her ass up and carried her up the stairs. When we got into her bedroom, we both began coming out of our clothes, sharing kisses here and there when we could. Once we were ass naked, I laid her down and put her legs on my shoulders. As soon as my head touched her opening, I felt like I would nut right away.

"Bellaaaa," I moaned as she whimpered.

I gripped the headboard as I moved in and out of her slowly with no cap. I never got tired of feeling her raw, and lately that was how we'd been doing it. Biting down on my lip, I watched her face twist and ball up cutely, as she cooed and sniveled while running her soft hand up and down my abs. I wound my hips into her slowly, enjoying how wet and tight she was.

"Mmmm," she cried out, lips tucked in. Her body jerked once she released on my rod, and that was when I decided to tear her shit up. "Ahh! Ahh!" she screamed damn near, as I slammed my dick into her pussy.

The feeling was indescribable, and had me moaning just like her ass. I didn't give a fuck who heard, because if they were experiencing what I was, they'd be hollering like a bitch too.

"Fuck, Bella, I'm about to nut," I growled, playing with her nipples as I beat it up.

She came on my dick again, and after that I was blessing her with my seeds. Collapsing onto her, I kissed her sweet smelling neck while

I let it sit inside.

"Wanna bathe before they get back?" she asked in her sexy little voice.

"Yeah, come on."

After showering, we got back in our clothes, and laid down on top of her covers. When I saw her texting, I took her phone and set it on the dresser closest to me.

"I'm sorry," she half smiled.

"It's cool. Have you heard anything about Huelo?" I asked her. Bella knew more people than I did at UNLV. It was mainly because niggas were on her bumper, so they always tried to find reasons to talk to her. That shit kind of pissed me off, but right now it may come in handy.

"Why would I know anything about his ass?" she frowned, sounding a little angrier than I expected.

"What's your beef with Huelo?"

"That nigga tried to rape my friend, you didn't know?"

"Fuck is your friend?" I sat up, astonished by what I was hearing. We had to be talking about two totally different niggas right now.

"Khyle. He came to her room like he was in need of their class notes, and when she was getting them, he tried to force himself on her."

"Huelo?" my brows dipped.

"Yes, *Huelo*."

"What the fuck? That nigga didn't mention that shit to me." I stared off at Bella's light purple walls in deep thought. It seemed like no one was who they said they were.

"Why would he?" she sucked her teeth.

I fell back, pressing my head into Bella's thick pillow. Something was not right, and I needed to figure out what the hell had happened to my homie.

CHAPTER FOUR

Tasmine

Louisville, Kentucky…

"What is it that you do again, son?" my father asked Anton for the hundredth time.

He was over for dinner, and right now my parents, sister Tasia, and my cousin Mia were all here. He'd been over all day, and my dad had barely let me spend any time with him alone. I felt so bad for Anton by this point, but it was almost over.

"I'm a club owner, and partial owner of Brown Sugar Bourbon. I'm not sure if you've heard of it."

I smiled because Anton answered my father's repeated question calmly as if it were the first time, every time.

"Right, right."

"He's already told you that, Daddy," Tasia chimed in, rolling her eyes.

"You know your father's memory is bad." My mom shook her

head as she put a forkful of mashed potatoes into her mouth.

"My memory is not bad, Junie. I was just making sure he wasn't lying. That's how you tell, keep asking the same question over and over," my dad explained.

"Myron," my mother shot him a look and he just shrugged.

"Now, how old did you say you were again?" My dad's brows furrowed as the whole table let out exasperated sighs.

For the rest of the dinner, my dad interrogated Anton, asking the same shit over and over. Of course, Anton stayed coolheaded, and didn't show a hint of frustration once. It was torture however, because my dad wouldn't allow any other conversations to go on while he got in Anton's business.

Dinner had finally come to an end, so Anton was going to his hotel and I was coming too. I'd already cleared it with my mom, and she said she would handle my dad. We were almost out the door, when my father came out of the downstairs bathroom, eyes squinted.

"And where are you going, Tasmine?"

"Daddy, I wanna go with Anton," I whined like a little child.

"Myron, let her go. It's not like she's not alone with him over in Nevada. Tasmine has been raised well," my mom buttered my father up as he stared deeply into Anton's eyes.

My dad wasn't as tall as him, but he acted as if they were equal in stature.

"Fine, but be back here by 9am, Tasmine."

"Okay!" I squealed as Anton and I left the house.

I wasn't coming back until I was good and ready.

"I'm so sorry about that, baby," I rubbed Anton's hand once we were in the car. "I've never brought a guy home before, so I didn't know what to expect."

"I'm the first to ever meet your parents?" he glanced at me while driving towards his hotel.

"Yep, you're the first one."

"Damn, I like that. I wanna be your first everything; well, everything that matters most to you," he replied, making me feel giddy inside.

"You will be."

He parked his car at the hotel, and went around back to get my bag that I'd put in there earlier. I didn't want my dad to see me leaving with it, so I made sure to have it put there while he was busy earlier.

Anton's room was inside of the Marriott hotel downtown. It was pretty nice, actually very nice, but it wasn't over the top.

He set my bag down when we got into the room, and then he closed the blinds so I could get undressed. He finished before me, so he sat down on the edge of the bed in his boxers, just watching me.

"I can't believe I'm only the second guy you've been with," he spoke lowly.

"Why is that?"

"Because you're so bad. Usually women as fine as you have been around the block a little bit. They got niggas hollering at them every time they look up, so they're bound to fuck some of them. Shit adds up over time, you know?"

"Well not me. I'm too picky. Well, I wasn't at first, but after the first guy played me, I decided to tread more lightly."

I was about to pull my nightgown down over my head but he stopped me. Pulling me closer, he surveyed my body with his lids lowered. I only had on a thin pair of panties, but I felt comfortable with him. I always thought it would be weird to be naked in front of a guy unless we were having sex, but Anton made me feel different. I didn't mind letting him watch me step out of the shower, or change clothes. He acted as if my physique was a work of art, and that in turn made me feel flawless in his presence.

Leaning in, he pecked my flat stomach while holding a handful of my ass. His lips were cold for some reason, but so soft. His hands rubbed up and down my back as his kisses became deeper and less gentle. Throwing my head back, I caressed his fresh haircut, while enjoying his touch. He laid me on my back, and cut the lamp off to make the atmosphere a bit more romantic. It was dark, but we could still see each other… and only each other. I couldn't even tell you if someone was in the corner watching us, because my eyes were fixated on him.

"I love you, Tasmine," he whispered, kissing down my collarbone until he reached my perfect C cups.

I was stunned hearing him say those words. I knew we were close, but I had no idea that he felt this way about me already. I felt like I loved him too, but I assumed it was just me being my same stupid self.

"I love you too, Tony," I moaned, feeling his lips grace my waistline, while he tugged down my panties.

When my underwear passed my ankles, he immediately propped

my legs up on his shoulders. His mouth latched onto my clit, and he began sucking gently while caressing my thighs. I loved the way his tongue flicked over my clit, moving faster than a muthafucka. That shit always made me cum hard, and I think he knew that.

Scratching his scalp, I whimpered like a wounded animal as I reached my peak. As usual, he kept licking and sucking my middle, so I began to grind against his mouth.

"Oh, oh my gosh!" I called out, gripping the sheets with one hand, and rubbing his head with the other. I didn't know what to do with myself as he pulled that second orgasm right out of my body.

Sitting up, I pushed him onto his back, and then mounted him backwards. This was his favorite position, so I made sure to put it on him every now and again.

I started slowly, moving up and down with precision, allowing myself to adjust to his size. His soft grunts were a turn on, and made me want to do more. Leaning forward, I gripped his kneecaps and began bouncing on it, causing him to grip my hips and scream out. I loved making him moan like hell, so I kept my movements up.

"Fuck, Tas, damn," he whined in his deep voice, as I continued to guide my sopping wet center up and down his long, thick dick.

Every time I came down, he hit my spot, taking me over the edge. I bit down on my lip to muffle the moans that were attempting escape, but they eventually broke free. All you could hear was our skin smacking together, and us calling out in unison like we were a part of a church choir.

"Ahh! Ahhh!" I cried when he spanked me and gripped my ass

roughly in his big ass hands. He then trailed them up my back, before sitting up to kiss my shoulder blades.

We intertwined our fingers as I bounced in his lap backwards, calling out loudly over the room. My inner thighs were wet as hell from me cumming so many times, but I didn't even care. A few more pounds into me, and we were both exploding together. I love when we came at once.

"Fuck, baby, you trying to get a nigga to propose right now?" he panted against my back. The warmth of his breath felt so good against my skin.

We gained our composure, and then he lifted me off of him. We took a bath together, then climbed into the bed naked, cuddled up and shit. I get could used to stuff like this.

"You really love a nigga?" he asked, nuzzling his nose into my hair.

"Yeah, I do. I did before you told me, but I didn't want to say it because I thought I was being my usual emotional self."

He laughed lowly in his deep sexy voice.

"Well, I want you to know that no matter what happens, and no matter what I say or do, I love you more than anything, Tasmine Randall. I want to marry you and all that other shit niggas do when they're pussy whipped."

Giggling, I replied, "Well I'm happy to hear that." There was a moment of silence. "You know I used to dream about being with you."

"When?"

"Before I started school in Vegas. I came to visit one weekend, and my sister and I attended one of your parties. That was the first time I saw you, and I'd been smitten ever since."

"Damn. I wish you would have said something to me then, or gotten my attention."

"Why?" I picked my head up off of his strong chest to look up into his alluring chocolate face.

"Just because I feel like I could have spent more time with you if we had have started earlier, you know."

"But we have forever together, so it all works out."

"Yeah," he mumbled, staring up at the ceiling as if he were in deep thought. "You're right." He grinned as if he'd realized he was going into a zone, but snapped himself out of it.

"You okay, baby?" I toyed with his chin hairs.

"I'm great."

We stayed up talking for a little bit longer, before we both drifted off to sleep.

***

The next morning…

"Almost ready?" Anton called from the bathroom. He was about to take me out to eat lunch, and then shopping. We wanted to spend some more time together before we went back to my house. Also, I wanted to show him around Louisville without my family.

"Yes, worry about yourself," I replied, spreading lotion over my feet. He was still in the bathroom getting ready, yet he had the nerve to check on me.

I finished putting on my lotion, so while I waited I grabbed my phone. I tapped the Instagram app, and liked a few pictures on my timeline of Khyle, Bella, my cousin, and a couple other people I knew from high school and college. When I was done, Anton's ass still wasn't ready, so I went through the explore page. While scrolling, I saw a girl that looked like that bitch Violet. I enlarged it, and then chuckled when I realized it was her. Being my usual nosey self, I clicked her page and almost squealed when I saw it wasn't private.

While casually gliding my thumb up the screen to scan the many pictures on her profile, I spotted a dude holding a baby. He looked a lot like Anton, and was wearing a hoodie that I knew all too well. I tapped the picture and sat up on the bed. The caption read, Father and son bonding moment.

Clenching my jaw, and blinking back the tears waiting to fall, I rose to my feet and darted to the bathroom.

"Damn, you look radiant," Anton grinned as he brushed his fade while looking into the large horizontal mirror. "You like that, baby? Radiant? I'm trying to find new words to impress your pretty ass with."

"You lied to me," I whispered almost.

"Lied? About what?" His hand lowered slowly until the brush was on the sink counter.

"This." I showed him the picture. "Her baby was yours and you told me that it wasn't."

Inhaling and holding it in for some seconds, he finally let it out and said, "Tasmine, I can explain—"

"No, there isn't anything to explain. I asked you what the results were and you told me the baby wasn't yours." My voice was shaking, which pissed me off because it made it obvious that I was about to cry. "Stay back!" I hollered when he started towards me.

"Tasmine, I lied because for one, I'm still skeptical and because I knew you would leave me!"

"That's the thing! You don't know shit! Why the fuck would I leave you over a baby you made *before* we got together, nigga?"

"I— shit, I don't know, I just thought—"

"No, you don't fucking think! You're so used to doing what the fuck you want, that you don't *think* about other people and how they fucking feel, Anton!"

"I *was* thinking about you! You're all I fucking think about when I should be worried about my son! I'm over here stressing about telling you this shit, when I should be focused on him!"

"Well guess what, nigga? Now you have all the time you need to focus on your new family. I hope you guys stay blessed." I turned to walk off and get my duffle bag but he grabbed me.

"Tasmine, don't do this. Like you just said, the baby was made before you. Don't do me like this. I'm sorry I didn't come clean, but now you know. Let's work through it."

"Don't want to." I snatched from him and stormed to get my bag.

"You said you loved me last night. How can you leave me if you love me so much?"

"Like this." I shoulder checked him, well more like torso checked him, as I walked towards the door of his hotel room.

"Tasmine. Baby, please," he begged, gripping my waist from behind, and kissing my temple gently.

"No, stop! When you grow up and learn how to deal with your shit like a fucking man instead of a little ass boy, then maybe we can talk. But right now, I never wanna see you again," I cried.

Fuck, I didn't want to cry!

"I don't need time for that, baby—"

I cut him off when I ripped my body from his arms. Snatching the door open, I rushed out, ignoring his calls to me.

This was the last time I would allow Anton to play me for a fucking fool.

CHAPTER FOUR

Truman

Pilar was sleeping on my chest after I'd just gotten done dicking her down. It was about a quarter 'til 1am, and I'd been with her the whole day. We had breakfast, went shopping, had dinner, and then came back to her place to have the most mind-blowing sex ever. But for some reason, despite the day being so phenomenal, I couldn't get Chiina off of my mind.

Since that day she told me she was pregnant, I hadn't seen her. I told her I would be home the next morning, but I never went. I just stayed with Pilar, dodged Chiina when I went to work, and then came home to Pilar… or other women. I'd been doing that for the past week, and when I stopped by my crib yesterday, Chiina had left me a note basically saying that she was done with me. I didn't believe her ass, so I hit her up. I'd been texting her on the low all day, and she didn't reply to not one damn message.

"Fuck," I mumbled to myself.

I couldn't even sleep because of that damn girl. Here I was, lying in bed with the woman who was supposed to be the love of my life, yet

I was missing my sidepiece. Nah, she wasn't a sidepiece. I hated to even call her that, or think of her like that. I loved Chiina, and she had my baby, so she was no fucking side chick.

Carefully removing my body from under Pilar, I sat up on the edge of her bed. Grabbing my phone from the nightstand, I hit the home button to see if I had any texts. I had plenty from a couple of birds I'd been fucking, but none from Chiina yet. She was pissing me off. Pilar hadn't even done me like this before. At least Pilar would answer, just with rude shit. Chiina wasn't giving me anything and it was killing me.

I decided I would call, so I headed to the bathroom, turned on the shower so that Pilar wouldn't hear in case she woke up, and then I dialed Chiina; yep, at almost 1am.

"Can you leave me alone?" she finally answered.

"You ain't seen me fucking texting you! I texted you 10 fucking times today, Chi! What the fuck is wrong with you!"

"No, what the fuck is wrong with you, nigga? You should never text someone that many fucking times, ever; especially if they haven't answered not one! I left you a letter explaining that I was done with you. If you want to be in the baby's life you can be, but as far as being with me, that's done."

"Bit— yo, who the fuck do you think you're talking to, Chiina?" I had to stand up off of the closed toilet for this shit. I had never in my life had a woman I cared about talk to me like this. I was beside my damn self.

"You're the only muthafucka on the phone, right? Or am I on

three-way with you and another one of your bitches?"

"Aye, in a minute I'm gonna find yo' ass and fuck you up. You're fucking with the wrong—hello?" I pulled the phone away to see she'd hung up on my ass. "Did this bitch really…?"

I went ahead and got into the shower, washed off quickly, and then brushed my teeth. I then put my same clothes back on, and left out to go see if Chiina was up in the strip club portion of Palace.

When I got there, the shit was packed the fuck out, line around the damn corner of the building, and muthafuckas looking like a can of Vienna sausages on the inside.

I entered through the back, and then went down into the strip club area before heading towards the back where the ladies were.

"Aye, is Chiina here?" I barked over the locker room.

"No, she called in sick today," one chick with fire red hair responded to me.

"Fuck!"

"Why? I can help you the same way she helps you," she added.

Usually I would have been down, especially seeing how fat her pussy was in them short ass spandex shorts, but I wasn't interested right now. All I wanted to do was make Chiina forgive me and agree to fuck with me again.

Instead of responding, I just continued down the long hallway, leading to the floor of the strip club. When I was about to step foot on the floor, someone blocked my way… that someone was Marie, Billz' wife. She was looking good as hell in some tan one-piece shit, and I saw she didn't have any panties on because the lips of her pussy were on full display.

"Long time no see, Tru."

"Ain't you married?"

"Yeah, so? Me being taken ain't never been a problem before, so don't act like it's one now, baby."

"I'm not, but I just thought after that nigga gave you his last name you would get some act right."

"And I did, but I still have a taste for you on occasions."

"Anton too?" I raised a brow, staring down at her cleavage. Got damn this bitch was bad, especially when she wasn't running her fucking mouth.

"I fucked him one damn time, and the dick was aight, but nothing like yours."

Taking her hand into mine, I pulled her inside of the unisex bathroom, locking the door. She already knew what was up, because as soon as I started unbuckling my pants she was on her knees, tongue out like a thirsty dog.

"Damn," I exhaled when her wet mouth wrapped around my dick.

I had to close my eyes because it was feeling good as fuck. Palming the back of her head, I began humping her face feverishly, pounding her tonsils. Any other bitch would be gagging like crazy, but Marie was a professional hoe. Bitch could 'bout suck two dicks at one time. I wouldn't know though because I ain't into that train shit. It was kind of gay if you ask me.

"Oh fuck!"

My breathing became shallow as she used her jaws of fucking life on me. She was damn near slurping the nut up of out my dick like she was drinking a milkshake or something. Before I knew it, I was nutting all in her sexy mouth, and she was taking it down like a baby did a damn bottle. I stuffed myself back into my boxers as she rose to her feet.

"I can't get no dick?" she frowned.

"Man," I sucked my teeth and looked off. "Bend over the sink." I hadn't planned on fucking her, but I changed my mind.

Before we could even walk over to it, the door was broken off of the hinges by some buff ass nigga. I was about to get in his ass, but Billz walked in behind him, holding a .45.

"William!" Marie shrieked.

How did this nigga even get into Palace?

POP! POP! POP! POP!

The bullets tore through my body as screams came from every damn where. The whole club was in a panic as I dropped to the floor bleeding out. Scott came running in after Billz, Marie, and his bodyguard had bolted out. I could hear Cara's voice as she called 911 for me, just before I completely blacked out.

I was always told my dick would get me into trouble, but damn…

***

Around 9am that morning…

Opening my eyes, I could see the bright lights of the hospital. I remember slipping in and out of consciousness when I was being wheeled in, and when they brought me back from surgery. My body felt sore, and it almost felt like I was paralyzed. When I looked to my left, I saw Oden and Chiina, which prompted me to try and sit up.

"Relax, man. You want some water or something?" Oden offered.

I nodded and waved him over to me. When he got there, I asked lowly, "Where is P?"

"She had some work event in New York. She said you knew about it and she couldn't miss it. Do you remember her telling you?"

"Yeah," I replied, slightly bummed.

When Oden left the room, my eyes landed on Chiina. She was wearing some black tights and a black top with no straps that showed her stomach. Her hair was in a ball at the nape of her neck, and she had them big ass gold earrings hanging from her ear. Her skin was glowing, but I don't think it was because of the pregnancy, because her skin always beamed like that. She looked beautiful as usual, and I missed her.

"I only came to make sure you were okay," she neared my bed.

"Thank God I am. How are you?" I grabbed her small hand.

"I'm okay, Truman." She took her hand from mine.

"Chiina, I miss you, baby. I love you. I've been going crazy not talking to you. I know I shouldn't have left after the baby news, but I

104

couldn't deal."

"And what am I supposed to say to that?"

"That you forgive me," I grinned but her face was stale, unenthused.

"No. I'm tired of dealing with you and your female addiction. I deserve better than what you're willing to offer me. I'm smart, I have ambition, and I'm pretty easy on the eyes. I can get a man that's not gonna lie to me, and one that is gonna respect me as his woman, and as a woman period. You have no respect for the female specie, which is why you do what you do. Pilar is good for you because she's willing to deal with your immature ass ways. I may be only twenty, but I don't have time for it, especially not when I'm about to be a mother."

"So what, you're just gonna raise my fucking baby alone?" I felt myself getting angry. I didn't like this newfound woman she was becoming.

"No, we don't have to be together for you to be a father, Truman. If you want to help me with your baby, I will allow it, but I won't be with you."

"What will make you be with me?"

I couldn't believe I was asking this shit. However, I was desperate, and I wanted Chiina more than I thought I did. Somehow, Pilar had become the least of my worries, and I didn't understand why.

"If I were to decide to give you another chance, which I probably won't, you would have to prove to me that you can be with me and only me. Prove that you can love one woman, and make her feel like no other female matters to you. If you could do that, which I don't even think you can, I would consider us being together."

Once she said her piece, she grabbed her purse and left the room. Oden walked in as she walked out.

"How are you faithful to Khyle?" I asked him once he set the water pitcher next to me.

"What, nigga?" he chuckled a little as he sat down after handing me a cup of the water.

"How are you able to only be with one woman? Chiina said I need to be able to be faithful in order to get her back, but I don't know how to do that shit, O. I love pussy way too much, and I like having different kinds."

"It's not a science, Tru. You have to want to be faithful to do it. I mean I'm a man too, so I love pussy just as much, but I love Khyle more. I'm not gonna lose a woman I love over one night with some random hoe. Is that hoe gonna be there when you're sick, when you need someone to talk to, when you want your head rubbed while you complain about life, or if you happen to lose everything you've worked for? Hell nah she's not. Most of these bitches only fuck with us because we have money, and our name means something when brought up."

"You right."

"And Chiina? I thought you loved Pilar, nigga."

"I do, I do love Pilar. But it's something about Chiina and the way she's been acting towards me lately that has me feeling differently."

"She ain't a doormat, that's why."

"Huh? I love doormat bitches," I joked, and we laughed heartily in unison.

"To fuck yeah, but by your side, you want a woman who is gonna keep your ass in line. That's why you're feeling her. Only weak niggas fuck with weak bitches the long way."

"Makes no sense though. You should hear the way she's been talking to me. If I were a different type of nigga, I would have choked her ass up a wall."

"Yeah, she got yo' ass. I always told you that Pilar was too soft for a nigga like you. I mean that was before she put a cap in my ass, but still. Niggas like us need to be tamed, and it ain't gon' happen with a meek female."

I nodded in agreement as I let his information sink in. Was I really falling for Chiina because she was bossing up on my ass? I needed to get my shit together.

CHAPTER FOUR

Oden

That afternoon…

"I'm gonna wait until you get here to tell them," Khyle said. I had her on speakerphone while I got dressed.

"That's fine. Just a few more days, baby, and I will be out there. I have to tie up a few loose ends before I can leave."

"I know." Her voice was low. "You're going to lunch today?"

"Yeah, I am. Don't worry about it. We're just gonna eat, chat, and then go our separate ways. She already knows about you and everything. Soon as she stepped foot in my spot I showed her your picture."

"She was in your house?"

Fuck.

"Well, when I got here she was already outside waiting for me, Khyle. It's not like I picked her up and brought her back here or anything."

"Just making sure. You tend to not understand unspoken

boundaries."

I just laughed as I buttoned up my burgundy quarter sleeved top. After I fastened my watch and chain, I grabbed my phone from the dresser.

"Aight, baby, I'm about to go okay?"

"Okay, and don't let her touch your hair." I could hear that she was smiling. "I'm serious, Oden."

"I know, and I won't. We won't touch at all. I mean nothing more than some head, but I will let you know how it goes."

"Oden!"

"I'm kidding." We laughed together. "I love you, Khyle."

"I love you too."

I spritzed my cologne on, and then grabbed my keys and left. Hopping into my Porsche, I sped out, headed to Naomi's hotel room, inside of the Monte Carlo. I called her when I was near, so when I pulled up to where valet was, she was already standing outside.

"Damn," I sucked my teeth at how good she looked, before getting out of the car.

Why couldn't her ass wear some sweats and a big t-shirt? Nah, instead, she was rocking some short ass shorts that had her pussy on full display damn near. Her shirt was short as fuck, showing off her flat stomach, and her golden locks were hanging down, sweeping the top of her fat ass. My dick seemed to get harder and harder as she switched towards me, looking thicker than a fucking Snicker.

"Hey," I smiled as I opened my passenger door for her.

"Thanks, babe." She hugged me, and then tilted her head back to smile up at me.

"Aight, I see you, Oden!" some random hollered, making Naomi giggle.

"Fuck out of here," I mumbled to myself as I closed the door and then rounded the back of my car to get in on my side.

"Damn daddy, you're still out here dressing to impress, huh? That's what I've always loved about you, you stayed clean even when dressed down," Naomi commented, brushing her small hand down the front of my chest. "And feeling like steel. I see you still work out."

I just nodded as I pulled out onto Las Vegas Boulevard.

"Ya man didn't dress like this?"

"He did, but he didn't know how to switch it up like you and wear a three-piece suit. I feel like I compare everyone to you." She touched my chin hairs but I moved my face, making her chuckle. "Sorry, I forgot you had a little girlfriend."

"Where do you want to eat?"

"Let's go to Hexx Kitchen. I heard it's pretty good. I don't remember that being here when I lived in Vegas."

"I think it was something else when you lived here."

Since Hexx was right down the street, on the strip, I made it there in less than a minute; I was already headed that way anyhow. I parked my car with the Paris Hotel valet, and then helped Naomi out of the car. It was a nice ass day, not too hot, with the sun shining brightly. It was one of those days where you just knew it would be a good ass one.

"I feel weird walking next to you and not being able to hold your hand. It's like I need to find something to do with my hands," Naomi said as we walked alongside the restaurant before making it to the entrance.

I didn't respond because I didn't care and I didn't have shit to say to that.

We were seated immediately since it was the middle of the week, and the Vegas vacationers weren't here. The waitress gave us some ice waters, took our alcoholic drink orders, and then left to give us time to look over the food menu.

"I bet you I can guess what you're gonna order," Naomi smiled. She was fucking beautiful.

"Okay, what?"

"The pasta; the scampi."

"You right," I nodded slowly as we both laughed.

"Of course I am. I know you. I remember everything about you, Oden. I never stopped thinking about you, ever."

"Is that why you got married four months after we broke up?" I sipped my water.

"Someone is still salty I see. And no, I married him because he wanted me and you didn't. Well at least that's what you told me."

"I mean, if we're being honest here—"

"Sorry to interrupt, sir, but are you guys ready to order yet?" the waitress appeared.

"Yeah, I will have the filet mignon, medium please," Naomi

ordered. "Oh, and he'll have the scampi."

"Great choices. That will be out fairly shortly."

"Now, what were you saying before she came over babe?" Naomi sipped the 18-dollar glass of champagne she'd ordered.

"Don't order for me, Naomi."

She was smiling until she saw that I wasn't returning the same gesture.

"I'm sorry, I was just trying to be quick so we could get back to our conversation, that's all. I didn't mean it in anyway."

"You know better."

"I do, which is why I'm sorry. Can you forgive me and finish what you were saying? You were talking about not wanting me, which is why I'd gotten married."

"I was just gonna say that I didn't want to be in a relationship with you, but I still found it odd that you got married so soon. A new relationship is one thing, but a marriage?"

"Kenneth got a good job in Durango, so he asked me to move to Colorado with him. I told him the only way I would go is if I were his wife, so he asked me. I knew I couldn't be with you, so I accepted."

"No need to explain yourself."

"Yeah, but I feel like if I do, maybe you will forgive me."

"Ain't really nothing I need to forgive you for, Naomi. I broke up with you, so what you did after that wasn't any of my concern. I was simply expressing to you, that for you to still be thinking about me, it was odd for you to get married."

"So let me ask you, if I hadn't have left, do you think we would have gotten back together?"

"Can't say," I shrugged.

"Fair enough," she chuckled. "Do you still think about me? Like, do you miss the time we had together? Do you regret breaking up with me?"

"I think about you, but only when a certain memory crosses my mind. I don't necessarily miss the time we had together. I mean, when we first broke up, a little, yeah, but now, not at all. I don't even think about it. And do I regret breaking up with you? No. At that time I wasn't happy with you, and now I'm with somebody that is more befitting in my opinion."

"Why weren't you happy with me?" her brows dipped and her head cocked.

"You know why, Naomi. You were breathing down my neck every day about women that I wasn't even fucking with."

"Can you blame me? Look at you. Any woman would act like that in a relationship with you, Oden, get used to it."

"Not Khyle."

"She's an 18-year-old girl, Oden. She doesn't know any better."

"She doesn't know any better, yet you were the one accusing me of shit I didn't do? She's smart enough to know that I love her genuinely, and would never step outside of what we have. The only person that doesn't know any better, or didn't know any better was you. If you knew better you'd do better which wasn't the case, right?"

"You love her?"

"Yeah, I do."

"So that's it, you're off the market now?"

"Yeah, Naomi. Fuck shorty, what's your problem?" I grinned.

"Nothing. It's just when we were together you made it seem like I would be the only woman to ever have your heart."

"That's because I thought you were someone that you weren't."

"Here we are," the waitress beamed, setting our plates down in front of us. Naomi didn't acknowledge her, she just kept her eyes on me with a sad expression.

We ate our food in silence because I guess she was angry with me. I didn't really know what to say to her, and I wasn't about to coddle a bitch that wasn't mine. Yeah I cared for Naomi, meaning I didn't want her to die or anything, but the only woman I was gonna focus on making feel good was Khyle Luke.

I paid the bill once we were done, and then drove her back to her hotel.

"Come up for a little bit, Oden."

"Naomi—"

"I'm probably not gonna even see you again for a while since I'm gonna be busy condo hunting. Please, just for a little bit."

"Okay, 20 minutes."

"That's fine, just 20 minutes."

"Only 20, Naomi."

"Alright!" she giggled as we both exited my car. I waved the valet attendant over, and took the retrieval ticket he gave me.

Naomi and I made it up to her room, and as soon as she got in, she removed her heels and went into the bathroom.

I scanned the area, walking in slowly, before finally sitting down on the edge of the bed. Realizing that this was a bad spot, I hopped up and sat in the chair instead to wait. About 10 minutes went by, meaning I only had about 10 left, before she emerged from the bathroom naked as the day she was born. How did I fall for this shit?

"Wait, tell me you don't love me and that you never want to be with me again, and I won't bother you." She moved closer to me, and my dick seemed to get harder with each step she took.

"Naomi, I don't love you and I don't want to be with you. I have a girlfriend, shorty. I love her, I really do," I pleaded, looking up into her eyes as she stood over me. If I looked anywhere else I may bend her ass over and fuck.

She just stared down into my face, before walking to the bathroom and grabbing a robe. She covered herself as I stood up and neared her. Kissing her forehead gently, I hugged her lightly and then left.

Hopefully that would be the last time she embarrassed herself for me.

CHAPTER FOUR

Bella

Tonight, my distant homegirl, Allegra and I were gonna go out. I call her distant because we weren't best friends or anything, but we hung out occasionally. I didn't have many friends in high school because girls were jealous that I was with Santino. Then when we broke up, no one really wanted to be cool with me because they thought I was a slut or something. Anyway, Allegra had lived on my street since I was 12 years old, so we hung out when we could. We went to different schools, so she mostly chilled with her school friends.

Her older brother, Alondro, was throwing a party tonight because he was going off to the Navy. Since I'd been away from UNLV and wouldn't be back for a month, I was craving some sort of turn up. I knew Santino wouldn't take me to a party because he hated for niggas to be in my face, and with his temper, it was best he didn't witness something like that.

"So Khyle and Tasmine are your best friends?" Allegra quizzed as she drove towards her brother's home.

"Yeah."

"You just met them, Bella. How is it possible that they're your best friends?"

"Just like with romantic relationships sometimes, it may not take long for you to realize you and another person mesh well together."

"I bet you haven't even talked to them since you've been back."

"Actually I have, Allegra. We text one another all day in group message, and FaceTime a lot too. We're thinking of getting an apartment together when I go back to Vegas."

We had planned to get an apartment, but Khyle found out she was pregnant, so we decided to hold off for now. Allegra didn't need to know that though.

"How would y'all pay for that?"

"Our parents agreed to pay our share of the rent."

That part was true too. Our parents liked the idea of us having our own space, away from our co-ed dorm. I think my father felt like boys could just walk into our rooms anytime that they wanted, so he was happy to get me away from that. And I didn't bother telling him that wasn't the case either.

"Oh," she raised both of her brows and sighed.

"Why you wanted to be my best friend?"

"Girl, bye! I was just making sure you weren't out there in Vegas being blind to fake bitches. I ain't trying to be anybody's best friend. It don't mean shit anyway."

I shrugged it off and just looked out the window for the rest of the ride. She had her music blasting, so we swayed a little, singing along until we got there. A gang of people were standing outside of Alondro's place smoking, drinking, and playing cards in the yard. This shit was so ghetto, but I think that's what I needed right now; a good ghetto ass party that could tide me over until I got back to school.

All my ladies in the club with their own money. Now grab your girls and tell 'em he ain't getting shit from me…

You could hear "Nothing" by Mase and Eric Bellinger playing from inside of the house. The niggas playing cards in the front were eyeing Allegra and I like we were big ass pieces of meat as we walked by, and I was kind of scared to make eye contact with them.

"Damn, baby, I ain't seen you around Alondro's before," one reached for my hand, but I coolly moved it away. He looked dirty as fuck, and his breath was one of an old man.

Allegra and I continued into the house, swaying to the music and just checking out the scene. This was the first house party I'd been to where the lights were on and bright as fuck. Usually back at school, it's somewhat dark, with only blue, yellow, purple, or red lights going everywhere. But not here, nope, you could see every damn thing, even the shit you didn't want to see.

"Want a drink?" Allegra offered.

"No, I have my own." I reached into my purse to pull out this drink I'd gotten from the store. Santino told me about it, and said just one would have me drunk. I didn't believe his ass, but after we had one together one night and I damn near passed out, I knew I'd found my new favorite drink.

"Wait, hold up, ain't that your old nigga?" Allegra tapped on my arm as she sipped the punch she'd gotten from the bowl. I didn't understand how she could trust it, but then again, this was her brother's shit.

I followed her pointer finger to figure out what the hell she was talking about, and saw Dean smiling all in some bitch's face who was sitting in his lap. I wasn't jealous or anything, I was just a little perplexed. He'd been begging me all summer so far to give us another chance, but he and old girl looked pretty cozy to me. She didn't seem like someone he'd just met at this party, but who knows? I was gonna find out though.

"Where are we going?" Allegra shrieked as I tugged her ass with me. I wasn't about to go alone and look dumb.

"Hey, Dean." I stopped right in front of the ugly ass couch they were sitting on.

"Be-Bella," his eyes opened wide which alarmed me. Now I really wanted to know who this bitch was.

"Dean, who is this?" the girl frowned, and when she turned her body to face me I saw a small belly poking through her shirt.

"Hi, I'm Bella. Dean and I *just* broke up some months back. You are?" I grinned, as Allegra's dumb ass laughed.

"Excuse me? Dean, what the hell is she talking about?" she looked at him, then back up at me. "Dean and I have been together since last September!"

"Oh, only a month after I left to go to school in Vegas, huh Dean?" I smacked him upside the head.

"Ah! Bella, baby, let me explain. This shit with her went too far," he begged, while the dumb girl stayed put in his lap. If she opened her mouth any wider, her jaw would part from her face completely.

"Went too far?" the girl finally spoke up.

"Trish, calm down—"

"No, I'm happy for you and the new baby coming, Dean."

"Baby!" Trish barked. I guess she was just fat around the stomach. Her frame was small everywhere else, so it was an honest mistake on my part.

"Oh shit, this bitch is just fat," Allegra instigated. I couldn't help but to laugh because I for real thought she was pregnant.

"Ah!"

Dean screamed as I emptied my drink over his head completely.

"Have a nice life, bitch ass nigga. Allegra, can you please drop me off at Santino's?" I started off and she was right behind me.

"Bella!" Dean called after me.

"What the fuck are you calling her for?" I heard Trisha grit from afar, before Dean started to explain himself.

"What about his parents?" Allegra inquired, referring to Santino.

"They're not home. They traveled up to Washington State to design some big wig's house. Who gives a fuck, just take me, please?"

"Aight."

Seeing Dean tonight was bittersweet for me, but mostly sweet. It bothered me to know that he'd been cheating on me damn near ever since I went away to school, but I was no angel either. On the flip side, it was sweet as fuck because I no longer felt bad about leaving him behind for Santino, and I was actually kind of happy to see he had someone. Hopefully, now that I knew about her, he would stop chasing me and let me be happy with Santino.

When Allegra pulled up to Santino's, I handed her some gas money and then blocked Dean in my phone because he kept texting me. I waited for Santino to let me know he was coming outside, and then I exited the car.

"Thanks, Ally," I said.

"Hey Santino!" she stuck her arm out of the window to wave to my nigga. He was so sexy with the way he walked out of his house in gray basketball shorts, socks, slides, and no shirt.

"What's good?" he responded before placing his hand on the small of my back and kissing me on the lips.

"Guess who I saw tonight?" I giggled because he scooped me up bridal style to carry me up his driveway and into his home.

"Who?"

He carried me to the big backyard where the heated pool was, overlooking the city. His parents' house was really the shit.

"Dean."

"Oh." He began helping me out of my clothes. I guess we were gonna go for a naked swim like we used to back in high school.

"He had some girl in his lap. He's been with her since September of last year. I thought she was pregnant, and she wasn't so she got mad."

"So does this mean that I will never have to hear about that nigga again?" He stared down at me as he stepped out of his bottoms, socks, and shoes.

"I don't talk about Dean a lot."

"I know. I wouldn't let you. But I don't want you talking about him at all. You know I get jealous. I'm stingy with you, baby." He lowered his voice on the last part and pecked my lips.

"I'm stingy with you too."

We stood there kissing for a little bit, nice and slowly. It wasn't rushed at all, just romantic. We were allowing each other to really feel one another's lips. Finally we pulled away, and got down into the heated pool water.

"When you gonna marry me?" he asked, circling me in the pool.

"Whenever you ask me."

He nodded and kissed my collarbone as I cupped the back his head.

"Be ready," he winked.

CHAPTER FIVE

Anton

$\mathcal{E}$ver since that afternoon in the hotel room, Tasmine hadn't said shit to me. I tried calling her, texting her, dropping by her parents' home and everything, but she wouldn't even acknowledge me. I knew I'd fucked up but damn, did she have to go this hard? She expressed her loved for me already, so it couldn't be this easy to just break up.

Eventually I had to leave Kentucky and come back home to Las Vegas. I'd been here two days, and Tasmine still hadn't hit me up. She didn't even tell me to have a safe flight.

Me: *Talk to me, Tas.*

When I saw she'd finally responded, I almost crashed my car.

Tasmine: *How much do I owe you for my plane ticket to Vegas in two weeks? I'm not coming but I want to pay you back.*

Me: *Just come, Tasmine.*

Tasmine: *Tell me how much or don't get your money.*

Me: *You're good.*

No response after that of course.

Speaking of us breaking up, I was currently on my way over to Violet's house to spend time with my son. I needed to change my mood really quickly so that I could focus on him and nothing else. I didn't want to have Tasmine on my mind when I was supposed to be paying attention to my kid.

My phone buzzed in my hand at the red light, and I instantly looked down at it hoping it was Tasmine. When I saw it was just my baby's mother, I sucked my teeth.

Violet: Hey can you get some more diapers, onesies, bibs, a few blankets, new bottles, and some caps?

Damn!

Me: Yeah.

I stopped at Target to get the shit Violet asked me to, and then went straight over. Before getting out of the car, I tried calling Tasmine, and to my surprise she picked up.

"What, Tony? Fuck!" she shouted. I wasn't a bitch by any means, but her tone low-key hurt a nigga's feelings.

"Just promise me when you come to Vegas we can talk. No—promise you'll use the plane ticket and come out here in two weeks, baby."

"Why?"

"Besides the fact that I want to see you, we need to talk. I know you're mad about me keeping a secret, but I want a chance to explain myself. I had good reasoning for doing what I did, and I want you to see that. I can't do it over the phone."

"If you think fucking me is gonna solve it, think again, Anton Gregory Nickerson."

I chuckled lightly at her, but not too loudly because I didn't want her to think I was taking this shit for a joke.

"No, I don't. I just want to be able to talk to you in person. And then when you forgive me because you understand, we can live it up until school starts."

"I will think about it."

Click.

She hung up.

I couldn't do shit but laugh at how mean her otherwise nice ass was. That shit kind of turned me on to be honest.

I grabbed all the bags from Target and got out of the car, slipping my phone into my pocket. When I got to Violet's door, I knocked and just waited patiently. She answered in no time, smiling widely at me like she always did. It did feel good to have a better relationship with her, because I felt kind of bad about my initial reaction to the paternity test.

"Thank you so much, Tony. I wouldn't have asked if he really didn't need it."

"No need to thank me, Violet. I'm his father so this is something I should be doing anyway, you know?"

"True. Are you hungry? I'm making baked chicken wings."

"Yeah sure, I can eat."

Picking my son up, I kissed his small cheek and laid him back in my arms. He gripped my thumb in his hand as he made small noises. I could feel myself getting attached to him more and more, and that shit was definitely softening me up.

I would be lying if I said I didn't like the idea of having a child. The circumstance wasn't preferred, but he was here, he was mine, and I loved him. I would do anything for him.

"I see you've gotten more comfortable," Violet returned and sat on the other end of the couch, watching us with a smile.

"It's time for him to eat if you don't mind." She reached her hands out for him, and after a few short seconds I passed him over to her.

"Yeah… go 'head."

She'd breastfed in front of me so many times that I was used to it by now, so I didn't feel the need to find something to do with my eyes.

"So what's wrong with you, Tony? You seem so quiet these days."

"I do?"

"Yeah. Before when you came over, your energy was different. Now you seem to be a little bit glum."

"I'm fine, everything is gravy."

"You sure?"

"Very."

"What did your girlfriend say about Athen being your baby?"

"It's complicated, Violet, that's all I'm gonna say," I sighed, falling back against the couch. "Just complicated."

"So she's not with the idea of you having a baby with someone that's not her?"

"No, no, it's the way I went about it. I kept it to myself for a little bit and she found out before I could tell her."

"You kept him a secret?"

"Sounds shitty as fuck, I know, but that wasn't my intention at all, Violet. I felt like I just needed some time to adjust to the shit myself before I told her, you know? But that wasn't the right move."

"You have to do what's best for you, Tony. If you weren't ready then she should be able to understand that, especially if she loves you."

"So I'm not a complete asshole?"

"No. I think because she's so young she probably doesn't understand some things. But that's none of my business."

"She's pretty mature for her age."

"I guess."

Once Violet got Athen to sleep, she and I sat in the kitchen to have dinner. The conversation was nice, and I'd realized that I never took the time to converse with her when we first met. She was smart as fuck, beautiful, and an all around good catch. If my heart wasn't already with Tasmine, I might have wanted to give us a try.

"This was okay, right?" Violet grinned as she led me to her front door. Time had flown by and it was now nighttime.

"Yeah, it was. It's important for us to get along." I hugged her lightly, and we made eye contact for a little bit when I pulled back. "Oh, almost forgot." I rushed to Athen and kissed his small cheeks as Violet giggled.

"See you later, baby daddy."

I left out of Violet's spot, and as I approached my car I heard screeching tires.

"Punk ass nigga!"

CRASH!

A brick flew right through the front windshield of my car, and when I looked at the other vehicle speeding by, I saw Amethyst hanging out of the passenger window throwing up her middle fingers.

"It's a wrap for you!" I shouted, perplexed by my fucking shattered window on my Lamborghini.

"Fuck you, you bitch ass niggaaaaaaa!" she screamed as the driver peeled down the street with her sticking out.

I swear, if it wasn't one bitch it was a fucking 'nother. All the women in my life seemed to only want to give me a hard time. Even my fucking mother was stressing me out, because I knew her ass was back on drugs. I guess the fact that she had HIV already didn't matter to her junkie ass.

"Fuck!" I yelled loudly as I locked my fingers on the top of my head. "Calm down, Anton," I mumbled to myself.

Life just couldn't seem to stay afloat.

CHAPTER FIVE

Shayne

"Don't take too long, Shayne. We have to be at the airport in two fucking hours, aight shawty?" Lloyd looked down at me with his fine ass.

"Yeah, I know. Chill."

I left out to get into my car, and then sped off to my destination.

Today, Lloyd and I were going to his hometown, Birmingham, Alabama, because he wanted me to meet his people and shit. I was a little bit nervous, which was rare for me, but I think it was because I loved him and I wanted them to like me. He said his family meant a lot to him, so I knew shit wouldn't work too well between us if they didn't fuck with me. I was gonna be on my best behavior, and since Lloyd said they didn't know much about me other than the good shit, I felt I should be cool.

Right now, I had to run out and get a few toiletries, you know travel-sized stuff, so that I would be fully prepared while away for four damn days in the country. I heard they didn't have curbs out there, which I found to be odd as fuck.

I walked down the aisle at CVS, looking for the shit I needed, and since I wasn't paying attention, I bumped into someone. Picking my head up, I realized it was Alanna's ass. I had damn near forgotten about her because she'd been missing for so damn long.

"Well, look who it is," I smirked, folding my arms across my breasts.

"When you're done, I wanna talk to you." She bumped my shoulder with hers, and proceeded down the aisle until she was outside.

"Bitch," I grumbled.

I finished shopping, while wondering what the hell Alanna needed to talk to me about. Shit, I needed to talk to her come to think of it. Her old bitch ass nigga tried to push up on me, and she needed to check his ass for it, or I would have my man do it. The only reason Lloyd hadn't killed Earl Jr.'s ass was because I begged him not to, and convinced him that it wasn't a good idea to murk a public figure.

Walking outside with my bags, I spotted Alanna standing there with her face balled up.

"Talk," I said, hitting the alarm on my Range Rover and continuing to it so I could put my bags up. Alanna was right behind me, but hadn't said a word.

"Why did you try to fuck Earl?" she questioned as soon as I closed my trunk.

I immediately burst into laughter because this shit was for real a damn comedy. I mean, I knew I didn't have the best track record when it came to loyalty, but I would never fuck that nigga. Not necessarily because he was the love of her pitiful life, but because he was so whack. Good looks and money could only get you so far with Shayne Luke; you needed to have swag and have some personality. Earl Jr. was a weak ass nigga, and I would never open my legs for him.

"Boo, your man popped up at my old apartment that I used to share with Pierce trying to fuck. Nigga would have raped me if I hadn't clocked his ass over the head."

"Wow, because he told me that you called him over there, making him think you wanted to squash shit but really you wanted him to fuck you."

"Alanna, do you hear yourself? How would I call him? I don't have his fucking number. And do you think I'd wanna squash shit with him?"

"No, but I think you're a hating ass hoe who is so jealous of me that you would fuck the man I love to hurt me." Her mouth was all twisted up, as if she were about to move something. Her ass knew better though. I would fuck her ass up in under 10 seconds.

"Alanna, I have a man that I love and that loves me. I ain't worried about you, or your man that ain't even really your fucking man. He has a fiancée, Alanna Benson! Wake the fuck up and smell the damn coffee!"

"Mind your fucking business you slut!" she shoved me backwards, and that's when shit hit the fan.

Punching her right between the eyes, I sent her stumbling backwards, clutching her face. I was about to go in on her ass, but I suddenly remembered this was just Alanna. She wasn't a fighter at all, hell, she was barely confrontational. She was a sad woman who didn't know how to stand up for herself whether it was against her friends or the man she loved. The urge to drag her ass all around this parking lot had abruptly vanished.

"I'm sorry, Alanna," I spoke lowly as I neared her, trying to help her with her bleeding nose. I felt guilty for punching her so hard, when all she did was push me.

"Move, Shayne!" she cried, waving me off.

"Alanna, I'm sorry I hit you, but you can't keep doing this to yourself! There is someone out there for you that will treat you better than Earl Jr."

"You think so?" she inquired and I nodded. "Even though you think I'm meek and without pride?"

"I know I was harsh, but it's true, Lana. No man is gonna treat you right if you don't demand that from him. I mean, look how Oden treated me? It was because I let him disrespect me. You have to exude confidence for him to treat you right."

"Thanks," she whispered and started off. I grabbed her arm and pulled her into a hug because I did in fact miss her.

When I let her go, she turned around to leave. I watched her for a little bit, and then got into my car to head home. I hoped to God that I'd finally gotten through to her.

***

Birmingham, Alabama…

"Why the hell are there so many damn trees and shit? I feel like I'm in a forest!" I turned my lip up as Lloyd and I walked through 100 yards of grass it seemed.

His mother had a pretty big home in the middle of fucking nowhere, and there were big ass trees on each side of the house. Alabama was nothing like Vegas or Los Angeles. It was so quiet, and there seemed to be flying bugs of all kind every damn where. But, I was not gonna complain. This place birthed the man that I'd fallen in love with, so it couldn't be all that bad.

"I'm used to it, but now that you mention it, there are way more trees and grass than on the west, huh?"

"Damn right."

Before we could even make it up the rusty red colored walkway of his mother's home, she was bursting through the netted screen door with a smile on her face. She was very fair skinned, and had long curly hair that was 60% gray. I knew she was his mother because he looked just like her, only he was dark skinned.

"Baby!" she rushed to him and hugged his body. She was no bigger than a minute, and pretty skinny too.

Not knowing what to say or do, I just stood there smiling a little, waiting for what would happen next. After pulling Lloyd's face down to hers to kiss his cheeks one million times, they both turned to me.

"Mama, this is Shayne, my girlfriend."

"Shayne, wow," she hugged me tightly, before pulling back and nodding her head approvingly. "She is gorgeous, Lloyd. Are you a model?" her brows dipped.

"Oh, umm, no, no, I'm not a model. I dance, in the umm, Vegas shows. And it's nice to meet you, Mrs. Gardener."

"Call me Marta, or mom if you'd like. But a dancer? No wonder you have that cute little body. It's looking perfect for making my grandchildren."

"Ma, come on, man," Lloyd groaned as she and I shared a laugh.

"Well, come on in and get settled because dinner is almost ready. I made neck bones just for you, Lloyd."

"Thanks," he sighed.

"Is that all your hair?" his mom whispered to me while touching it. I laughed while shaking my head 'yes' as we entered the home.

From looking at the outside of the house, I thought the inside would be somewhat shoddy, but boy was I wrong. It was so beautiful, with pristine brown laminate flooring, and pure white furniture. It was obvious his mother loved the clean look, because most, if not every piece in the home was white. I didn't see a stain anywhere either. The kitchen was beautiful too, from what I could see as I passed, with granite countertops, and beautiful, fresh white tile.

"Your mother's house is beautiful, honey," I commented as Lloyd and I entered his old bedroom.

The room had been redone since he moved out years ago, and it was obvious. Everything was white except for the dressers and the nightstands. The comforter on the bed was white, with a yellow sham thrown over the bottom. Mrs. Marta had taste, that's for sure.

"Told you they had nice houses out here in Alabama."

"I know. I didn't believe you until now," I smiled, still admiring the bedroom.

"You think you can be quiet tonight while I'm fucking you?" He pulled me into him and started to kiss on my neck.

"If we only do missionary," I giggled at the feeling of his soft lips on me.

"I don't know about that, maybe."

"Come eat!" his mother banged on the door, startling us.

Lloyd and I shared a couple kisses before he opened the bedroom door for me so that we could go eat. It was early for dinner in my opinion, 6pm, but Lloyd said they'd eaten dinner at that time all his life.

When I got into the dining room, my stomach immediately began growling at all the wonderful ass smells in the kitchen. The middle of the table was filled with different kinds of foods that you only had for Thanksgiving and Christmas dinner. And lately, I'd been eating lighter because I had to stay in shape for work, so you could imagine my excitement at seeing all of this.

"Wow, son," Mr. Gardener eyed me, licking his lips until his wife elbowed him in the ribcage. He was tall, very dark and very handsome like his son.

"Okay," I sighed, sitting down next to Lloyd. This dinner was gonna be interesting.

CHAPTER FIVE

Lloyd Gardener

That night…

"Mmmm, ah!" Shayne hollered out as I pounded into her from the back in the shower.

We chose to do it in here because I knew her loud ass would wake my parents up, and I didn't feel like having to explain to my mom that I was grown and could fuck when I wanted to. In a black home, being an adult didn't mean a damn thing until you moved out and got your own shit. So even though I was just visiting, I still had to abide by parents' rules if I was gonna sleep here.

"Damn, you stay wet as fuck," I growled, still slamming into her.

Shayne had the best pussy I had ever encountered, and that was the honest to God truth. It wasn't because she was my girl either. The first time I fucked her, I only planned to make her a fuck buddy, because I knew what type of girl she was. However, what she had between her legs was way too good for me not to want to lock it down.

Between me and you, I was in love with her, but I didn't feel comfortable telling her that shit yet. Her past, meaning fucking Oden, still bothered me, and a part of me wanted to hurt her because of it.

"Tell me it's my pussy, Shayne."

"It's your pussy, baby!"

"My name ain't baby," I hissed as I thrust into her, pulverizing her tight, wet, middle.

"I-it's your pussy, Lloyd!" Her hand slid down the shower wall as a high-pitched moan burst through her sexy lips.

Gripping a handful of her long ass hair, I pummeled into her until I was cumming all inside of her body. I knew I should have been strapping up, but once I felt it raw I couldn't stop.

Standing up and turning around, she stood on her tiptoes and draped her arms around my shoulders to hug and kiss me.

"I love you Lloyd Gardener," she whispered against my lips before pecking me again.

My hands moved up and down her sexy, slippery back as I indulged in her perfect mouth. Kissing Shayne did something to a nigga, had me feeling shit I'd never felt before, and that was how I knew that I loved her. I'd been with plenty of women in my day, a few girlfriends here and there, but none of them had my nose wide open like shawty right here. A little bit of me hated that she had such a trashy ass track record because she was better than that.

"I know," I responded instead of telling her how I really felt.

I could see in the way she looked at me that my reply kind of hurt her feelings. She'd told me she loved me three times already, and either I wouldn't respond or I would say 'I know'.

We washed up for real, and then I dried her body off before doing my own. I sat in the chair in my old room, checking my messages as she spread some sexy smelling lotion on her body. It had to be what she wore all the time, because it was familiar. I wasn't sure what it was, but it was soft, sexy, and sweet.

I'm telling you, everything about my shawty was A1 except the shit she had done. She was fine, smart, had ambition, phenomenal hygiene, and she could be the sweetest girl ever when she wanted to. She played hard, but when it came to me she was soft as pound cake.

"Ready for bed," she smiled, standing to her feet and rubbing the rest of the lotion into her hands.

She had on some top that she told me was a bralette, and silk pink shorts. I examined her body for a few moments, just taking in the perfection of her smooth vanilla skin and tones physique.

"Yeah, let me reply to a few messages."

Hesitating for a minute, she nodded and then peeled the covers back. I felt her watching me, moving her long hair back every now and again.

I shot off a reply to the message I'd been leaving in the shadow for a minute, and then grabbed some boxers before sliding into bed behind Shayne, planting kisses on her supple shoulder.

An hour and a half later she was asleep, so I crawled out of bed and put on a t-shirt, some sweats, socks, and slides, before grabbing my hoodie. I left out to get into the rental I'd booked, and sped off towards

Elodie's house.

Elodie was my girlfriend for a long ass time, and we didn't break up until three months before I moved to Las Vegas to work for Oden. I had love for Elodie but she lacked hustle. She was nothing like Shayne. Shayne would get her money by any means necessary, whereas Elodie would just sit in a corner and cry as her car got repossessed.

When I first met Elodie, she wasn't like that at all. In fact, she was quite the opposite, working three jobs, living in a nice ass house, and driving a fresh Toyota Corolla. If you haven't noticed, I'm attracted to women who have some hustle in them. I'd rather date a stripper that's a go-getter, than a businesswoman with no ambition.

Anyway, when Elodie and I first got together, she had her duckies in a row as my mother would say. But after about a year and a half of being a couple, all she wanted to do was lay up under me, and chill with me. It was to the point where she'd gotten fired from two of her jobs from calling out so much. Eventually, she became this bum bitch that I was no longer attracted to. But because I had love for her and liked fucking her, I kept her around.

"I thought you got to Birmingham earlier," Elodie rolled her eyes when she answered her door.

She had gained some weight for sure, because her stomach was no longer flat. I didn't care though. I wasn't picky like that when it came to women's bodies. As long as she had a pussy between her legs and some titties, she was alright with me. However, Shayne's impeccable ass body was nothing to shake a stick at. Damn, she consumed my mind with her fine ass.

"Had to have dinner and spend time with my parents, Elodie. I mean that *is* who I came to see." I locked the door behind myself.

"So those are the only people you came to see, Lloyd?" her lip trembled, making me want to slap the shit out of her. Luckily for her, hitting women wasn't my thing.

"I really don't want to argue, shit, I don't even want to talk. Right now I wanna fuck, are you cool with that? It's late, I'm tired as hell, and I don't have the energy to debate with you about why I'm just now coming over after 1am."

"Sorry," she whispered sadly.

Elodie stayed on that woe is me bullshit and I hated that. Weak bitches were not my style, which was all the more reason Shayne was perfect for me. She was everything but weak, yet she knew how to bow down to a king when she was supposed to. Elodie, on the other hand, was meek and docile all the damn time.

 Walking up to me, Elodie hugged my body and stared up into my face. I leaned down to kiss on her neck while unhooking her bra. Once it was off, I threw it to the side, and then yanked my hoodie and shirt over my head. She pushed me down onto the couch, and stepped out of her shorts and panties before straddling me. Her hand went down into my jeans after unbuckling them, and for some reason no matter how much she stroked my dick, I couldn't get hard. She finally noticed it, and stopped to look at me.

"What's wrong, Lloyd?"

"I can't, shawty," I sighed, moving her out of my lap and dropping my face into my hands.

"Why not? You don't find me attractive anymore?"

Here we fucking go with the sympathy tour.

"No, I do. Of course I do, what the fuck?" I frowned, picking my head up out of my hands to glance at her stupid ass for a few moments. "I just—"

"What, Lloyd?"

"I'm in a relationship, Elodie, and I love her ass. Fuck!" I shouted, shaking my head and looking off at the wall.

I planned to fuck Elodie to hurt Shayne. I brought her here to meet my parents, but I also wanted to make her feel some type of way about me fucking another bitch while she was down here. Childish as fuck I know, but it seemed like the best way for me to get over her letting Oden smash, and stringing me along while she kept her fiancé in the background.

"Who? Please tell me it's not that bourgeois hoe you've been fucking with back in Las Vegas, Lloyd."

"Watch your mouth, aight? Her name is Shayne, and she ain't no damn bourgeois hoe."

"She's not? She was fucking you while she had a fiancé at home, and you mean to tell me she's not a hoe? She's gonna do the same thing to you, that she did to that nigga." Elodie lit a blunt that was sitting in the ashtray next to her. With it hanging from her lips, she grabbed her panties and shorts, sliding them on.

"Nah, she won't."

"How do you know? Did you get her to sign a contract saying she wouldn't or something?"

"Nah, she just won't. She and I are both different for each other, something neither of us have had and that's why we're in love."

"Ha!" Elodie laughed loudly, making me jump a little. She took a pull and blew out smoke before saying, "Lloyd, that bitch is gonna chew you up and spit you out. That's how they are; girls from Las Vegas that is."

"Take care, Elodie."

I rose to my feet, snatched up my t-shirt and hoodie, then made my way out of the door. I quickly put my shit on when I got inside of the rental, and sped back to my parents' house.

I crept inside to the bedroom once I'd arrived, and quietly undressed down to my boxers before getting back into the bed with Shayne. Wrapping my arms around her body, I pulled her into me before kissing her shoulder again.

"Who is she?" Shayne asked, breaking the silence in the room. I thought she was asleep.

"Who is who baby?"

"The bitch you got out of bed to go see."

"I didn't see any bitch. I went to handle something real quick, and got caught up in conversation with one of the homies," I quickly lied.

"I smell her on you," she began sobbing which caught me off guard.

"Shayne," I mumbled, turning her onto her back so that I could see her. When I did, she covered her face as her body jerked lightly.

Now I felt even worse for what I'd tried to pull tonight. "Baby—"

"Don't touch me," she sniffled, nudging me off of her.

"I didn't sleep with her. I went there to do so, but I couldn't do it."

"Why?" This time she was looking at me, and her face was drenched already. I leaned in to kiss her but she turned away.

"Because I wanted to get back at you for all the shit that went down with you having a fiancé and that shit with Oden." It sounded dumber every time I ran it through my mind.

"You're a little ass boy."

"I know, I agree. But I didn't do it and I couldn't, you know why?" Instead of speaking she shook her head 'no'. I'd never seen her this vulnerable, and it showed me that she really did love a nigga. Not that I didn't believe her before. "Because I'm in love with you. And I told her that too."

"You are? I thought you said you didn't know." She wiped her face.

"I am. I've been in love with you for a long time, but I didn't want to tell you that because I was angry with you deep down."

"How can we be together if you're mad at me? I told you Oden was a mistake, and you know the situation with Pierce, Lloyd. You said you—"

"It's fine. I'm not mad anymore. Let's make right now the beginning of everything, okay?"

"K," she sniffled again as I gripped her face to pull her in for a kiss.

"I'm sorry, shawty, aight?"

She nodded just before we went back to kissing hungrily. Maybe I needed tonight to happen in order for us to move forward.

CHAPTER FIVE

$\mathcal{I}$ was sitting outside of my parents' Beverly Hills home, just watching the streets. The neighborhood was quiet, because only doctors, lawyers like my parents, and dentists, and shit lived over here. Some had kids too, but they were either gone off to college, or stayed inside of the house on their computer and stuff like me. A few cars, expensive ones, drove by slowly and I just watched them, giving my eyes something to look at as my brain went crazy.

I felt scared, very scared about having to tell my parents that I was pregnant. Not only did I feel afraid, but I felt like a failure. I'd gotten pregnant twice in less than a year, and I was only 18 years old. Sometimes I hated Oden for doing this to me, but then I had to remember that I was a willing participant in our sex life.

It wasn't that I didn't want to have a baby with him because I did, just down the line. I was too young, and I wanted to experience life some more before I became someone's mother. However, I refused to get an abortion. I needed to be held accountable for my actions. This child didn't deserve to die just because I wasn't careful in the bedroom.

"Dinner will be ready in about 30 minutes, okay?" My mom peeked out of the large wooden front door. She was a beautiful woman; Shayne and I looked exactly like her.

"Okay," I said, barely above a whisper.

"You okay, honey? You seem to be down. Let me guess, you miss Oden. He'll be here later tonight." She rubbed my hair and pushed it behind my ear. I hated when she did that usually, but right now I didn't mind.

"Yeah, I miss him, that's all. But I will be in when it's done, okay?" I looked up at her with the best forced smile I could provide.

"Okay." She went back inside.

I pulled my hair from behind my ears and when I did, I saw Emery walking up my parents' driveway. I hadn't spoken to her ass since I put her out of my house, and frankly, I hadn't missed her. I mean, some things I did miss, like the memories we made together, but other than that, I couldn't care less about this grimy bitch.

"Long time no see," she smiled, sitting down one step lower than me.

"So." I rolled my eyes and looked off.

"I know you don't miss me, but I miss you. I don't know if I ever apologized for sleeping with Oden but I'm sorry. I knew it wasn't okay, but the shit you used to tell me about him had me interested."

"Oh, poor Emery, couldn't hold back because she was interested. News flash, I told you that shit because I thought you were my best friend, not to intrigue you."

"I know that already, Khyle. He just sounded so bomb, and then when I saw him I couldn't help myself."

"Cool."

"So how have you been? I see you have some new friends and shit. It's like when you went to Nevada, you stopped giving a fuck about Brian and I."

"No, I stopped giving a fuck about you when you fucked Oden, and I stopped giving a fuck about Brian because I'd had an inkling that he was cheating on me."

"How are you doing though, that's what I really want to know? I haven't been the best at showing it, but I do care about you, Khyle."

"I've been good."

I purposely didn't ask how she'd been.

"You look sad though. It's understandable that you don't trust me anymore, but believe it or not you can still talk to me."

I laughed.

"Right."

"I'm serious, Khyle. I know you like the back of my hand, and something is wrong with you. I've never heard you talk this low."

"I'm having a baby, Emery."

You could hear her gasp a mile away.

"With Oden?"

"Who else?" I turned my lip up. "Not everybody fucks random niggas all damn day like you baby girl."

"I deserved that," she chuckled lightly. "So what did your parents say? I'm honestly surprised you're still alive and well."

"They don't know yet. Oden is coming here, and we're gonna tell them together so I'm waiting."

"You think that's a good idea, Khyle?"

"What?" I turned to face her. I'd been looking off this whole time, only turning her way periodically.

"I don't think you should tell your dad you're pregnant with Oden around. Your father is crazy. He rarely lets it out, but he's off, and so is Oden. You know your pops is gonna try and fuck Oden up, and Oden isn't gonna back down."

"He likes Oden," I assured her, even though everything she'd said was right.

Emery may have been a shady bitch, but we'd been friends for a long time. She knew my parents as well as I did. My dad was much more poised now that he was a father and lawyer, but my mom had told me plenty stories of him fucking people up for her and other reasons. I would hate to see the two men I loved the most go at it.

"I'm sure he does, but if I were you, I would tell my dad by myself first. He's gonna go ape shit, but at least Oden won't be around for him to take his anger out on."

"Thanks… Emery."

"No problem."

"Dinner is ready, honey. Oh Emery, I haven't seen you here in a while. Did you want to stay for dinner?" my mom smiled.

"Uh no, my mom actually cooked so I'd better go. See you later, Khyle."

I nodded and got up to go inside and eat.

For dinner, my mom made steak with a side of shrimp pasta and greens. She was a great cook, and had passed her talents down to Shayne and I.

The three of us said grace, and then began eating. It was silent at first like always, before my dad decided to talk.

"You know I planned to get you a car because of your good grades sweetheart, but since Oden beat me to the punch, what else did you want?"

"I don't really know, Daddy. If I think of something I will let you know."

"Very nice vehicle he got you too, honey," my mom chimed in.

"Yeah, it was my dream car. I told him about it one day, and I guess he remembered, right down to the interior."

"He loves you, that's why, so he listens. Remember when you would listen to me, James?" my mom joked with my father.

"I don't listen anymore because we've been married so long that I've heard everything you've had to say, Marissa."

"James," my mom giggled, just before he kissed her lips.

"Please you guys," I begged.

It got quiet again as we continued eating our food. I knew Oden would be here in about two hours, so I wanted to get this shit over with.

"Steak is good, baby," my father said, chewing the food.

"Mom, Dad, I have to talk to you about something." They both set their forks down and stared at me. I'd never been so scared in my life. "I want you to know that while in Las Vegas I have been working very hard, as you can see by my grades. I plan to finish college and get my degree, then get my Master's. I'm gonna be a parole officer no matter what."

"Khyle," my dad said before sipping his glass of wine. He was telling me to get to the fucking point. For some reason right now, he seemed so intimidating.

"I…" Tears formed in my eyes.

"Oh, sweetie," my mom started to get up to console me but stopped once I finished my sentence.

"I'm gonna have a baby."

"Excuse me?" my dad looked at me with squinted eyes, hand firmly grasping his wine glass. If he squeezed any tighter it would break.

"I'm pre—"

"How in the fuck did you get pregnant, when you're supposed to be studying and most importantly, not having sex?"

"James, calm down."

"No! I'm not gonna fucking calm down. I sent you to that damn school to get a muthafucking education, not for you to be opening your legs for any man that smiles in your face and says nice things to you."

"Daddy, I didn't!" I cried.

"Then how the hell do you have a baby in your body, Khyle? Huh? What happened to waiting until marriage?" His stare was so intense.

I'd never seen him so angry. The veins in his forehead were popping out, and his handsome face was contorted.

"Is Oden the father?" my mom inquired.

"Yes," I whispered.

"So you let that thug convince you to have sex with him, and then he got you pregnant? I did not raise you to become some hoodlum's baby mother, Khyle Luke!" My dad slammed his hand onto the table, making the silverware clink and me jump.

"Daddy—"

"No, just stop talking." He stood from the table. "Where did I go wrong with you?"

"James, it happens all the time—"

"Not to my daughters! You wait until I see that motherfucker you call a boyfriend, Khyle. I'm kicking his ass."

Before I could respond, he left the dining room.

Sobbing, I dropped my head down to let it all out. I wished I could take it all back. If I would have told Oden to use a condom, or gotten on birth control, none of this would be happening to me right now. I'd never been so irresponsible in my life.

"Khyle," my mom kneeled down in front of me. "You don't have to keep the baby if you don't want to. I don't care what Oden says. It's your body and you can get rid of it if you want. If he doesn't want to be with you because of that, then he was never the one."

"I want to keep it, Mom," I cried.

"But think about the sacrifice you will have to make if you do, honey. All those college parties you wouldn't be able to go to. All the sleepless nights you'd have to endure, missed classes, and your body is gonna go through a lot. I just…" I looked up to see she was teary eyed. "I just want you to be able to experience this part of your life freely, Khyle. You have plenty of time to have children."

"Would you kill me?" I questioned.

"What? Of course not."

"Exactly, Mama. I don't want to do that to my child either. I love it already, even though it hasn't been here that long."

Her expression turned sympathetic as she rubbed her hand down my hair. She kissed my forehead on her way to standing up, and then left the kitchen to get my father.

I finished my food because I was hungry, but I couldn't ignore the fight my parents were having upstairs in their room about me. I never thought I'd see the day where my mom defended me and my dad was against me, but it was happening. I always thought my mom would be happy to see me make a mistake, but I was wrong. She loved me more than I thought.

I scraped everyone's plates, and then washed the dishes before going upstairs to my room. As I was getting my stuff ready for a shower, my phone chimed.

Oden: On my way to your house.

Me: Don't come in, just wait outside and take me to your hotel.

Oden: I thought we were gonna talk to your parents.

Me: We have to talk first.

Oden: *Aight.*

As soon as I locked my phone, another message came through.

Brian: Damn, I was trying to make you a queen but you let that nigga turn you into a fucking baby mama. Make better choices baby girl. Lmao

"Fucking Emery," I mumbled.

I held back the tears as Brian's mean ass message circled my mind, and proceeded to take a nice hot shower. I cried for forever before I even cleaned myself.

When I got out and put my clothes on, I saw that Oden was outside. I stuffed some things into my Louis bag that he'd gotten me, and then left out without saying anything to my parents. I knew I should have, but I didn't want them to know Oden was here.

CHAPTER SIX

Oden

$\mathcal{I}$ sat in my car, bobbing my head to an old Dom Kennedy mixtape, while waiting for Khyle to come outside. I was a little confused about the sudden change of plans, but I guess she'd tell me the situation once she got into the car. I had my damn speech prepared and everything for her parents, but I guess now I just had more time to go over it in my head.

"Hi." Khyle got into the car smelling good as fuck as usual.

"Come here," I leaned over into her seat and kissed her lips. I held mine against hers, and then slipped my tongue into her mouth. We began kissing hungrily, causing our breathing to become shallow.

"Oden, stop." She nudged me off of her and looked away. She quickly swiped the tear running down her cheek, before folding her arms. "Can we just go, please?"

Declining to say anything, I peeled out of her driveway, going towards my hotel. I was staying at the Beverly Hills one again, so it wasn't too far from her house. We didn't say a word to each other during the ride, while I checked into my room, nor when we walked down the hallway to my door. When we entered, I set our things down and then sat on the bed. She started to walk past me, but I pulled her down into my lap.

"I told them," she whimpered lowly.

"But I thought you wanted to wait for me?" I kissed her cheek. The room was dark, but we could still see one another pretty well.

"I did, but I talked to Emery and—"

"Who the fuck is Emery?"

"My ex best friend that you fucked! Have you forgotten? Do you remember sleeping with my sister too? Or do you not remember her either?" She shot up from my lap.

"Whoa, whoa, calm the fuck down coming at me with all that bullshit, Khyle. Sorry if I don't remember ya fucking friend. Wouldn't it be more of a problem if I did?"

I didn't know what had gotten into her, but it clearly made her forget that I wasn't the one. In love with her or not, she wasn't gonna be talking to me any kind of damn way.

"Anyway, she told me it was a bad idea to tell my dad about the baby with you present and she was right."

"So you told him already."

"Yeah, I did. I knew if you were there, he would come after you, and I didn't want that to happen. I didn't want to see you guys fight."

"I wouldn't fight your fucking father, Khyle."

"So you'd stand there and let him fuck you up?" I just sighed and she said, "Exactly." She continued pacing the room, letting tears cascade down her cheeks.

"Well, what did they say?"

"My mom told me to get an abortion, but passive aggressively, and my dad basically told me he was disappointed in me. He was so angry, Oden, and the look he gave me was just… I have never upset him."

"What did you tell your mom when she suggested such a thing?"

"I told her I wasn't going to. I almost let her know that I'd had an abortion already, but I felt like that was too much."

"Khyle, what do you want to do? If this is too much, I won't hate you for getting an abortion."

She stopped pacing and looked down at me angrily.

"You don't care if I get an abortion, Oden? Really? I guess I'm the only one who cares about this baby. I guess you have to see it to care about it!" She was crying harder than I'd ever seen her cry. "You just don't fucking care, do you?"

"Khyle! Calm the fuck down, aight!" I got up off the bed. She was working my fucking nerves. I was trying to be calm even though she was on 100, but I realized I was gonna have to stop protecting her damn feelings. "I wanted the first fucking baby that you decided to run off and kill without telling me! I do care about this one, but I'm not gonna force you to do some shit you don't want to do! Sorry if I love you and understand why this situation is not the best right now! You need to wake the fuck up and realize when someone cares about yo' stupid ass! A nigga can't even be there for you because you're too busy running your mouth about dumb shit like why I can't remember your hoe ass best friend! I know you're 18, but if you plan on being with me, and especially if you plan on being somebody's fucking mama, you need to grow the fuck up!"

I started off towards the bathroom, and when she grabbed my wrist I snatched away. I was gonna keep going but I stopped. Us arguing was not the best thing right now. Everybody she loved was mad at her, and I didn't want to add myself to that list.

"I'm sorry," she wept as I hugged her close to my body.

"Khyle, I love you and I'm just trying to be there for you. I need you to understand that, baby. We're in a partnership, which means that we have to support one another, even if we may not necessarily agree. You have to know that I care about you more than my own life. How could you even come out of your mouth and say I don't care about something that we created together, shorty?"

"I know you care, I'm just upset about my parents' reaction. I'm sorry, Oden." She looked up into my eyes.

"I accept your apology, but Khyle, don't you ever in your life talk to me the way that you did tonight. I don't accept disrespect from anybody. I never have and I won't start now. When you talk to me, no matter how angry you are, make sure you're respectful. I love you but I won't tolerate the bullshit."

"Can I have a kiss?"

I laughed a little before pressing my lips against hers.

We continued kissing as we undressed each other. Once naked, we fell down onto the bed, with me between her thighs. Placing her legs in the nooks of my arms, I forced my way inside of her tight, wet opening. A soft moan came from both of our mouths just before we resumed kissing passionately.

"We're gonna ha-have a baby," she whispered against my lips as I glided in and out of her slowly.

"I know."

Pinning her hands above her head, I continued to pump her center. She was sopping wet, and moaning softly in my mouth every time my full length entered her. She felt so amazing, and knowing we were starting a family together meant something to me.

I never really expressed to her in detail how low-key depressed I got knowing she killed the first baby, but that was only because I didn't want her to feel bad. Khyle was my other half, and I understood her like no one else did. She was young, still is, and at that time she did what she felt was best. I could never hate her or blame her for doing what she felt was right. I loved her too much and would never want her to carry such a burden.

The only reason I broke up with her after the abortion was because she kept it from me, and had planned to never tell me, even down the line. Then to make matters worse, she'd insulted me as if she'd met me outside of some prison or sleeping in an alley.

"Ahhh, mmm, ahhh!" she cried, pulling me from my thoughts. My thrusts were faster, and her pussy got gushier as she released for the second time.

I stared down at her, admiring her beauty as I fucked the shit out of her. Taking her nipple into my mouth, I sucked it hard, switching back and forth between the two. Sex with her was like a drug, and she was the only one I wanted to do it with. That was odd for me, but I was with it.

Grasping the headboard of the bed, I lifted myself up and began beating her pussy up with precision. A few moans escaped my lips from the feeling as she sniveled.

"I love you, baby. I love you," I growled, feeling my nut rise as I slammed into her snug and drenched pussy. I loved listening to how slippery it was as I watched myself pound her.

A few pumps later, I was shooting up the club.

I kissed her lips while caressing her trembling legs, and once I caught my breath, I pulled out of her.

"You wanna take a bath or are you too tired."

"No, let's go baby daddy," she grinned, crawling to the edge of the bed with her sexy ass.

"You better stop crawling like that. That's how I got yo' little ass pregnant twice." I grabbed her up and kissed her lips as I walked to the bathroom.

We sat in that hot ass bathtub until our fucking fingertips were wrinkled, then cleaned up in the shower. After slipping on some fresh boxers, I laid a towel down in the middle of the bed for her, and then grabbed her favorite oil from her bag. It smelled good, but I couldn't quite pinpoint what the fragrance was.

Pouring some into my hands, I began massaging her whole body, starting from her small shoulders. Her long hair was piled on top of her head, and her eyes were closed as she enjoyed the feeling. Once I'd gotten her completely covered in oil, she put on her short, silk nightgown, and we got under the covers.

"I know I shouldn't be, but I'm happy about the baby, Khyle."

"Me too at times. When I'm with you, and when I talk about it with Tasmine, Bella, and even my sister, I feel happy about it. They make it seem like a good thing."

"It is a good thing; a great thing. It may be the wrong time, for sure, but it's a great thing. And after we get married we can have some more." I pushed a lone piece of hair from her face.

"I can't wait to marry you, and live in a nice house with our children and stuff." She smiled and looked off a little bit as if she were imagining it. Her smile soon faded, and I knew why.

"Don't worry about your parents, they'll get over it and accept it soon. They're good people, Khyle."

"Yeah."

I prayed to God that I was right. If her people tried to cut her off, I would definitely feel like the shit was my fault.

CHAPTER SIX

Santino

Scottsdale, Arizona...

Since I didn't have to be back at school yet, I made sure to keep in shape at home. I went to the gym about four times a week, just enough to keep me at a point where when I went back to hardcore training, I wouldn't feel like dying.

Being in this gym made me think about Huelo though. My nigga had just dropped from the face of the earth and it bothered me. Not to mention the whole rape shit Bella told me about was disturbing.

"Damn," my homie Caesar commented.

I looked to see what he was watching while biting his lip, and saw sexy ass Crystal doing squats. She had on some small ass tight shorts, and a sports bra that her titties were spilling out of. Licking my lips, I watched her for a minute right along with Caesar. She saw us too, and kept strong eye contact with me as she squatted her body slowly and repeatedly. All I saw was her doing that on my dick.

"I ain't never seen her before, bro," Caesar grinned.

"Go holler at her," I laughed to myself. "She's a friend of my old thang, Leena."

I knew Crystal would turn him down because she was hot for me, but hey, maybe I was wrong. Ain't shit I could do with her because I had Bella. I wasn't about to lose my girl for no bitch. I didn't care how fat her ass was or how big her titties were.

"Old thang? Nigga, in Leena's eyes you're still her man."

"Nah, I'm Bella Bacigalupi's man," I corrected him as I used the leg machine.

"Belllaaaa," he sang her name. "You're lucky you got to her pretty ass before I did because I would have had her ass pregnant by now."

"Caes…"

"My bad, I forgot about y'alls little mishap back in the day. I'm happy you got her back, though. I was tired of hearing about her and seeing you obsess over her."

"I ain't even talk about her that much, and I was not obsessed," I chuckled, knowing I was lying like fuck.

"Nigga, what? How long did it take Corey and I to talk yo' ass out of getting her name tatted?"

I shook my head with a half smile as I recalled the day. Bella and I had been broken up for a minute at that time, but I was still in love with her like I'd always been. She was already with Dean, and I had my few bitches that I was fucking with, but I wanted to get her name tattooed somewhere my parents wouldn't see. Corey and Caesar talked me out of it, but if I had have gotten it, I wouldn't have regretted it.

"Whatever," I finally said after traveling down memory lane.

Caesar got on the leg machine next to me and began working out, and after about 40 minutes of that, we were ready to go. Standing up, I scanned the gym with my eyes, wondering where Crystal had gone. I had no business looking for her, but it was just a reflex.

As Caesar and I said our goodbyes in the parking lot, and headed our separate ways towards our vehicles, I heard someone running up behind me. You already know who that was.

"So you're just gonna leave and not say a thing? Shit, not even a hi when I know you saw me earlier."

"My bad, Crystal. I was more focused on my workout than anything, you know?"

"Yeah, I do make niggas lose focus, so it was smart of you to pay me no mind." She ran her tongue over her full lips.

Adjusting myself, I cleared my throat and said, "Well aight, it was nice seeing you. You have a good evening."

"Uh uh, nigga, you're not about to leave me just yet. I never have you alone and I want to take advantage of it," she giggled, showing all of her pretty white teeth.

Fuck yo, why was God testing me? There was no way I could fuck with Crystal because not only would Bella stop messing with me, but I would hurt her and I couldn't do that shit again.

"Crys, come on, baby girl. I'm in a relationship, and we can't—"

"Leena told me you dumped her ass because you claimed you

needed to focus on school and not her. So y'all are back together?"

Leena had to lie to kick it.

"Nah, we're not back together, I have someone else."

"That was fast."

"No, we dated, and then broke up for some years, and now we're back together."

"Fuck, Santino," she grinned, shoving me lightly. "You better promise me that if shit doesn't work out with this new slash old girl, you will let me know."

"I definitely fucking will, but I doubt she and I will part, you know? We have history and this time around we're sticking it out."

"Damn, okay. Well like I said, in case you're wrong, call me, Facebook me, Instagram me, shit, send a message in a bottle; I will get that shit."

We shared a laugh.

"I got you, baby girl."

I licked my lips as we stared at one another lustfully. As attracted to each other as we were, this right here alone was cheating.

"I will let you go then." She checked me out from head to toe one more time and then turned on her heels to walk away. And damn did she look good walking away.

"Damn," I mumbled, climbing into my car and pulling off.

I stopped to get myself a protein shake, and then went straight home so I could shower and go see my baby. I missed her and I hated that we had to sleep separately most nights. Occasionally, Bella's parents would ease up and let her sleep over with me, but it was rare as hell and only when my people were out of town.

As I walked up the stairs of my parents' home, I saw my bedroom door was wide open. Furrowing my brows, I slowly neared it and heard a lot of rustling. I could already tell someone was in my shit, and deep. Walking in, I saw my parents going through my stuff like they were a part of the damn police department.

"What are y'all doing?" I shouted.

"Are you dating Bella again?" my mother cocked her head, folding her arms.

"Why does it matter—"

"Because we specifically told you that you were to never see her again. All she wants is to live off of you! That's been obvious since she tried to trap you!" my father barked.

"Trap me? Ain't nobody tried to trap me, aight? And why are y'all in my shit!"

"I got your credit card statement and saw that you've been sending a lot of nice gifts to the Bacigalupi residence," my mom responded.

"Fuck you in my mail for, huh? Ain't like you pay that damn credit card bill!" I was hot. I'd never cursed in front of my parents before but they'd pushed me over the edge with this bullshit.

"Watch your mouth." My dad walked up on me like I was supposed to be scared. I simply laughed at his ass and snatched whatever the fuck of mine he had in his hand.

"Get out my room," I gritted.

"How about you get the hell out of my house?" my dad replied.

"Luca," my mom tried to interject.

"Oh, get out your house? You want me out?"

"No, Santino. Luca, tell him that's not what you meant—"

"No Bette, that is what the fuck I meant. Get out of my damn house. I don't want you living here if you can't act like you have some sense and respect me. This is my home, and my rules are to be abided by. And one of those rules is you are not to see Bella."

"I'm gone then."

"Santino!" my mother grabbed on my shirt as I bolted past her and my dad to get my duffle bag.

I snatched down whatever I needed from the hangers, and then went to grab shit from my drawers. I stuffed the bag to the point where it wouldn't zip, as my mom ran off at the mouth about something. I was tired of this shit. I refused to let them ruin my relationship like they'd done in the past.

"I'm out," was all I said before going down the stairs and walking out the door. I climbed into my car, and sped off towards Bella's home. Since I was already going to see her, I decided to do so right now. I just wished I were able to shower first.

When I arrived, I put my bag into my trunk, and then walked up to her door. After ringing the doorbell, I saw her dad's big ass shadow walking up through the window. I took a deep breath, and waited impatiently for him to answer.

"Good evening, Mr. Bacigalupi," I smiled.

"Sup. Come in. She's in the den." He stepped back and gestured for me to come in.

The whole way to the den, I kept thinking about what the fuck I was gonna do about my living situation. I just thank God that I paid my own car note, and got it in my name. My parents offered to buy it for me, paying cash in full, but because I wanted to boost my car credit, I declined. I had never been so happy about a past decision in my life.

"Surpriiissse," I sang as I slid onto the couch next to Bella. The room was dimly lit as she watched some TV show. She was wearing a bathing suit, so I guess she'd been swimming earlier.

"Hey," she whispered lowly, before leaning forward to see if anyone was coming. When she saw no one was, she straddled my lap. "Why do you look sad?" she pecked me.

"I'm straight."

"Santino."

"I got kicked out of my house today… Bella."

"Why? Oh my gosh!"

"Because they're on that same bullshit they were on years ago. Trying to run my life and tell me who to be with. That shit ain't gonna work no more. I can do okay until I have to go back to the dorms."

"Santino, maybe you should—"

"No. I shouldn't. I would live in a damn dumpster before I go back there with them muthafuckas."

"So where are you gonna stay?"

"Don't know, but you think you can ask your parents if I can use the shower real quick? I feel disgusting, and I didn't get a chance to clean up before I left."

"Sure."

She climbed off of my lap, and as soon as she left, I dropped my face into my hands. I didn't know what the hell I was gonna do. I still had a couple weeks before I went back to UNLV to start football training. I would just have to sleep in my damn whip, and shower at the gym. I nodded my head at my thoughts.

"Okay, they said you can use the guest bathroom, and that you can stay in the guest bedroom until you go back to UNLV."

"What?" I picked my head up from my hands. "Bella, no, all I wanted was a shower."

"You need somewhere to stay, baby, so I asked." She neared me, placing the towels in my lap. She was kneeling down, and looking up into my face with her beautiful one.

"I have a car."

"I don't want you sleeping in a car, Santino. Not when my parents have an extra bedroom that you can sleep in. It has a bathroom in it. And just think, I will be here."

"Mmm, that last part sounds nice."

"I know. We can sneak around and have sex. Doesn't that sound fun?"

"It does," I chuckled, staring down at her. "I love you, baby. You're too good to me." I grabbed her face gently and kissed her lips deeply.

"I love you, too, but I will love you more after you take a shower."

"Right," I laughed. "Let me go get my bag from the car so I can shower and thank your parents."

We both rose to our feet at the same time, and before I left out, I had to kiss her again. Every day she proved to me why she deserved to be my wife, and she would be.

CHAPTER SIX

Tasmine

"So you're really going, huh?" my sister Tasia walked into my bedroom.

I was currently packing up my stuff to go back to Las Vegas tomorrow. All of the appliances I had were stored at Anton's place because it was too much to fly back with, so all I had to come bring were my clothes. I'd gotten a lot of new stuff when he visited me, so he of course bought me a new luggage set. Now that I think about it, his ass was probably doing all of that because he felt guilty for lying.

"Yeah, he wants to talk face to face." I zipped the suitcase and then sat it upright before pushing it against the wall.

"I mean why though? What could he possibly say to you in person that he couldn't say to you on the phone, Tas?"

"Tasia, I'm wondering the same thing. But he's claiming that he can better explain it with me there. I already told him if he thinks sex is gonna fix it, it won't."

"Ugh, you'd still sleep with him?"

"I mean, I don't plan on it, but I have been missing it. It's better to hop on the same one than to go out and get some new dick."

I didn't like that 'ugh' comment.

"Sleeping with him is a bad idea, Tasmine. We're not like niggas. When we sleep with a man our feelings get deeper."

"I know that already, but I don't think my feelings for him could get any stronger."

"You love him?"

"Yeah, I do."

"Oh wow. Yeah, that's why he wants to see you. It's gonna be easy as pie for him to convince you to get back with him. Tasmine, I love you, but you're really naive and he's well… not."

"I've actually done some growing while away at college. I'm surprised you can't tell."

"I can, I can. I'm just saying, one year away at college with girls who gave you a little bit of advice does not put you on the same level as a nigga like Anton. This is a game he plays daily, boo."

"I can handle myself, Tasia. I promise you I will do my best to refrain from sleeping with him, but if I get real horny, I will have to," I laughed, and thank God so did she.

"So it's really that good? I've never heard you say anything about being horny."

"Girl, it's beyond good. Ugh," I sucked my teeth and groaned. I hated him right about now, but I was definitely interested in seeing what the fuck he had to say.

"Well good luck, I will be praying for you."

"Thanks."

***

Las Vegas, Nevada...

I was finally here, and on my way to my room inside of the Bellagio hotel. I was originally supposed to stay with Anton, but since he'd lied to me, shit changed. I told him the only way I would come is if he paid for me to stay in a room until I either forgave him or school started, whichever happened first.

I did feel bad using up all of his money, but I was furious with him. He had messed up so much that it was keeping us apart more than together. I wanted him to take our relationship more seriously, meaning that he needed to be honest with me about everything. I mean how long did he think he'd be able to keep a baby from me? The only explanation I could think of was that he didn't see us being together for very long, so it didn't matter and he could hide it for the time being. Honestly, what the hell else could it be?

"Thank you," I smiled at the Uber driver as I scooted across the back seat and got out. I had him stop at a drive-thru and he'd paid for my food. I think he wanted my number but that wasn't happening so he played himself.

Walking into the hotel, I was in awe. It was so beautiful that I just had to stand there for a little bit and take it all in. I looked around the hotel lobby with my eyes, and spotted Pilar, Truman's girlfriend, waving me over. I sauntered over, and when I got close enough she smiled.

"Your room keys," she reached them out to me from behind the big counter.

"I didn't know you worked here."

"Yeah I do, have been for a while. I'm a manager."

"I see. So, Anton hit you up for a discount?"

"No, he asked me to hold the keys to the side for you because he was sure you didn't want to see him just yet. You guys good?"

I guess she didn't know he and I had broken up.

"I don't know yet, we will see. For now, we're not together. You and Truman okay now? I heard he got shot."

Sighing while scratching her neck, she said, "Yeah, we are. I mean, he's been acting a little funny lately, but I think that's just because he's been injured you know."

"Yeah, something like that would damper your mood a bit."

"Exactly. Well, you're all set. You're in the penthouse suite."

"Oh my gosh, really? He's so ridiculous," we chuckled in unison.

"Aren't they all. The room number is on the inside of the cardholder. Enjoy your stay, Tasmine."

"Thanks, Pilar."

I made it up to my room, well suite, and it was very nice. I think even after Anton and I make up, I will still stay here. It was that nice, and spacious too. Wait, what am I saying? I'm already telling myself I'm gonna forgive him.

I sat down in the living area to eat my food, and as soon as I was done, I passed the fuck out. It may have been the middle of the day, but that food coma was no joke.

BZZZZZ! BZZZZZ!

I woke up to the sound of my phone going crazy, and when I looked I saw it was Anton calling. It was dark outside from what I could see through the window, and the lights on Las Vegas Boulevard were already popping.

"Hello?" I answered, reaching over to turn on the lamp.

"Open the door, Tas."

"Damn, shouldn't you have called before you came? I didn't ask you to get me a room so that you could just pop up whenever the fuck you wanted."

"Aye, open the damn door and quit being disrespectful, Tasmine."

His tone was stern and authoritative, so I didn't argue. I just sucked my teeth so I wouldn't sound like I was backing down, and sashayed to the door. Hanging up as I looked through the peephole, I scanned Anton's sexy ass. He was wearing a red sweater, dark jeans, and some red shoes that appeared to be Adidas.

"Hi," I stated dryly, opening the door for him and walking off.

"I thought you were gonna hit me when you got here, Tasmine."

"I planned to, but I had some food so I ate that and fell asleep." I stretched out on the couch and just stared at him, as he nodded approvingly at the room. "You didn't have to go all out."

"I wanted you to be comfortable."

"I would have been comfortable in a regular room. I hope you're not thinking—"

"Tasmine, can't I just do something nice for you? Fuck. I have money and no damn body to spend it on, so yes, I do like to get nice things for the girl I love when I can. I ain't trying to get back with you by getting you a nice room."

"Good." I felt a little stupid for assuming. "So talk, Anton. That's what I came out here for, for you to explain to me *in person* why you lied."

"Okay," he sighed. "I'm just gonna come right out and say it, not beat around the bush or anything, baby." He sat down at the other end of the couch.

"Well." I wound my hand to let him know to get a fucking move on.

"I didn't tell you because I really don't think the kid is mine."

I sat there, waiting for him to add something else to that pitiful ass excuse, but after a while, I realized he was done talking.

"Please tell me you have more to say."

"No, I don't. I have nothing to say other than I feel like the baby isn't mine, so I didn't want to tell you about it."

"But wasn't there a DNA test done?"

"Yeah, but—"

"And didn't it come back saying that you were the father? You used your own people, so it's not like she could have faked the results."

"I know that, Tasmine. I used a condom with her."

"Condoms break, nigga!" I'd never been this angry in my life.

"You fucked her and the condom broke, or yo' ass probably didn't use one!"

"Who's fucking side are you on?"

"I was on yours but you're acting stupid as fuck right now. That fucking baby is yours and you just need to accept the shit and grow the fuck up, Tony! The least you could do is come in here, act like a man, and admit that you lied because you were scared. Instead, you make up some lame ass excuse about the boy not being yours. You make me sick like for real."

"Wow," he laughed, nodding slowly.

"Wow all the fuck you want. I knew I shouldn't have come out here. I knew you were gonna be on some bullshit. You've been on bullshit since I've fucking met you, yet I still tried to give you the benefit of the fucking doubt. And for what?"

"Because you love me and I love you. Tasmine, I swear this is not just some excuse. I honestly don't believe the kid is mine. I mean, wouldn't I have some sort of connection to him? I don't, and I feel like I'm forcing myself to. I'm getting attached to him, but not in a fatherly way."

"I want you to leave."

"Tasmine."

"Leave, Anton."

I couldn't even look at him right now. He was so fucking childish that it made me sick to think about. Why couldn't he just accept that little baby as his and step up? Why couldn't he just admit that he'd lied because he was afraid that I would leave him? But no, typical Anton always trying to make himself look like the victim somehow. I was done with his ass.

"Baby, what do you want me to say? I'm being honest here. Okay, yes, I was afraid that you would leave me, but if I'm being all the way 100, I didn't believe the results so I kept it from you."

"Bye, Anton," I started to cry.

"Baby—"

"No, don't touch me!"

I tried to push him off of me but he was way stronger than I. He hugged me tightly and kissed my temple longingly as I sobbed. I felt like I'd invested so much into this relationship, and now it was for nothing. Not to mention I felt dumb for falling for him.

"Please leave," I begged through tears.

He didn't say anything; he just scooped me up bridal style and carried me to the bedroom. We laid down on top of the covers, and he hugged me into his chest which smelled so good. I continued to cry as he held me, until I fell asleep.

CHAPTER SIX

Truman

"How are you feeling?" Pilar watched me as I got dressed in all black. She asked me that shit about 100 damn times a day, and I was tired of it.

"I'm good, just like I was an hour ago, Pilar."

I am not sleeping at her crib tonight, I said to myself.

"Right. So can we talk when you get back, baby? I can set it out for us. I think we need to spend time together."

"Yeah. See you." I leaned down to kiss her cheek and bounced.

I loved Pilar, but my mind was always on Chiina. She still wasn't fucking with me, and only talked to me when she had a doctor's appointment. I'd sent her flowers, jewelry, clothes, shoes, tipped her at work with a suitcase of money, and she still wasn't giving me the time of day. I didn't want her stripping anymore while pregnant, but when I said that shit she basically told me to suck her dick. I just missed her like crazy, no matter how hard I tried not to.

Getting into my car, I cranked it and let it warm up for a little bit before driving over to Oden's. Tonight, we planned to off Billz' ass since we had a location. Actually, we'd had a location on him for some weeks, but because I didn't want Oden and Anton handling him without me, we waited until I recovered fully.

"You good?" Oden slid into the car.

"If one more person asks me that shit, my fucking head is gonna explode, dog."

"You've been real irritable lately," he chuckled.

"No, I haven't. I just don't like being asked the same shit all day. Pilar questions me about how I'm feeling all damn day long, so please, if you can, don't ask me."

"Shit, I didn't *want* to ask you, I just felt sorry for ya lovesick ass," he said, making me chuckle a little.

"Ain't lovesick."

"Nigga, you brought a suitcase of cash and basically gave it to Chiina. And she still treated you like a bum ass customer."

"Was just being nice that day."

There was silence before we both started cracking up. He knew I was full of shit and so did I. We continued talking about random stuff until we made it to this shopping center. It was small and somewhat abandoned.

"He's in that spot with the *For Rent* sign," Oden said, twisting the silencer onto the front of his gun.

"Why though?"

"Plays cards here every Thursday with his homies. Nigga makes a lot of bread off of people at these card games."

"How are we doing this?"

"Anton is already inside, little does that nigga know. It's a cool 15 people in there. Anton could have been killed him but you wanted in. So we're gonna come through the back, and spray them niggas. I will do my best not to hit Billz so you can take him."

"Make sure you don't hit Anton."

"I won't. Our informant already gave us the rundown of how the spot is laid out. Anton will stick by the door, and once you and I come in he's gonna get in line."

"Cool."

I was ready to kill that nigga Billz. Granted he had every right to get at me for fucking with his wife, but shit, shoot that bitch not me! She came after me, I didn't come after her. And he had some nerve showing up to our club knowing we were looking for his ass.

Oden and I went around back, and I parked my car a little ways down. I'd changed the license plate earlier, so I wasn't too worried. And no one would snitch if they knew what was good for them.

Oden and I crept to the wooden door and knocked three times like we'd been instructed. Some big nigga opened the door, then smiled when he saw us.

Gay ass, I thought.

We entered and I immediately spotted Anton, chilling off to the side and bobbing his head to the music. Billz was sitting at this black card table, smiling and shit, so I knew he was winning. The carpet was red, the walls were too, and the front door and window had some deep black tint. Because there were a nice amount of people here, music playing, and plenty of conversation, Billz dumbly didn't pay attention to who came and went. Oden and I looked at one another, and before we could make a move, Anton started popping niggas near him.

PHEW! PHEW! PHEW!

Oden and I began icing muthafuckas as we neared the table Billz was sitting at. I thought this shit would be a mess, but we each gravitated to our own sides of the room to blast so we weren't hitting each other. I ain't know if these niggas lacked heat or if they were just too slow, but these muthafuckas were dropping like flies.

Billz tried to get up but fell out of his chair. Attempting to crawl away, he kicked the table over as if that would help him stall me.

Only living people here were Anton, Oden and I, since Anton popped the informant that let us in.

"Come on, let's talk about this," Billz damn near cried once I flipped him into his back.

"Ain't shit to talk about, bitch. This was long overdue," Oden spat.

"We can all get money if we just stay out of one another's way—"

POP! POP!

I didn't have my silencer on because I wanted to hear when I killed him.

On our way out of the door, Oden placed a call for our clean-up crew to come through. I realized Anton was right behind us, so I hit the alarm on my car from afar to make shit go faster.

"Nigga, how did you get here?" I questioned Anton as I sped out the back.

"Hitched a ride," he replied, texting on his phone in the back seat. Ain't no telling what that meant. "Aye, they took care of Pablo's body." He was referring to the doorman who let Billz into the club that fateful night, knowing he was banned.

I pulled over in an abandoned area, and removed my license plate while they played lookout. When I was done, I got back in the car and headed to our townhouse community. After dropping them two niggas off, I sat in my car, not wanting to go inside my own spot. I dialed Chiina, and when she didn't answer, I knew she must have been at work.

I was immediately pissed off by the thought, so I drove over to Palace. I barely parked my shit before I was out of the car and rushing inside, passing the bouncer at the door who I ignored when he spoke to me. Scanning the room, I searched for Chiina and found her little ass in some nigga's VIP, smiling all in his face. She was dressed in little to nothing, showing off shit I no longer wanted other niggas to see.

"Aye, let me talk to you for a minute," I called out to her. She looked over her shoulder at me, rolled her eyes, and then went back to talking to old boy. "Chiina, it's about your job."

"Give me a second, sexy," she chuckled, coming down towards me. The disco lights were beaming down on her golden complexion.

"I'll wait here for as long as you need me to, baby," the patron responded.

I was tempted to kick his ass out, but I'd seen him before and he always spent a lot of money while here.

"What did you need, Tru?" Chiina asked, folding her arms as soon as we got into my office. I wanted to wring her neck, but kiss her at the same time.

"I don't want you here while pregnant, Chi."

"I'm not even showing, Truman! When I get to be three months, maybe four, I will stop. But for now I have bills to pay."

"I already fucking told you I had you. I will pay your damn rent, and I will pay for your schooling."

"No. You want me to live with you, and I'm not gonna do that."

"Why?" I walked up on her, and I saw her tense up. That shit made me smile inside, because it told me she still loved me.

"Because I don't want to. You just want me to live with you so you can watch me, and then turn around and cheat on me."

"No, baby, I want you to live with me because I love you." I held the sides of her face, tilting her head back.

"I know you've been with her this whole time, Truman. I'm not stupid. And then you just got shot over another woman. I don't wanna be with you, it's too much of a hassle."

"It doesn't even have to be that way though, Chiina! I've learned my lesson now, and if you give me a chance I will show you that."

"How?"

"Huh?"

"How will you show me?"

"I will pay for you to get your own condo, away from me, a car because I don't like you riding in Ubers with my baby, and—"

"Money will not do, Truman."

"Let me finish girl, damn," I frowned, and she smiled for the first time in a long time. "And I will focus on only you."

"You swear?"

"Yes, I swear. I will be all about you, our baby, and my work. I'm gonna cut all these other girls off, and spend my free time with you so I won't be tempted."

"Okay, I can give you a trial run."

"But can we stop working here while you have my baby? Just go to school right now, love. I don't like you in other nigga's faces and swinging around a pole for money. Especially not when your nigga has enough coins to fund your lifestyle."

"No, I don't trust you yet, Truman. If you can find another position for me here at Palace, then I will quit dancing."

Damn, this little girl was giving me a run for my fucking money.

"Okay, you can help Cara with booking VIP tables for the club area, not the strip club down at the bottom. She's been saying she needs help because we have hundreds of requests a night, so you can assist her. It pays $19 an hour, and you can do it on weekends only."

"That's fine. Thank you," she tousled her hair.

"I love you, baby." I moved in close to her and kissed her lips. "You love me?" She simply nodded. "No, tell me."

"You don't deserve to hear it yet."

"So I'm guessing we won't be fucking either?"

"Hell no! You won't touch me until I see progress. Get to work. I'm gonna go change my clothes, and tonight I want you to stay with me."

"I will."

I let her walk out of my office and stood there cheesing like fuck. Chiina wasn't all the way mine just yet, but she would be. And I planned to make good on every promise I'd made to her.

CHAPTER SEVEN

Pilar Abraham

The next morning…

I'd just finished washing my body, and I was simply letting the water rinse all the soap off. I knew it was all gone, but the feeling of the hot water beating against my body felt really good. It helped to ease my mind about the fact that my man decided he wasn't going to come home last night.

Truman stood me up even though I'd told him that I was cooking for him. You'd think that I'd be ready to leave his ass, but no, all I kept doing was silently praying that he walked through that door. I missed him, and hated how I felt when we were apart… sometimes. I wished he didn't have such a fucking hold on me, because at the end of the day, he had so many skeletons. I had my secrets too, but he knew nothing about that, so I wasn't sure why he was acting funny.

I stepped out of the shower and grabbed the big pink towel I loved to wrap my body in. In the middle of me brushing my teeth, I heard my doorbell sound off, so I quickly rinsed my mouth and sipped some Listerine. Rushing to the door, my heart fluttered when I saw it was Truman.

He came back, I smiled on the inside.

"Hey," he walked in, smelling so good and looking even better.

I didn't respond right away, I just rushed off to spit the mouthwash out. When I returned to the living room, he was sitting on the couch looking through his phone like always. I couldn't imagine always having messages and shit like him, but he'd been that way since I met him—a popular guy.

"So what happened to you last night?" I sat down next to him, prompting him to put his phone away and adjust his hat to the back.

"Pilar, I need to talk to you."

This did not sound good, and I was super scared to hear what he had to say.

"Okay," I adjusted my towel. I probably should have gotten dressed, but I was so elated that he was here.

"When I got shot this last time, do you even know why?"

"No, I—"

"You didn't even ask me. You left the state, and didn't even hit me up until a couple of days later."

"I had to work, Truman. You knew I was going to New York in the morning, and you chose to skip out of here and get shot."

I knew not calling to check on him was fucked up, but I was angry at the fact that he'd left out of the house while I was asleep. We were supposed to wake up together, especially because I was gonna be out of town for some time. And shot or not, I wasn't gonna cancel my trip to New York.

"And it's obvious your work is more important than me."

"No it's not. But your work is definitely more important than me, nigga," I spat.

"No, it's not. Anytime you needed me, I've always dropped whatever I was doing to help you, as long as it wasn't no bullshit."

"Whatever."

"Anyway, the reason I got shot was because Billz Montgomery caught me with his wife, Marie. She'd just gotten done giving me head. I'm telling you because I feel like I should come clean."

"Are you fucking serious, nigga! After all of the shit we've been through, you left me in the bed to get your dick sucked by another bitch? I'd just sucked your fucking dick all night!" I swung on him but he caught my wrists.

I couldn't believe this shit. It's like he went from being the most perfect man in the world, to being some philandering ass nigga. I was starting to believe all the shit my homegirl Adira pumped into my fucking head about him. I didn't know this Truman, and I definitely wasn't sure if I loved this Truman.

"Chill, Pilar. I was on one that night and was just fucking up. I've realized now that I need to do better, and that has to start with me being honest, mature, and disciplining myself."

"I feel like I've heard you say this same bullshit before."

"Before it *was* bullshit that I was feeding you because I wasn't ready to do what I had to do."

"So you promise to be different this time?"

What was I saying? I should have been chucking picture frames and knives at this nigga, yet here I was trying to give him another chance. I'd been with him for so long and I didn't want to just throw away what we had because he couldn't get it right just yet. I believed he could do better, and if I just gave him some time he would.

"I promise myself that I'm gonna be different, not necessarily you."

"What?"

"Pilar, after doing some thinking, I've realized that it's best if I let you go. You're a good woman and you deserve a man who treats you as such. I've done so much shit to you, that sometimes I can't even look you in the eye because of it. I see my mistakes when I look into your face and that's not an insult to you, it's one to me. In order for me to start fresh, and for you to do the same, I think we need to do it apart."

Shaking my head 'no' as tears spilled down my cheeks, I said, "What the hell are you talking about, Tru?"

"I can't be with you anymore baby. And since I'm being honest, I've fallen in love with someone else."

"Fallen in love? So that means you've been dealing with this person for a fucking while?" I bucked my eyes, still in disbelief. I almost wanted to let him know what I'd been up to.

"Yeah, I have, and I love her. We're having a baby too, P."

"Get out."

"Pilar, I—"

"Get the fuck out of my house right now nigga!"

He stared at me and rose to his feet slowly. He opened his mouth to speak again, but when I turned my face away, he walked out. As soon as the door closed, I balled up on the couch and began sobbing. Why didn't I just leave him when I had the upper hand?

Later that evening…

I woke up from a much-needed nap to my phone ringing loudly. Groaning, I reached onto my dresser and grabbed it to see it was Theo, my boyfriend. Yes, I said boyfriend.

If you remember, Truman broke Theo's nose after he caught us at TAO nightclub that one time. Theo was from New York, and he visited me a lot down here in Vegas. That night Truman hit him, he and I made shit official. I actually met him before Truman and I broke up at a work event, but it was just a friendship. When I became single, he and I became closer, and eventually got into a relationship.

When Truman came begging for my forgiveness, I agreed to work with him because I did truly miss him. However, I had deep feelings for Theo so I never broke it off.

That business trip while Truman was in the hospital? Yeah, it was just a little getaway I planned so I could see my man. I knew he couldn't come out here because it would blow my cover, so I went there instead.

It was fucked up of me to go see another nigga while Truman was laid up in the hospital, but now that I knew the reason for his stay, I didn't feel so bad.

"Hey, baby," I answered, sipping the warm glass of water that I'd set next to my bed before knocking out.

"Hey, did I wake you?"

"Yeah, it's okay though. I don't mind. I miss you."

"I miss you too. We need to start looking at some places out there in Vegas together."

See, what I loved about Theo was that he was a man and not a little boy like Truman. Truman had that gangster swag, but Theo was sweet and romantic. Truman could be that way too at times, but not enough for me. I had the best of both worlds when they were both my men, but now that Truman had moved on, I admit I was a bit sick. Regardless of what he had done, I loved him.

"Or maybe I could come to New York," I giggled, placing him on speakerphone.

"Aye, that don't sound too bad, you know? I would love to be able to stay in my hometown, but it's up to you. I will go wherever you go, ma."

I loved that shit. Truman would have told me to either move to New York or be okay with a long distance relationship. He only cared about himself.

"So what are you doing?"

I went onto Truman's Instagram as Theo told me about his day. He was a hotel manager too, so we bonded a lot over work.

When Truman's Instagram loaded up, I tapped the latest picture since it was of some girl, and saw he uploaded the shit just 10 minutes ago. I guess now since he dumped me he felt like it was o-fucking-kay to spread the word about her.

The girl was cute, but she looked young in the face, maybe 19 or 20. She was wearing some jean shorts and a tube top, showing off her small but shapely frame. She was actually beautiful, definitely Truman's type, but I didn't understand how her young ass had made him fall in love.

When I clicked her profile and it uploaded, it suddenly hit me; this was the bitch that I'd caught him with twice. She was at that Christmas party, and she was in his office that night.

"Wow," I ended up saying out loud, feeling my blood boil.

"Wow, what?" Theo asked.

"Nothing, baby. Now what were you saying?"

Oh, this bitch had me fucked up. New boyfriend or not, she had no right to take Truman from me and I was gonna let her ass know that.

***

It'd been about a week since Truman decided to leave me for that little baby bitch, and I'd been following them almost ever since. The hoe basically lived with him, even though I believe he bought her, her own spot.

This morning, I followed her from that nice ass townhouse he most likely paid for, and saw that she stopped by UNLV for something.

I wasn't sure why because my friend went there and school didn't start for three more weeks, but who knows. All I cared about was getting in this bitch's ass for taking my nigga… well, one of them.

I watched her switch to her fresh ass Lexus that I assumed Truman bought for her. It didn't have plates yet, and had the same flashy ass rims that he had on a couple of his cars.

"Pilar, this is so stupid. You have a good man in Theo, just let it go," my friend Adira sucked her teeth.

"Let it go? I have dedicated years to this nigga!"

"I know you have, but you need to realize that he's not worth it, Pilar. How many times does he have to do you dirty? I mean, he did you dirty and broke up with you. Where they do that at?"

"Adira, just hush."

Placing my hand on the door lever, I waited until Chiina got close enough before I hopped out abruptly, causing her to look my way. And can you believe the hoe had the nerve to suck her fucking teeth like she was so damn tired of me?

"Hi," I folded my arms, leaning up against the hood of my car, which was parked right next to hers.

"Bye," she waved me off.

"Look, I don't know what you think you have with Truman, but he's playing you just like he plays everyone."

"Talk about what you know, sweetie."

"Sweetie? Girl, you're probably half my damn age, what are you, 14? Don't address me like that. I'm trying to help your naive ass."

"I don't need your help. I have Truman right where I want him and right where he needs to be. Ain't my fault you couldn't make him become a man so he left you."

"Oh, and you think *you* made him a man?" I laughed.

"Yeah, I did. Now he comes home to me every night, he pays the bills, and he's preparing to become a father. Not to mention he cut off all the women that don't matter to him, including you."

"You feel good about that? You like being a home wrecker, bitch?"

"I'm not a bitch, so don't address me like that. When I got with him, he told me you and him were not together. Had I known he was lying, I wouldn't have messed with him. I won't apologize for something I didn't know."

I glared at her, breathing heavily but lowly. It was taking so much out of me to keep from rocking her shit in this empty parking lot. I didn't know if I was angry because I was jealous of her, or because I believed that she didn't know that Truman and I were currently exclusive when they started fucking around.

"You know what, you can have that nigga. Gon' head and dedicate years to him just so he can ditch your ass like he did me."

"He won't." She hit the alarm on her car and opened the driver's side door.

"How can you be so sure, Ms. Chiina?" I mocked her, smiling to myself a little bit.

"Because he's doing things for me that he's never done for any other girl. You know it, I know it, and he knows it. Have a good rest of your day, Pilar," she fake smiled and slid into her car.

Do not bang your fists on her hood, Pilar.

"And now you look stupid," Adira said to me once I got back into my car.

"Shut up, damn."

I planned to get in Chiina's head and have Truman without either of us, but this shit had backfired. I wanted to get over this relationship and just focus on what I had with Theo, but I wasn't sure if I could.

CHAPTER SEVEN

$\mathcal{I}$t'd been a few weeks since I told my father about the baby, and during that time, I've been staying in a hotel with Oden. I hadn't been home once, and every time I was going to visit, I got scared and changed my mind. It hurt that my father hadn't even tried to talk to me until recently, but I was happy that he seemed to be coming around.

He wanted to have a sit down with both Oden and I, and I was scared as hell. I didn't know what would happen at this meeting, but I hoped it didn't end in a brawl. Oden swore it wouldn't come to that, but I knew he had a temper and so did my father, so there was no way to really predict how this shit would go.

"Are you ready?" Oden asked, walking out of the bathroom.

He looked nice, in a black quarter sleeve button up, light blue jeans, and all black Chuck Taylors. His black diamond chain hung around his neck, matching his watch, and although very nice, it wasn't too flashy at all. His beautiful head of wild curly hair was voluminous and healthy looking. His facial hair was trimmed neatly, and he smelled like a million bucks. The more I looked at him the more attracted to him I became. I thought it was impossible, but clearly it wasn't.

"Yes," I finally replied.

I checked myself out in the full-length mirror close to the bathroom, admiring the red tube dress that stopped mid thigh. I didn't get to take many clothes, but Oden fixed that by taking me shopping at the Beverly Centre. I got so much shit, that the living room of the suite was still swarming with my shopping bags. Oden loved to spoil me, and even though at first I felt bad, I was now used to it.

"You look perfect," he rubbed my lower back.

I ran my hands down my flat stomach, and cocked my head, letting my long hair fall to the side. I was still in a little bit of disbelief that I was gonna be a mother. Later down the line would have been better, but I would be lying if I said I wasn't happy about my baby. It was better than never becoming a mother, is how I looked at it. Plenty of women couldn't even bear children, so I was blessed that I could.

"Thank you," I smiled, looking up at him. He planted a deep, longing kiss on my lips, and then I grabbed my purse so we could leave.

I was perfectly calm until we pulled into my parents' driveway. I felt like I needed to have security on standby just in case these niggas got into it. Because if they did, there was no way my mother and I would be able to peel them off of each other.

"Don't be nervous, Khyle. All we're gonna do is talk, answer any questions he has, maybe eat some food, and then leave."

"I definitely could use some food," I chuckled nervously.

"I know." He kissed the corner of my mouth before getting out.

Coming around to my side, Oden opened the door for me and helped me out of the car. We walked up the long wide driveway, until we were met with the large wooden double doors. Slipping my key in, I walked in first and then once Oden was inside, I closed and locked it.

"Follow me," I told Oden, starting off towards the den.

When he and I got there, we sat on the couch near the glass coffee table outlined in gold. I retrieved my iPhone, and texted my parents to let them know that he and I were here and in the den. I knew that was informal as fuck, but I was too scared to look into their faces at the moment.

Oden and I waited in silence, until finally my mother walked in wearing a sympathetic smile. She looked beautiful as always, wearing a dress similar to a maxi one, with her hair hanging down her back. A few moments after she hugged Oden and I, my father walked in and it seemed like a dark cloud had suddenly covered the room.

"Hi, Daddy," I stood up, hoping he would acknowledge me.

"Khyle," he stated dryly before giving me a loose hug.

"Mr. Luke," Oden stuck his hand out to shake my father's, but my dad just turned away and sat down next to my mother, across from us.

Oden didn't say anything as he and I sat back down, staring at my parents. No one knew where to start, and the harder my dad glared at us, the more difficult it became for me to think of something to say.

"So what are your plans, Khyle?" My dad squinted his eyes at me, clasping his hands in front of himself.

"Well umm, I plan to still finish school and on time while—"

"How?" he cut me off, one brow raised. He was so angry that you could almost see steam coming from his ears and nose.

"My counselor said the classes I need for junior year will be available online. So I plan to take online classes for my junior year while the baby is still young, and then maybe for my senior year, I will look into a babysitter. I'm not sure."

"What do you plan to do while she's making all of these sacrifices, Oden?" he turned his attention to my baby. Oden was nowhere near as nervous as me.

"I plan to help her in anyway she needs me to. When she needs to study, do homework, take tests, or anything like that, I will watch our baby. I'm graduating this fall semester, so that will free up a lot of my time."

"You're in college?" my father frowned, but more so like he was confused, not upset. Finally, an expression that wasn't an angry one.

"Yeah, I'm in college studying business. I will be getting my degree in business with a minor in foreign language."

"Really? I guess that was one of the questions we forgot to ask during Christmas and Thanksgiving dinner," my mom grinned. "That's fantastic, Oden."

"And you plan to use that to further your businesses?" my dad inquired. I smiled seeing that he was softening up.

"Exactly. I know a lot about the business arena already, but having that degree gives you an insight on things that the average mind wouldn't know. The foreign language part will assist me in making business deals with people overseas."

"I see," my dad nodded.

"Do you speak any foreign languages?" my mom asked.

"No, Mama," I spoke for him, chuckling.

"Actually, yes. Spanish and French only. I was gonna add more, but that's all I can handle right now with everything else going on."

I stared at this nigga because I had no idea he was so well rounded. Well I did, but I guess he was just more accomplished than I thought.

"Oden, my problem with Khyle and you having a baby is not you necessarily, young man, it's the fact that she's only 18 going on 19, and I fear a child will stop her from pursuing her dreams. I want Khyle to be her own woman, not someone who depends on her husband or significant other to provide for her and do for her," my dad explained.

"Exactly. We raised both of our daughters to be independent, well at least we tried to. And like my husband, I want to see Khyle come into her own, making something of herself before starting a family," my mom added.

"And she will. I love Khyle, and I want the same things for her that you do. Would I rather be married to her already, and we both have our degrees before having a child? Of course, but that's not the hand she and I were dealt. You did a good job with her because she's very independent, and very focused on school. I mean, you saw her grades," Oden assured them.

"And Oden makes all A's too," I grinned, making my mother and Oden chuckle lightly.

"Just know that your daughter is great and in good hands. She will graduate from school in three more years, all while being a great mother."

"Do you plan to marry her?" my dad quizzed.

"Yeah, I do. I would marry her this second, but I want things to settle down a bit before all of that."

My father nodded slowly as he looked over at my mother. She touched his hand and mouthed something I couldn't quite understand.

"Well son, I'm gonna hold you to that promise you just made me. I wanna see Khyle prosper, and I want a healthy grandchild."

"I got you," Oden smiled.

He and my father rose to shake hands, before my dad pulled him in for a hug. Oden then hugged my mom again, before we all shared low laughs. I could tell we were all happy this went well.

"I have dinner ready, so is everyone hungry?" my mom inquired.

"Yeah," we all answered simultaneously as we headed out of the den.

My father grabbed me back as Oden and my mom left. He pulled me into a tight hug, and then kissed the top my head.

"I missed you, sweetheart, and I'm sorry for how long we went without talking."

"It's okay, Daddy, I should have called too."

"No, I'm your father, and you're my child. You shouldn't have to hunt me down. But listen, no matter what happens between you and him, you can always talk to me, okay? I can't promise that I won't shoot him, but I do promise to be there for you."

"Thank you, Daddy," I giggled because he was so crazy.

We left the den to join Oden and my mom for dinner. They were already joking and talking, which was good to see.

I couldn't be happier about the way things had gone down.

CHAPTER SEVEN

Oden

Khyle and I were back in Vegas just for the weekend, because I had some business to handle. I told her I would be back soon, and that she could stay in the suite I had booked, but she wanted to come with me. I didn't mind though; I honestly loved spending time with her, and hated when we were states a part. Look at her got me sounding like a bitch, but I guess that's how you act when you're in love. She had me open for real, and it was low-key scary.

"So what do you do in here?" Khyle ran her delicate fingers across the edge of my expensive cherry wood desk.

It was in the middle of the afternoon, and since I had some shit to do inside of Palace, Khyle agreed to come. The club wasn't open yet, so I felt it wouldn't be any harm having her underage ass in here with me. We'd be gone before it opened up anyway.

And after doing all this damn paperwork, I planned to go home and lay up with my baby.

"I mostly handle paperwork for the club, or other businesses."

"Like the employees paychecks?"

"No, not paychecks. My club manager, Cara does that, but she sends it through Anton for approval first. I mainly deal with how much liquor is ordered, food, supplies, and events that people may want to throw here."

"So can I ask you something?"

"Course, baby," I furrowed my brows as I typed on my computer.

"How much do you make just from the club? Not including Anton and Truman, just you, how much do *you* make?"

"Like in a month?"

"If you can figure it out, yeah. But yearly is okay, too."

"Club is just now creeping up on a year, so I guess we'll go with monthly. I make about $80,000 a month from the club. Sometimes $120,000 if we have a lot of events, birthday parties, and holidays."

I laughed when her mouth dropped.

"Okay, I will no longer bitch and moan about you buying me expensive things."

"Finally," I chuckled. "But it's two clubs in one, a strip club and a regular club, so we make a lot of money here."

"Maybe I should open a club."

"I think you have to be of drinking age at the least to open a club, baby."

"I'm old enough to have your baby, but I'm not old enough to open a club of my own. This world makes no sense sometimes."

"Tell me about it."

I scooted back from my desk so she could sit in my lap. We kissed for a little bit, and I ran my hand up her smooth buttery thigh.

"You hungry?" she inquired. My bottom lip was tucked in my mouth because my mind was still elsewhere. "Earth calling."

"Oh shit, yeah. I am."

"Want some In-N-Out Burger?"

"Yeah, that's cool."

She got up from my lap, and rounded my desk to get her purse. I noticed her body was filling out some more, and it kept me horny 24/7. Her thighs were a bit thicker, and her butt was a bit plumper. She was perfect before, but somehow she'd improved on perfection.

"Be back in a little bit." She switched out in them little ass jean shorts that had me ready to bang her out.

I closed my eyes and took a deep breath to calm myself down, just as my phone rang. When I looked down, I saw it was Giovanni, the guy I'd made a deal with in Modena.

"Hello?" I answered, still typing on my computer.

"Bishop, how are you?"

"Alright. What did you need, Gio?" I sat back in my chair, placing my hand over my eyes since they were starting to hurt from looking at the computer.

"I just wanted to make sure we were both holding up our ends of the deal. You're selling the cars I give you for no more than $250,000 right?"

"That's what we agreed upon, so yeah. Why?"

"I was informed that you were selling them for a little over half a million. Now I didn't believe it, but I wanted to ask and be sure."

"Who told you that?"

Laughing, he said, "It's fine, son. Just—"

"Cecil," I chuckled angrily. Giovanni's silence told me everything. That nigga was trying to throw me under the bus in hopes of me losing my deal with Giovanni.

"Have a good day, Oden."

"You too."

I hung up and shook my head, thinking about Cecil. I didn't work with him because I didn't want to kill his ass, but it looked like I was gonna have to do so anyway.

I continued working, putting a dent in all of this shit, and by the time I was done, Khyle texted me that she needed help. I didn't want that stinky ass food in my office, so I told her I'd come down to meet her so we could eat at the empty bar and then go home.

Cutting my computer off, I made sure everything in my office was locked up, before I left out, locking my office door. I made it downstairs on the side of the building where I'd told her to go, but when I opened the door she wasn't standing there. I stepped out of the door, and right when I did, I heard her laugh. Looking to my left, my heart dropped as I watched her interact with my bum ass father.

"Khyle, what are you doing?" I rushed over, looking from her to my dad nervously.

"Baby, he says he's your father," she grinned as if this shit wasn't weird.

"Khyle, go inside."

My father just stood there, face long as fuck like he'd expected me to have a better reaction. This muthafucka was out of his finger-licking mind.

"Oden—"

"Go inside! Here—take the damn key!" I barked at Khyle's ass and she rushed off. After making sure she was inside of the club using the side door, I turned back to my father. "Fuck are you doing around here, huh? Did you forget that it's not winter time?"

"I've been getting clean, Oden, and I wanted to talk to you."

"You can't even spell the word clean, Ossie!"

"Look at me, son! Do I look the same? I took that money you gave me and got help! I finished a program, and now I'm back. I'm good, and I want to be in your life."

"Nah, no," I shook my head repeatedly. "You have to go, man. I can't do this right now. I have my girl, and we have a baby coming. I'm finishing school. I-I have too much shit on my plate for this."

"Oden, if I didn't need you I wouldn't ask. The only people I have in my life are drug addicts. If I go with them I may relapse. Please, son." He had his hands in the prayer mode.

Looking off, I ran my hand down my hair before turning my attention back to him.

"Okay, look. Go to the Caesar's Palace hotel and tell the manager

Roscoe that you're my father and you need a suite. Tell him to charge me for it. If he needs confirmation he will call me," I said as I dialed on my iPhone. I was gonna have one of my people's come pick this nigga up and drive him.

"I can walk, the strip is right around the corner."

"Nah, someone is coming. Stay here, and my boy Sirio will be here in five minutes. Remember, Roscoe the manager. I will check on you later."

He nodded as he blew out hot air, so I went back inside of the club. I saw Khyle eating her food at the bar quietly, so I came up to her slowly.

"I'm sorry, baby, I was caught off guard."

"It's fine. Is he really your dad?"

"Yeah, unfortunately." I sat down.

"Why haven't I met him?"

"Because he's a fucking junkie and I didn't want you around him. I don't acknowledge him like that."

"He doesn't appear to be on drugs."

"Well he is. *Was* I guess. He says he's clean and wants me to help him. I'm gonna see what I can do."

"Aren't you happy he's clean, baby?" she rubbed my back as I sipped the drink from In-N-Out.

"He's sang this same song before, Khyle, and then played me. If he were being for real this time then yes, I'd be happy, but I just don't know."

"Be positive. Maybe now he finally sees that he should change. You have this club and you've made something out of yourself. He's proud of you and wants to be a part of your life."

"We will just have to see."

***

That night...

I stood outside of my dad's suite, hesitating. I wanted to leave, but I also wanted to talk to him; look into his eyes to see if he was being honest.

"Hi son." He answered the door for me, and I immediately began scanning the living room area with my eyes before sitting down. "Thanks for all this. It's really nice."

"So what, you serious this time or are you on that bullshit again?"

"I'm serious. I hadn't planned to use that money you gave me to get clean, but the way you looked at me that night made me feel like shit. That's when I decided I was gonna at least try. And now, here I am, feeling 100 times better."

"My life is good, Pop, and I don't need you coming in it and fucking my head up."

"I know, son, I know." He scratched his head. "She's beautiful."

"Who?"

"Kylie, she said her name was?"

"Khyle."

"Oh, yes. I thought she said Khyle, but since that's a guys name I assumed I'd misheard. But yes, Khyle is very beautiful. Us Bishops have always been suckers for pretty women."

"She's nothing like mom."

"And that's a good thing; a great thing."

"So you'll be staying here until you get on your feet. Here is a phone with my number in it already so you can call me." I stood up.

"Thank you. Will I see you sometime soon?"

"Maybe. In the meantime, look for work or something. I will send someone over to take you shopping for clothes."

I walked towards the door and he followed me. As I pulled it open to leave he said, "I love you, son."

I kept my back to him as I stood there for a few moments, and then just walked out without another word.

CHAPTER SEVEN

Bella

"Oh Mama, I can take care of the dishes," I smiled at my mother.

Surprised, she asked, "Are you sure, mija? It'll only take me a second to do."

"Yes, I'm sure. It's just a few dishes. You already made the meal so go ahead and lie down. Goodnight."

"Goodnight, sweetheart, and thank you."

I watched my mother leave the kitchen before a huge smile burst through my face. I needed her and my father to go to sleep so I could creep with my baby.

"Fuck you got planned?" my brother Brandon walked in.

I hated when he came to visit from Oakland at times. I have no idea why the hell he moved over there, but it wasn't for anything good. He still called home for money and everything else, so it couldn't have been a damn job he left for. I loved my brother for real, because he was my blood, but damn did he annoy me with his mooching ways.

"Nothing, what are you even talking about?"

"The fact that as soon as mama turned her back you were looking all giddy and shit. Let me find out you're sneaking to the guest room."

"So what if I am? It's not like I haven't had sex with Santino before."

"How could I forget? He sexed you then dogged you."

"No he did not, Brandon!" I sucked my teeth and placed the dish into the drying rack. "You know why we broke up so don't even make it sound like that."

"What happened to the big angry nigga you started fucking with?" He opened a can of soda and sat down at the kitchen table.

"His name is Dean, and we broke up. He's gotten somebody else already. Actually, he had her since September of last year."

Dean's ass had finally stopped trying to contact me via every social media site around. And recently, I saw that his little bitch Trish was pregnant by him, so I guess I spoke it into existence.

"Damn, I never liked him anyway."

"How is Tamia?" I inquired about his girlfriend of forever. He was never going to be faithful to her, but I guess she was the only one who couldn't see that.

"She's good like always because she got me."

"Oh my gosh."

We laughed in unison.

He talked to me until I finished washing the dishes, and then we hugged before going our separate ways. When I got up into my bedroom, I took a hot shower and then spread lotion all over my body.

I sprayed a little spot of perfume on my neck and collarbone, and by that time, it'd been a good hour since I'd finished the dishes, so my parents should have been asleep.

I came out of my bedroom quietly, and then went downstairs and to the back towards the guest room. I walked right in, and saw Santino was lying down in the dark. His chest was moving up and down slowly, so I guess he was asleep already. He always said my mother's good food made him tired. I didn't care though; I wanted some dick. I'd been seeing him all day and I could barely touch him.

"Baby, baby, wake up," I shook him lightly, getting into the bed.

"Bella," he grunted lowly, rubbing and squeezing my inner thigh. That only made me wetter. "Give me 10 minutes," he whispered, drifting back off to sleep.

I got up, pulled my nightclothes off, and then got back into his bed naked. Lying on my stomach, I got in the doggy-style position, with the side of my face pressed into the pillow. I was looking his way, so I ran my finger over his full sexy lips.

"Santino," I mumbled.

"Bella—" he stopped talking to eye me in position, and then immediately sat up. I chuckled as he pushed his boxers down with the quickness and got behind me. "You're soaking already with your freaky ass."

"I know… I want it," I whined.

"You know I like when you talk nasty like that."

He forced his way inside of me, prompting me to grip the sheets in my hands. Santino was blessed down below, and he never let my pussy forget. He moved in and out of me slowly, getting me wetter and wetter with every thrust. I was so full of him, whimpering every time I hit the base of his long, thick dick. His strong, rough hands rubbed up and down me slowly as he wound his hips into me, making me cry out like a little child.

"Ahhh, I'm gonna cum."

"Cum on it." He spanked me, grabbing my ass roughly once his hand landed.

Chills ran up and down my spine every time he smacked my ass and grabbed on it. I could see him out the corner of my eye, biting his bottom lip while watching himself work. His motions were slow, steady, and driving me crazy. The sweet pleasure he delivered by stroking my walls, mixed with the pain I felt here and there was what I loved about sexing him.

"Mmm," my voice shook violently along with my body as I spilled my nectar on his thick pole.

"Fuck," he panted, referring to how hard I came.

Holding my hips tightly, he started to pound me from behind, making me yell. I tried to muffle it at first, but the way he had me ready to burst was too much. Not to mention it felt so good that I didn't care who heard. If my parents walked in right now they would just have to stand by until I got my second orgasm.

"Damn, shit, Bella."

I scraped my nails down the wooden headboard, just before Santino pushed my face back down into the pillow. He didn't lose his stride, as he continued to pummel me with force and precision. I was about ready to cry because of how good this felt.

"Ahhh! Ahhh! Ahh!" my moans became high pitched, right along with his, and soon after we came simultaneously.

We stayed in position until he was finally able to pull out of me. He fell to the side, and after going to pee, I cuddled up next to him.

"I wish you could sleep in here with me."

"Me too, but my parents, especially my father, would go crazy."

"Don't I know it?" It got quiet for a few before he said, "When I get drafted, what are we gonna do, baby?"

"Well, that won't be until we graduate, right?" I looked up into his face as I laid on his chest. He didn't look at me, he just kept his eyes fixated on the ceiling.

"Nah, this will be my last year in school." He finally turned his eyes down to me, and I just looked intently into his face with my mouth slightly ajar.

"Do you know what team?"

"No, but a lot of teams from California are looking at me. They've been watching me since high school, so most likely I will be moving there."

"So what are we supposed to, break up when you get drafted?"

"What? Fuck no. I'm thinking about getting two spots; something small in Los Angeles, and something medium in Las Vegas until you graduate. That way I can have a home in California, but when I'm free or on off season, I can post up in Vegas with you."

"So that means I would have to live in Vegas permanently?"

"Yeah, you don't like that idea? I know your life is here in Scottsdale, but that's the best I can think of to be close to you. And you know, when you're not in school we can stay at the crib in California, or visit Scottsdale."

"My old life is here in Scottsdale, but the one I want to build with you can be in Vegas."

"Yeah? So you fuck with that plan?" he grinned, making me chuckle and do the same. I just nodded. "Cool. I promise, Bella, I will be around and with you any time I can."

"I know. We're gonna make it."

"We are. I just wish my homies could be around to see me make it, you know?"

I swallowed the lump in my throat because I knew he was talking about Huelo. He'd been stuck on him disappearing for the longest.

"Like whom?" I asked as if I didn't already know.

"Well, mainly, Huelo. Caesar and Corey are gonna be there to celebrate, but not Huelo and… I don't know. I guess because shit with him was so sudden and the fact that I have no idea what happened, I can't get over it."

"Santino?"

"Yeah?"

"If I tell you something, will you promise me that you won't say anything? This information cannot be spread around, or there will be repercussions for probably the both of us."

"Baby, what's up?" he turned his whole body to face me, removing his chest and arm from under me.

"Promise me."

"Fuck, you know I don't like promising shit when I don't know what the deal is, but with the way you're talking, it may be best I follow your instructions. So… I promise."

"Well, remember when I told you Huelo tried to force himself on Khyle?"

"Yeah, what happened with that exactly? Do you know?"

"I told you, he pretended like he needed her notes, and then came in her room and tried to rape her. She said she'd never seen him act that way, or talk so disrespectfully."

"I just can't see him doing no shit like that. I mean, Huelo was a good guy, and he had a thing for Khyle, but it wasn't deep enough for him to try and rape her."

"Well he did, and he was calling her a hoe, saying he knew how she liked to get down and—"

"Oh fuck," he groaned, closing his eyes.

"What?" I searched his handsome face as if it'd tell me what was going through his mind at the moment.

"Trevor told Huelo and I about how Khyle came to a party with one nigga and fucked a different nigga in the bathroom. Basically, he was saying she was hot in the pants, and Huelo was kind of disappointed to say the least."

"So what? That doesn't give him the right to rape her. A prostitute doesn't deserved to be raped, Santino."

"I know and I agree. It's just I think he assumed that she would sleep with him because of what she'd done at the party, and when she, resisted I guess he got angry… shit, I don't know."

"Niggas. And plus, she came to the party with her then boyfriend, and fucked her now current boyfriend in the bathroom."

"It was Oden she let hit in the bathroom?"

"Yes, nigga. But Santino, I'm telling you this because the only reason Huelo didn't succeed was because Oden walked in on him."

He looked at me, confused, before he finally understood.

"And Oden got at that nigga…"

"Exactly."

"Oden killed the homie?"

"Yes, but Santino, you promised. You must take this shit to your grave. I don't want Oden coming after you."

"Ain't nobody scared of Oden, Bella. And stop acting like I can't handle myself against him," he frowned.

You can't, babe, you can't.

"I know you can, but you need to focus on football and us, not Huelo. And do you really want to go around defending a man who would rape someone?"

"You're right. You're right. I really don't have the time or brain capacity for that shit. I miss the bro, but I have other shit to focus on, like you and my babics."

"What babies?" I giggled as he palmed my flat stomach.

"The one I'm gonna put in here down the line." He got on top of me, in between my legs. "Mmmm," he moaned as he made his way inside of me. I spread my legs wider to accept him.

I prayed like hell that he kept his mouth shut and moved on from this Huelo shit. It wasn't worth his life or mine. And I'm sure Oden would probably take both if Santino snitched.

CHAPTER EIGHT

Anton

One month later...

Tasmine hadn't spoken to me since she kicked me out of her hotel suite that I was currently paying for. I tried dropping by a few times, but she either wouldn't answer the door or she would already be out and about somewhere. Then I got an extra key so I could just come in, but she cursed my ass out and wouldn't let me get a word in edgewise. I knew I was about a millisecond from throwing her ass out of the window of the hotel, so I just decided to leave at that point.

I loved Tasmine… a lot. I loved her because she made me do shit, shit that I should have been motivated to do before meeting her but wasn't. Had we not gotten together, I'm not even sure I would have had Selinda and Kai's babies tested already. At this moment they probably would have still been harassing me, and I would have been planning to kill them instead of doing what I needed to do. As my mother would say, Tasmine put some fire under my ass. By saying that, in order to possibly get her back, I needed to put that same fire under myself. I was determined to get Tasmine and keep her, even though the shit seemed to be impossible right now.

Pulling up to Violet's home, I parked a little ways down like I always did. For some reason I didn't want my shit right in front of her house. Getting my iPhone out of my pocket, I dialed our nurse Pheobe's partner, Whitney. I didn't want to speak with Phoebe for good reason, trust me.

"Hey, boss," Whitney answered.

"Where are you?" I got right to the point. No need for the damn formalities.

"Oh, well I'm eating lunch right now at the Capital Grille. Did you need something?"

These nurses we hired lived the muthafucking good life. Since we needed them to be on call for us at all times, considering the fact that we could be harmed randomly, they didn't have another job with a hospital or anything. They had good relationships with people that got them the tools they needed and shit, but that was about it. What that meant was, whenever we didn't need them, they got paid to just be free and live life. We gave them a monthly lump sum, every month, whether there was an injury or not.

"I need you to do another DNA test for me, Whit."

"Wow, you're a busy man, Mr. Nickerson," she chuckled, but it subsided when she didn't hear me doing the same. "I'm sorry. Well, let me get a doggie bag for my food and I will call Phoebe."

"No! Do not call her. I need you alone for this."

"But she's the boss, and I have to—"

"She's the boss?" I asked, a little bit appalled that, that'd come out of her mouth. Oden, Truman, and I were the ones who broke her off, so I don't know what the fuck she was calling Phoebe her boss for.

"No, no, you are. I will take care of it. Where do you need me?"

"The same place that Phoebe read the results last time. Townhouse on Petricola." I looked out of my car window to see if Violet had come out.

"Okay. I should be there in—"

"Give me 20 minutes. I need you here in 20 minutes. When you arrive, text me and I will let you know when to come in, okay? And don't park right in front."

"Ye-yes sir."

"See you soon."

I got out of the car, grabbing the shit that Violet asked me to pick up. She always needed me to pick a gang of shit up, on top of the $8000 that I gave her every month. Blowing out hot air, I made it to her door and after knocking only once, she answered.

"Thank you," she smiled, hugging me in the process.

I scanned the spotless living room, wondering how the hell I was gonna get Athen to be tested without her seeing it. I took a seat next to him, since he was lying in some little pillow carrier thing. Nigga was always sleep, and made me realize how much sleep I was always losing.

"So how have you been, Violet?" I quizzed as she unpacked the shit I got her.

"I've been doing okay. I'm supposed to go back to work soon, but I don't know if I will. Athen needs me, and frankly child support pays all the bills and more."

Wow.

"Oh yeah? But don't you like your job?"

"I do. That's why I still haven't decided yet. Daycare isn't an option, so I'm not sure what I'm gonna do."

"Oh, alright. Have you been able to get out of the house, you know get your nails done and shit like that?"

"What are you trying to say?" she grinned, placing her small hand on her hip.

"I just want you to have some time to relax. You're here with the baby all the time, and I just want to help you. It's my kid too, and I get time to do me way more than you."

"I would like to get a massage, actually a whole spa day." She looked off, wondering.

"So go. I will even pay for it. About how much do you need?"

"And you will stay here with him until I get back?"

"Sure will."

"Wow, thank you, Tony. I guess about 300 would be good."

She was making me feel bad as hell for what I was about to do, but my suspicions had gotten the best of me, and I missed my shorty.

"No problem." I peeled off $300 in 20s and reached it out to her. She rushed over to me, and grabbed the money, cheesing like a Cheshire cat.

I waited in the living room with my 'son', while she changed clothes and got ready in the back. She came back to the living room about 10 minutes later, and that's right when Whitney texted me and said she was here.

Me: Wait for me to tell you to come in.

Whit: Okay.

"Okay, just call me if anything goes wrong. I should be back in about an hour and a half. Thanks again, Anton," Violet smiled and rushed out of the house after kissing Athen on the cheek.

I watched her close the door, and then shot up off the couch to look out the window. Once she sped off in that new truck I'd gotten her, I called Whitney to let her know she could come in. I waited by the door until she got close, carrying a big colorful bag, and then I opened the door before she could knock.

"Thank you—" I paused after I closed the door. I noticed when I got close to her she flinched and looked down. "You okay?"

"Ye-yeah, I'm okay. I-I just don't know why I'm here." Whitney looked young as hell, but she had to at least be in her mid to late 20s if she was a certified nurse already. I didn't even know women her age could be this shy.

"Relax, I ain't call you here to sleep with you or anything."

"You didn't? I mean I know you didn't," she laughed awkwardly before it faded out. I then noticed she had a little bit of makeup on.

"No, I didn't. I want you to test the baby again."

"But why? Phoebe already did it."

"I know she did, but I just need another test for confirmation. I don't understand how this is my baby, Whitney, so please."

"Phoebe is really good at what she does—"

"Can you just please test the baby again. If your results come back the same, I will leave it alone. But I ask that you complete the test yourself, meaning you send it to the lab, not Phoebe. I don't want her knowing anything about this."

"K," Whitney nodded.

She turned her attention to a sleeping Athen, and made her way over to him, setting her bag on the floor. She reached in and began setting shit up, before gently swabbing his mouth. He didn't wake up which I was thankful for. When she was done with him, she swabbed me, and then collected the sample.

"How long will this take?"

"About five days, Mr. Nickerson. I will see about a quick turnaround, but we don't like to put a rush on stuff like this."

"Thank you, Whitney."

"No problem." She started out with her head down.

"Aye!" I called out and she turned around. "And if I didn't have a girlfriend, I would definitely be trying to fuck you," I smiled widely and so did she.

Why not boost her self-esteem a bit?

"See you soon, Mr. Nickerson." She kept her smile on, pushing her hair behind her ears.

I closed the door and locked it, then made my way back over to the couch. I saw Athen's eyes were open, which made me smile a little.

"Hey man. I'm sorry I had to do this. If you really are my son, I want you to know that I love you and I didn't mean any harm." I brushed my pointer finger down his small nose. "You know what, even if you're not my son, I love you. And I will always look out for you, man. Whatever you need you can come to me, son or not, aight?"

I admit I'd grown close to him over time. Something was missing from our bond, but I did have love for him, and didn't want anything to happen to little homie. I would vow to look out for him for as long as I could, even though I knew I wasn't his dad.

I turned on the TV, but made sure the volume was low so it wouldn't disturb him. I moved his small pillow holder with him in it, into my lap. He appeared to be comfortable, and so was I, and after a while of watching TV, I dozed off.

Two hours later...

"Come here, baby," I heard Violet's voice. I opened my eyes to see her lifting Athen up from my lap.

"Is he alright? Shit, I didn't mean to fall asleep."

"Relax, Tony, he's fine." She rocked him before sitting next to me and grabbing her cloth to cover her upper body while she breastfed him.

"I have some stuff to take care of, so I'm gonna go. But let me know if you need anything, okay?"

"Yeah. Thank you for today."

"No problem," I kissed her cheek.

I left out of her home and jogged lightly to my car. Opening my glove compartment, I pulled out the box with the diamond necklace in it that I'd bought for Tasmine. I planned to give it to her a while ago, but with all the shit going on, I kept forgetting. It was around 6pm in the evening, and since school was back in session, I knew she was probably in her dorm watching all her shows that came on Monday nights.

Feeling good about the DNA test that was done, I decided to head over to UNLV to give her the necklace. I was hoping it would soften her up a little bit.

I made it there in about 15 minutes, and parked my car in the back. As I was coming around the front of the dorm building, I spotted a figure that I knew all too well, standing across the way.

"Amethyst?" I frowned.

As soon as I said that, she darted off, and I was right on her damn heels. I finally caught up to her, and gripped her body tightly from behind.

"Let me go or I will scream," she gritted over her shoulder.

"Either you bring yo' ass with me right now, or I will come get you later. And if I have to do that you won't live to see another day." I spoke with my lips right up against her ear.

She said nothing, which I took to mean that she would comply. We walked back to the car, while I made sure no one was outside that knew Tasmine.

Amethyst and I got into my whip, and I peeled out, shaking my head in frustration. I planned to give this gift to Tasmine and maybe get a damn kiss at the least, but this bitch had fucked it up. She'd been fucking up a lot of shit lately, and it was time I killed that. I didn't want anything else interfering with my relationship with Tasmine.

"I'm sorry, Anton."

"Fuck you." I continued to drive, not even looking her way.

"But you led me on, so you can't expect me to—"

"Bitch, what? I didn't fucking lead you on! I told you I didn't want a damn girlfriend and you acted like that shit was cool! Fuck out here with that bullshit! I should knock the shit out you for lying like that!" I roared so loudly my own ears rang.

This hoe had me hot. I was done, DONE fucking with these hoes. Yeah, it was easy pussy and they were down for anything, but all the fucking hassle that came along with it was never worth it. Once I got rid of Amethyst, I was getting Tasmine back and keeping on the straight and narrow. I was too old and too damn tired to keep dealing with this shit. It was nice while it lasted but I wasn't about the psycho fuck buddy life anymore.

"Breaking my muthafucking window and shit," I mumbled more to myself than her as I pulled up to a house my homies and I had far off. It was where we came when we were injured, or had to take care of business that was top secret in a way.

"Where are we?"

"My real house," I lied. "Get out."

We got out of the car and once inside of the home, I led her down to the basement. She was hesitant, but with a gun pressed to her back she couldn't do much.

"What are we doing here?" she began to cry.

"You know I don't like killing women."

"Then don't, Anton. I promise I will leave you and Tasmine alone. I swear, please!" she begged, crying hysterically by now.

"What did you think was gonna happen to you if you kept fucking with me?"

"I don't know! I didn't… I guess I thought you'd come back. But please, I promise to leave you alone and never come back. I will leave the state, change my name; whatever you want just please don't kill me, Tony! Please!"

"Hmmm," I hummed, clutching my gun tightly as I stared at her trash ass. "How do I know you're telling the truth?"

"I don't know how I can prove it to you, but I swear! Oh Lord Jesus, save me, please! Oh God forgive me, please! I promise—"

"Shut the fuck up! Damn!"

"Sorry," she mumbled before tucking her lips in. She was trembling, scared out of her damn mind.

It was obvious to me that she didn't believe the shit she'd heard about my crew and I. But now that she was witnessing firsthand that I wasn't the one to fuck with, she was shook.

Taking out my phone, I dialed Tasmine. As the line trilled, I put it on speakerphone and said, "Apologize to my girl."

"Yes, anything." She reached for my phone but I pulled away.

"Just talk, you don't need to hold it. Get stupid and watch me put a bullet in your head."

She nodded frantically just as Tasmine came through the phone with the driest hello known to man.

"Baby, please don't hang up. I have Amethyst here, and she wants to apologize to you for what she's done."

"Anton."

"Just listen dammit."

Tasmine sucked her teeth, but stayed quiet. I couldn't wait to get back with her and fuck the shit out of her for all that damn attitude she was giving me.

"Ta-Tasmine, I'm sorry for stalking you and throwing things at you. I-I'm also sorry for the things I've said. And I hope that you and Tony can move on from the bullshit I have caused. You won't hear from or see me ever again, unless it's in passing, but that's normal because we live in the same city and it's not uncommon for us to—"

"Shut the fuck up," I barked lowly, lip turned up. She stayed doing the fucking most.

"Right, sorry. Anyways, I apologize and it won't happen again," Amethyst finished up.

"I don't fucking accept, and you better pray I *don't* see you in passing bitch."

Click.

Amethyst picked her jaw up and shrugged. I didn't care if Tasmine accepted or not, I just wanted her to hear the apology.

"I don't want anymore shit from you or it's a wrap. And don't try to go to the police because most of them work for me."

"Got it."

I started to walk out and she was right behind me.

"Oh, and you're fired from Palace."

"Yes, yes, of course."

I was gonna let this bitch live because like I said, killing females wasn't my thing. But if she so much as bumped Tasmine on the strip, or looked at me too long, I was blowing her brains out.

CHAPTER EIGHT

Shayne

Marisol, Khyle, and I were out to lunch at this Italian steakhouse on the strip. I hadn't seen Marisol in a while, and I wanted to hang with my sister so I thought it was best to conjoin them.

Marisol was becoming a close friend of mine, so I wanted her and Khyle to meet. I know we're pretty close already, but I meant in a friendly way. I was strictly dickly, like Marisol, but we were slightly attracted to one another. I guess that's what happens when two pretty ass bitches start hanging out.

"You never told me how Alabama was?" Khyle said, gulping her drink down. Her ass had been a little hungry hippo lately, but it was justified.

"It was cool. It's so slow down there, which makes good for relaxing and shit. But when you're trying to turn up, nah."

"I'm sure there are some spots for all that, but you just don't know about it. That's not what you were there for anyway. You were there for your man," Marisol grinned.

"Yeah, I know. It was good for us."

Ever since that night Lloyd tried to cheat on me, he and I had been great. He was wonderful before, but I could definitely see the change in his personality now that he was over the grudge he had against me. I didn't notice it until after he explained it to me. Anyhow, I was just happy that I had someone like him, because he gave me everything Pierce couldn't; security, love, great sex, and excitement.

"Have you heard from Pierce?" Khyle quizzed.

"Nope. He texted me once or twice while I was down south, but I didn't respond. I guess he finally got the hint because it's been almost two months now, right?"

"Believe so. It's been a long ass time. I'm happy for you. And you, Mrs. Bishop," Marisol smiled at Khyle.

"Not quite yet, but maybe after I graduate."

"Can you believe your little sister tamed the beast? Girl, you need to teach a class because your man used to really be out there."

"I know, Marisol, but thank you, I guess," Khyle chuckled nervously. "I think you should check on Pierce, maybe see how he's holding up," she turned to me.

"Ugh, why?" I frowned.

"Because you guys were together for a long ass time, and you can't just leave him in the dust like that. You did do him pretty wrong, Shayne."

"I mean, I don't care for the nigga because he was a bitch, but I do agree with your little sister," Marisol nodded, shoving some potatoes into her mouth.

"I kind of wanted to be done with that part of my life, but I guess it wouldn't hurt to see how he's doing. Maybe we can be friends or something."

"Nah," Khyle and Marisol said in unison before laughing.

"Aight, maybe not friends, but I'd like to be cordial with him. You know if I see him out, I'd like for him to say hello or something."

I loved Pierce so I did want to see him happy. I thought I would enjoy him being miserable without me, but the truth was, that wasn't what I wanted. He needed to be happy and to find himself someone. Maybe a new woman could help him build his self-esteem and act like more of a man. Or shoot, maybe he'd find someone who was okay with a nigga that was on the softer side. Whatever the case would turn out to be, I just didn't want him to hate me. Like Khyle said, we'd been together for a long while and I didn't want any hard feelings between us.

"So are you still single, Marisol?" I inquired.

"Not really. Ever since you broke my heart, I had to get out there so I did meet someone. His name is Ivan."

"How did Shayne break your heart?" Khyle asked with furrowed brows. Oh Lord.

"I was just kidding because we have fucked around before." Marisol chewed her food. "Oh shit, you didn't know that, huh?" she asked when she saw Khyle's mouth open.

"Shayne!" Khyle shrieked with a wide grin.

"It wasn't even like that. We just had fun as close friends, nothing more, okay?" I laughed along with she and Marisol.

"Yeah, I was fucking around, but Ivan is really cool. He knows how to handle someone like me. I can be feisty at times, and niggas bitch up when they see that side of me."

"Tell me about it. That's what I love about Lloyd. He can check my ass while still allowing me to be myself. With Pierce, he just cowered under me and it was such a turn off," I groaned.

"I've never had that problem with Oden or even Brian," Khyle said. "But I will say that Brian let me get away with more slick talk than Oden does."

"I bet," Marisol and I said in unison. I think we both knew not to mention the threesome we had with Oden. We'd take that to our graves; at least I would. Khyle didn't need to know Marisol slept with her man.

The three of us continued to chat and eat, and by the time we were done it was around 7:30pm. I dropped Marisol off in my fresh ass Range Rover, and then on my way home I decided to take a little detour.

My sister and Marisol were right, so I was gonna make a little pit stop at Pierce's home. If he wasn't there already, I would just let myself in and wait since I was sure he'd be home soon. He got off work at around 7pm and was usually home by 7:25pm when he didn't have to 'work late'.

Pulling up to my old humble abode, I parked my car and slid out. Making my way to the door, I knocked lightly before waiting. I looked over my shoulder to see that his car was here, so I knocked again but much harder. There was no answer, so I used my key to let myself in. When I saw the bathroom light outlining the bathroom door, I knew that was why his ass hadn't heard me.

As I moved further into the house, I heard a female moaning. Anger took over me for some reason, because I guess I didn't expect him to already be fucking someone else.

Dropping my purse onto the couch, I rushed to the back where the bathroom was, and walked right in. My eyes literally rolled out of my head as I watched what was going on right here in front of me. Them in the bathtub fucking like they were in love. My breathing became heavy and I felt like my heart would beat out of my chest.

"Shayne, let me explain," Alanna stood up in the tub and got out. I backed away slowly, darting my eyes back and forth between she and Pierce.

"Explain what, you fake ass bitch!" I hollered. "How long have y'all been fucking?"

Pierce ignored me, picking up his blunt from a nearby ashtray and lighting it. He blew smoke out of his mouth, laughing at the situation at hand.

"For like a month, Shayne." Alanna grabbed a towel and wrapped it around her naked body. "I only fucked him because I found out that you tried to fuck Earl. Jr. And when I told Pierce about it, we just… it just happened."

"Yeah, it just happened, but now we're in a relationship," Pierce finally spoke up, stepping out of the tub and grabbing a towel as well.

"So I'm gonna need the key to my crib back."

"Really, Pierce? My close friend? You couldn't find anyone else?"

"Really, Shayne? You've been opening your legs to all of Las Vegas while I was busting my ass at work. You were fucking niggas that I knew and had talked to. Had them niggas laughing behind my fucking back and shit!" Pierce spat angrily, as the blunt hung between his fingers.

"Shayne, you don't even want him. You and I can be cool once you get over this—"

"Alanna, you and I will never be friends. I may have done him wrong, but I have never done you dirty. I tried to help you build up your self-esteem, and yet, you were still so fucking blind! You believed a nigga who didn't give a fuck about you over me? Why would I want to fuck Earl Jr. with as much shit as I talked about him, huh?"

Earl Jr. had left Alanna and finally married the girl he was engaged to. I knew this even though we hadn't been talking because it was front-page news on just about every magazine. His wife was a beautiful girl, dumb, but beautiful. Well, actually, I can't call her dumb because I'm not sure if she knew about Alanna, but I know one thing is for sure, Alanna's ass was stupid as hell. Here she was, dumped again and forced to take my sloppy ass, weak ass, punk ass seconds.

I may have been brash and rude with my delivery to her at times, but it was just tough love. I wanted her to see that being a man's doormat wasn't gonna get her anywhere but thrown in the trash. The sight before me hurt more so because I thought Alanna and I were closer than this. I understood Pierce because I'd fucked him over, but

Alanna? She may have been a fool, but deep down in her heart she knew Earl Jr. was lying about me coming onto him.

"Shayne—"

"Man, fuck her, Alanna! She ain't nothing but a hoe ass—"

"Watch your mouth before I have my boyfriend bust a cap in your whack ass," I threatened Pierce.

He knew from the calmness in my tone and the intensity of my stare that I was dead serious; and I was. All I had to do was point, and Lloyd would shoot. Plus, killing Pierce was probably something he wanted to do anyways.

"Leave my house, Shayne," he said, trying not to look like a bitch in front of his hoe.

"Gladly."

I tossed the key to his crib in his face and then turned on my heels to grab my purse from the couch and walk out.

I was sad about losing Alanna, but I had to charge that shit to the game. I'd done a lot of fucked up shit in my life, and I guess this here was karma.

Maybe Alanna would be just what Pierce needed and vice versa. He needed a meek bitch that didn't want him to do better, and she just wanted a nigga to love her. As for me, I needed more, and I had that with Lloyd, so I was good.

CHAPTER EIGHT

$\mathcal{S}$ophomore year was in full rotation, and I felt really good. I was in love with a man who loved me back, I had a baby that we made growing inside of me, and my grades were bomb; I mean they were going to be bomb. I was still living on campus in my same dorm room with my same bestie, Tasmine, right across from my bestie Bella and umm, Perry.

Although pregnant, I wasn't far along at all, so Oden and I agreed that it was okay for me to stay on campus. I only got one year to experience college life so far, and since this would be the last year I could, I wanted to take full advantage. Plus, most of the time I was with Oden at his place anyway.

I shook my head as I passed a piece of a flyer that I knew was posted in hopes of finding Huelo. It was so strange to see people looking for him, when I knew he was gone and never coming back. Oden assured me that his body would never be found, and not to be surprised if years from now they declared him dead from absentia. I didn't know how my baby pulled shit like that off, but it was scary yet sexy at the same time.

"Hey Khyle," one of my new classmates from political science named Amy waved. I waved back to her and kept it pushing.

As I kept walking towards my dorm building, I spotted what looked like Perry. She'd been dodging me and I wanted to talk to her ass. I think she knew that I felt like she'd done something to me, which is why she was never around. So now that I saw her headed to the dorm hall, I was on her bumper.

"Hey baby," some deep voice blared behind me, as some long muscular arms embraced me.

"Fuck off me!" I elbowed whoever it was, and then turned to look up into their face. "What the hell is your problem?" I barked.

Looking confused he replied, "Khyle, it's me, Edward."

"So! Who the fuck are you? I don't know an Edward, and even if I did, why would you think you could touch on me like that!"

"Are you okay?"

"Yes, I'm okay. Just don't do that shit again, or I will have you fucked up, okay?"

"A bit extreme, but okay. I wanted to know if you would be down to see a movie or not? I found a theatre that shows old films like you love."

"I have a boyfriend, Edward. And secondly, I don't like old films."

"But you told me that you did."

"Listen to me nigga, I do not know you, and I have no idea what the fuck you're talking about. I don't like old films, and I don't like random niggas hugging me from behind aight?"

"Random? We've been talking all damn summer!" He pulled his phone out and scrolled through the Facebook messenger conversation.

I took his phone and began reading some of the messages. I didn't have Facebook anymore, but that was definitely my name, and definitely my picture as the profile. The messages were pretty intense, and whoever this person was, was definitely very sexual. Not to mention they knew certain things about what Oden and I had done before, because they used it in conversation.

"Now do you remember me, baby?" Edward broke me from my trance. "I haven't seen you all semester because I know you've been busy, but today I decided to follow you from class."

"Edward, this isn't me. I don't use Facebook anymore because my boyfriend, Oden Bishop, he felt like it was too messy."

"Then who the fuck is this?"

"I don't know, Edward, but I'm sorry."

"Are you fucking serious?" he groaned, looking off for a few moments. He looked so disappointed, and I felt a bit bad for him.

"Yeah, and again, I'm sorry."

As he stood there pinching the bridge of his nose, I rushed off towards my dorm. Getting onto the elevator inside, I rode it up to my floor, and dropped my shit off in my room. The only thing I had in hand was my iPhone. I walked across the way and knocked on Bella and Perry's room door, hoping Edward didn't make me miss Perry. I had to catch her, because I needed her to talk to me, and tell me she didn't do what I think she'd done.

"Umm, who is it?" Perry called from behind the door.

"Perry, you know who it is, you can see me through the peephole."

"Actually, I can't reach the hole. So, if you tell me who you are, I can go ahead and decide if I want to open the door."

Inhaling deeply out of frustration I replied, "It's Khyle, Perry."

"Oh, Bella isn't here."

"I'm looking for you."

"I'm kind of bus—"

"Open the fuck up, Perry," I gritted up against the thick wooden door as if it were her. I wasn't feeling well, and I was in a bad mood over the fact that someone had used my picture to get with that Edward nigga.

Finally, she pulled the door open and I barged in, waiting for her to close it back.

"How are you, Khyle? Is something wrong?"

"Perry, why have you been avoiding me?"

"Avoiding you? No, I have much harder classes this semester, so I'm not in my room as much. I'm always out studying. Bella likes to talk on the phone with Santino, have you guys over, and listen to music, so I can't really concentrate in here unless she's studying too."

That sounded pretty legit, but a part of me believed her ass was lying.

"Perry, how did Raquel find out that I had an abortion?"

"How would I know?" she walked away from the door and stood by the sink. "Raquel does her own thing you know."

"Because you talk to her. Didn't you have some kind of deal with her that ended with Bella beating her ass?"

"Yes, but after that she hasn't talked to me. She doesn't really like me anymore because I came clean to Bella."

"And you promise you didn't tell her about me getting rid of the baby? Because Oden said she told him, and the only way she would know is if one of us told her."

"Well maybe Bella and Tasmine aren't as good to you as you think they are, Khyle. I mean, how can you be sure that *they* didn't tell Raquel?"

"Bella can't even be in the same room with Raquel without wanting to punch her face in, so I doubt she pulled her to the side to tell my business."

"And Tasmine?" she raised her thin brows. She definitely needed to look into getting them filled out with a good brow pencil.

"Tasmine is my best friend and so is Bella. They would never do anything like that to me. So that only leaves you."

"You've known us all the same amount of time, so why am I not your best friend?"

"I-I don't know, Perry. I mean I like you, you're cool, but I guess we never really clicked because you don't say much."

"I have a reason for that."

Who cares at this point?

"You do?"

"Yes." She moved closer to me, fidgeting. "I think that I love you, Khyle. And before you freak out, I'm not gay or anything I just… I just admire you. I love your personality and you're so beautiful." She touched the ends of my long hair.

"Perry, you don't love me, baby girl, I just think that you're confused right now."

She had to be out of her mind. We didn't even spend enough time together for her to be in love with me. I mean we did, but we barely said two words to one another during the time spent.

"Yeah, I do. My feelings started to arise during the second semester of freshman year, and over the summer they grew stronger. I think about you all the time, and while you were away, I stayed on your social media accounts. Khyle, if you just try with me, you may love me too." She grabbed my hands into hers.

"I'm not gay, Perry. I-I have a boyfriend that I love very much. And you, well you're my friend, and I don't see you that way."

"But you haven't tried, Khyle." She kissed the back of my hand and I felt like I was gonna throw up. Maybe it was because I was pregnant, but I had a strong feeling it was because I was repulsed by her actions.

"Perry—"

"Can we just kiss once? Maybe I will get over it. And this won't be new for you because you kissed Bella."

"I kissed Bella because I was drunk, Perry."

"We can get drunk. I stole some bottles of champagne from my father's cellar, and it's pretty expensive." She walked towards her closet, I guess to get the drink.

"No, Perry, I can't drink."

"Why?"

"Because I'm pregnant, three months to be exact. Oden and I are gonna have the baby this time."

"But you said the only way we could kiss is if you were drunk! How is this gonna happen now that you're pregnant!"

She was scowling at me, and I had never even seen her angry before, let alone *this* damn angry.

"Perry, I said the reason I kissed Bella was because I was drunk, not that I would kiss you if we were drunk. Look, I explained to you that I'm not interested in you like that. I'm not interested in any woman!"

"Leave my room!" she screeched with her eyes closed. Her collarbone seemed to cave in more than it already was.

"Perry—"

"Leave!" she hollered even louder with her eyes closed.

I rushed out, fearing that she would stab me in my stomach or some shit. When I got into my room, I saw Tasmine sitting on her bed. She smiled at me, but it quickly dissipated when she saw my expression.

"What's wrong?" she inquired, putting her laptop to the side.

"Perry, she's fucking crazy. She told me she's in love with me, and tried to make me believe that you or Bella told Raquel about the abortion."

"Perry and crazy in the same sentence sounds funny."

"Tasmine, she told me she loved me and tried to get me to drink so I could kiss her. Then when I told her I couldn't quite drink, she kicked me out of her room."

Tasmine stared at me for a few, before bursting into laughter, clapping her hands and all.

"Oh girl, I'm sorry, but come on now, Perry?"

"I guess you have to see it to believe it." I sat down at Tasmine's desk. "But how else would Raquel find out about my baby that I killed?"

"Didn't Oden say that Raquel told him she overheard us while in the bathroom?"

"Yes, but wouldn't she have told him then, instead of waiting until we got back together?"

"True, but then again, maybe she saved it up in case you guys rekindled the romance. And then when she saw you *did* get back together, she told."

"I don't know, Tas. Raquel is a messy bitch, and I can't see her being able to hold something like that in. She would have dangled that shit in my face as soon as she heard."

"You have a point there."

"And then some guy named Edward comes up to me today, hugging on me like I don't have a psycho ass boyfriend that would shoot us both."

"Who the hell is Edward?"

"That's what I was thinking when he told me his name like I was supposed to know. Then he shows me all the messages he and I have been sending back and forth to one another on Facebook."

"I thought you deleted yours?"

"Exactly, it wasn't me. Whoever the bitch was, knew a couple of things about me and my sex life though. Probably one of Oden's hating ass exes."

"Damn, a real live Catfish. He should call Nev," she joked, making us both laugh.

"What a damn day! I knew something was wrong when he offered to take me to see an old film, talking about I know you love them." I removed my earrings and grabbed my make-up removing wipes, before tying my hair up into a bun.

"Wait… old movies?"

"Yeah." I began wiping my makeup off.

"Perry is obsessed with old movies."

CHAPTER EIGHT

Perry Washington

$\mathcal{K}$hyle had pissed me off for the last time. I was officially done with her as a friend and as a lover. She knew I had feelings for her, yet she kisses Bella and then gets pregnant by that hood. But hey, maybe it was for the best.

I sat down at my desk and opened my computer. I went onto Facebook so I could delete the fake 'Khyle profile' I'd made. I told stupid Edward not to approach me in person because of Oden, yet I saw him talking to Khyle today. He was so dumb for blowing my cover. Now we could no longer talk because he'd found me out.

I know you're wondering why I used Khyle's photo to chat with a guy on Facebook when *I* loved her. Well, it was because I wanted to know what it was like to be her. She always had guys staring at her, and making comments about how beautiful she was. Sometimes she wouldn't even notice that a guy was watching her, which was amazing to me. I wasn't sure if I wanted to be like her, or if I wanted to be *with* her. She was right about one thing: I was confused.

KNOCK! KNOCK!

I jumped at the sound of someone banging on my door. Rushing to it after slamming my laptop closed, I jumped up to see who it was through the peephole, and saw it was Khyle again.

Maybe she's back because she realized she has made a mistake. I didn't really want a girl with kids, but I'd deal with it.

"Khyle, I'm sorry I yelled—"

WHAM!

All I saw was her fist before pain shot throughout my nose and whole face it seemed. I stumbled back, cradling my bleeding nose, as she entered into my room and closed the door. Her face was twisted up like crazy, as she walked towards me slowly with her fists balled.

"Please, not another one, Khyle!"

She was much stronger than she looked, unlike me. If I hit her she probably wouldn't even notice I had.

"You fucking lied to me, you little fake ass bitch," she growled down at me. I could barely see and think straight. Her punch was ferocious, and she'd broken my glasses.

"No, I didn't—"

She yanked me up by my collar, cutting me off. Where did all this superhuman strength come from? Khyle was small, obviously not smaller than me, but still little.

"You told Raquel about the abortion and I want to know why. Then I want you to tell me why you made that fake Facebook account." Her grip on my collar was firm, as I dangled from her hand like a rag doll.

"I promise I—"

"Lie again and I will bust your fucking face open, bitch."

Who was this person? I mean I knew she was no punk from the way she ravaged that stripper Keesha that night, but the look in her eyes was almost demonic.

Knowing I wanted no parts of her ass whooping skills, I said, "Okay. I told because I was upset about you kissing Bella."

WHAM!

She slapped me so hard that I spun like a ballerina and fell onto my bed. She had to have been a pimp in her former life, because that slap was of a professional.

"You watched me cry my fucking eyes out over him, and you didn't say anything, all because of your obsession with me! Perry, I swear if I didn't think that I'd kill you, I would stomp a mud puddle in your ass right now," she spoke closely into my face.

"I'm sorry, Khyle, I am! I was emotional and I acted out! Please forgive me!" I called after her as she bolted towards my bathroom.

I heard her banging on the door that led to Raquel and Siena's room, and luckily for them, they were gone. Today was Thursday, mostly every college student's weekend, so the girls had gone to California to meet some guys they said. They asked me to come, and after getting punched by Khyle, I realized I should have gone.

"Where the fuck are they?" Khyle came back out of the bathroom, pointing towards their room.

"They went to Los Angeles for the weekend," I mumbled, face in pain. "I'm sorry, Khyle, I am, really."

"Make that the last time you cross me, Perry. One more thing, and I will whoop your ass like you owe me money, hoe."

BAM!

I jumped from her slamming my door.

Dropping my face into my bed, I sobbed for a little bit, feeling sorry for myself. I always got the short end of the stick, and I was tired of it. I acted the way I did because I was tired of being Perry. I wanted to be like Bella, Tasmine, and Khyle. Shoot, I would even take Raquel and Siena, despite their promiscuity.

Stop always throwing pity parties, chica. Niggas don't like that shit, Bella's voice danced around in my head.

I stood up and grabbed some stuff so I could take a shower. Tonight I was gonna go out on the town; just walk the strip to get some fresh air. I'd gotten some contacts over the summer, so I was gonna wear those tonight, too.

After showering, I used some of Bella's lotion that Santino loved, and then her body spray as well. I then put on my undergarments and that dress Raquel and Siena convinced me to buy. My hair was so brassy and dry, so I used some of Bella's hair products and smoothed it through my hair. It curled up a little, so I just put it into a ponytail. Sliding on my boots, I grabbed my phone, purse, and keys before heading out.

Driving towards the strip, I decided to give my car to valet at the New York-New York Hotel. It was at the beginning of the strip, well, where the strip got exciting, so I felt it was best to leave my car there.

I crossed the street as I stuffed the retrieval ticket into my bag, and smiled at all the lights on the hotels. It wasn't too crowded just yet, but the vacationers were definitely here since it was Thursday. Today was a great day for me to do this, because tomorrow would be too damn hectic.

As I was passing Ross, minding my own business, some brown-skinned guy with a low fade, baggy jeans, and a white t-shirt caught my eye. He looked suspicious with his hooded deep brown eyes and full lips. Stroking his beard, he scanned me from head to toe, before looking around and leaning back up against the wall. He was bad news, a thug like Oden, which intrigued me. Thug guys seemed to be all the rage, so a part of me wanted to find out why.

"Can I help you?" he sneered, attitude dripping from his deep voice. And I guess he had reason to be that way since I'd been staring at him for some time now.

"Uh, umm, what are you doing out here?" I moved a little closer to him. He was kind of in the cut, almost like he was hiding.

"I'm working, fuck you staring at me for skinny?"

"Skinny?"

"Yeah, I don't know your name and that one describes you well."

See, thugs were rude and scary, so I didn't see the hype.

"I'm sorry I stared at you. I was just walking down and you caught my eye. In a good way though."

"Fuck happened to your nose, ma?" his accent was suddenly apparent, letting me know he was from the east coast.

"I had a rough night."

"Obviously. Someone knocked the shit out of you, B," he laughed, showing his perfect teeth. I didn't expect someone of such a low standard to have nice teeth like that.

"Yeah, I know," I sighed. "So can I stand out here with you, or are you trying to be alone right now?"

"I was actually about to call it a night, ma, so unless you wanna come to the crib with me and smoke, you're gonna have to find someone else to post up with."

I was still scared of him, but I wanted to have fun tonight.

"I-I will go with you."

"You sure?"

"Yeah, I am. Very sure. I want to smoke, I love to smoke cigarettes," I lied to sound hip.

"I don't smoke cigarettes, shorty. I have some granddaddy though." He licked his lips as he eyed my body, or lack thereof. "Yeah, one puff will have you walking on sunshine and shit for sure."

"Good!" I laughed, not knowing what he hell he'd said at all. I didn't know what granddaddy was.

"Aight, let me call an Uber."

"No need, I have a car." I dangled my keys. He was really tall, or maybe I was really short. He seemed to be shorter than Santino though, who was about 6'2.

"Damn, a beamer, son?" he beamed, staring down at my keys. "Aye, can I whip it?"

"Uh, sure," I shrugged.

We rushed back down the strip and then crossed the street twice to get to the New York-New York Hotel. We waited for valet to bring my car around, and then he hopped in the driver's seat. As I put on my seatbelt, he adjusted the driver's seat to his liking, and then peeled out. He was a wild driver, going about 90mph while trying to find a radio station. I assumed he was looking for rap, so I tapped the one Bella had programmed for the nights we went out.

"Thanks." He bobbed his head to the despicable lyrics as he swerved through traffic, cutting people off and almost side swiping others.

I wanted to break out in prayer when we finally parked at his apartment because I didn't think we'd make it here alive. His home was pretty nice, but it was rare you found a beat up spot on this side of Las Vegas anyway.

"This is your own place?" I asked, sitting down on his couch as he grabbed a bottle of Crown Royal vanilla and some glasses. The last time I'd seen Crown Royal was when I visited my uncle down in Arkansas.

"Yeah, it is. Took me a while to get my own spot, so I cherish it."

"Nice. I would live alone, but I like the dorms for now." I took the glass of brown liquor from him. When I sipped it, my insides immediately began burning. "Oh shoot, what's your name?" I coughed.

"Austin, ma, yours?" He glanced at me while rolling up one of those thingies that you smoke from. Khyle, Tasmine, and Bella loved them.

"Perry." I nodded for some reason as I watched him.

He cut on some loud rap music, and continued rolling two more brown things. I drank and drank while watching him, and I noticed I was starting to loosen up. When he finished, he polished off his glass of Crown Royal and refilled our cups. We downed those, and then he picked up one of the brown sticks and lit it. I watched him inhale, and then he held it in for a little bit before blowing out smoke.

"Okay, tuck your lips in when you do it." He reached it out to me.

I remembered the hookah, so I inhaled like I did with that, held it in like him, and then blew out the smoke.

"Ayyyye! You got it!" he nodded, smiling again. He had a really nice smile for a little hoodlum.

We smoked all three blunts and finished the rest of the Crown Royal. The bottle wasn't full to begin with, maybe halfway, but I still felt like a new person from what I'd had. I felt free, happy, and like life was extra good.

Austin cut the lights off in the living room, and led me to his bedroom. He left the lights off in there too, but just cut the TV on. Removing our shoes, we climbed into his bed, staring at the TV flickering. He searched for something to watch, eventually landing on some show that I didn't recognize.

After about 15 minutes, I felt his hand rub my inner thigh so I looked his way, unsure of what to say or do. His hand kept moving up until he was at my vagina. Sitting up, he yanked my panties down my legs, and then started pushing my dress up. I was still a virgin, but I was tired of being one. And since he was nice I thought… why not?

I laid there naked, feeling ashamed since his chiseled pecks were bigger than my breasts. He stepped off of the bed and removed his bottoms, before getting back in between my legs to kiss me. His lips were soft, and his kiss was sensual, not rough and sloppy like I assumed it would be.

"Ooh!" I jumped when I felt him touch between my legs.

"Relax," he whispered against my lips, while using his other hand to get a contraceptive from the drawer next to us.

He sat up and rolled it down his penis. It wasn't too long, but it was quite thick, which scared me. Lying back on top of me, he poked around at my hole before trying to plunge inside. It wouldn't go, so he lifted my left leg over his right arm, and pushed himself inside of me.

"Ah!" I screeched, feeling like he was completely splitting me open.

"Why are you so tight?" he bit down on his lip.

I was in too much pain to answer.

My body started to accept him more after a while, so he hugged me and began humping wildly. I was screaming at the top of my lungs in pain as he pulverized my vagina. He sucked on my bottom lip like it was a piece of candy, before shoving his tongue into my mouth. His thrusts slowed down, and suddenly I felt a sense of pleasure. Hugging his body tighter, I moaned softly into his mouth as we kissed. Suddenly, the pleasure from down below became overwhelming, causing a liquid to spill from my body.

"Shit," Austin groaned.

He sped up again, tearing me to shreds, and soon after I was spilling that liquid again. He kept going, slamming into me as I locked my legs around him and embraced his neck. After a little bit, he growled like a grizzly bear. His body jerked a couple of times, which worried me.

Lord, please don't let him be having a seizure.

"Austin! Are you alright!" I tapped his smooth back as he lay on top of me, still.

"Yeah shorty, chill," he chuckled, picking his head up and sliding out of me. I felt so sore down below that I couldn't move. "I'm more than alright. When was the last time you got fucked? A decade ago?"

He removed the condom, which held semen, and placed it in his trash. I wanted to throw up. I didn't understand how Bella, Tasmine, and Khyle said they'd swallowed that.

"I'm a virgin, Austin; well, was one."

"Oh shit, ma, why you ain't stop me?"

"Because I wanted it."

"Well, it was good as fuck to me. Did you like it?"

"I had an orgasm I think, so yeah, I did. It felt good at times," I nodded, covering myself with the sheet and half smiling.

"Damn, I'm your first." He stared off. "Let me show you what I can do in the shower." He grinned and scooped me up before I could protest.

Wow… what a night, huh?

CHAPTER NINE

Oden

My bedroom was pretty dark, only getting light from the moon outside. Khyle was straddling my lap as we kissed one another hungrily in the bed. I ran my hands up her sexy body, enjoying the feel of her smooth skin under my hands. My dick was deep inside of her wet pussy as she whimpered into my mouth innocently. Pulling my lips away from hers, I sucked on her nipple as I continued to bounce her in my lap slowly. She wound her hips perfectly, making sure my dick hit every part of her insides.

"Mmm, Oden," she cried, voice shaking like a leaf on a tree.

I brought my head back up to tongue her down nastily, as she grinded in my lap. Gripping her ass, I moved her up and down my pole fast, while sucking her neck like a vampire. Her nails dug deep into my back, but I didn't mind. Her tight wet pussy had all of my attention as it held my dick in a slippery chokehold.

"Fuck, I'm about to cum," I grumbled, flicking my tongue over her rock hard nipples. I loved her nipples.

"Oh, oh shit!" she hollered, holding the back of my neck firmly as I brought her down roughly.

"Fuuuuccckkk!" we called out simultaneously as we climaxed.

We immediately began panting heavily, holding one another firmly. Her body was sweating like crazy, but I loved that shit. After kissing her collarbone, I picked her up off of my dick and laid her down. I went to get us some warm wet towels to clean with, before taking them to the hamper and washing my hands. When she came back from cleaning her hands, we got into the warm bed together. I leaned down to kiss her stomach, and then brought the cover up over the both of us.

"That was so good, baby," she whispered, lying on my chest.

"Isn't it always?"

"Yeah, but I think being pregnant intensifies it."

"Yeah, your pussy definitely feels different."

It got quiet for a little bit, and then she asked, "Is your father still holding up? He has a job now and stuff right?"

"Yeah, been working there for almost two months."

I had to say I was happy my father had gotten clean and was doing better. I missed having a parent of some sort ever since my grandfather died. Ain't like I needed him to support me or anything like that, but I guess having someone around that was part of my bloodline made me feel good.

"See, I told you he'd be different this time," she brushed her small fingers down my abs.

I was about to speak but my phone started going off on the dresser. It was well after 1am, so I had no idea who the hell would be calling my phone at this time of night. Khyle was already burning a hole in the side of my face by glaring at it when I reached for my iPhone.

My own frown deepened when I realized it was Roscoe from Caesar's Palace hotel. I was praying that somehow my card declined or something, and that it had nothing to do with my father personally.

"Hello?"

"Hi, Mr. Bishop, I hate to trouble you at this time of night, but we need you to come down to the hotel."

"Tonight?" I sat up on the edge of the bed. "What umm, what happened?" I felt a queasiness in my stomach because I really didn't want the answer.

"It's regarding your father. We just need you to come down here, please."

"Alright, I will be there in about umm, 20 minutes. Cool?"

"That's fine, Mr. Bishop."

I hung up the phone and sighed heavily as I stood up. I felt Khyle's eyes on me as I paced the room for a little bit. I heard her about to ask me something, but I just left the bedroom and went to shower really quickly. When I was done, I slipped on some boxers, sweats, socks, and a t-shirt.

"What happened, Oden?" Khyle finally asked as I snatched up my hoodie.

"My dad, baby. I will be back."

I slipped out of the bedroom before she could protest, and headed out of the door. I made it to Caesar's Palace about 10 minutes later, and after parking my car off to the side, I rushed in and up to the front desk to look for Roscoe. I spotted him conversing with one of his employees, so I approached him. The expression he looked at me with had my heart racing like fuck.

"So just go ahead and process them, thank you," he finished up with his employee. "Mr. Bishop, again, sorry I had to bother you."

"It's cool. What's up, Roscoe?"

"Follow me."

I trailed him onto an elevator, and then we took it up to the suite floor. I felt like I was having a panic attack because of all the build up. Was my father dead? What the hell had happened? We stepped off the elevator, and then headed down the hallway until we arrived at my father's suite. Roscoe used the key card to open the door, and when he did, anger consumed me.

The suite was completely ransacked, and things had been stolen out of it. It looked as if some type of wild party had gone down, and then a robbery. Shit was ripped out of the walls, the furniture was stained, chairs, lamps, and the television were all broken. And of course, my father was nowhere to be found. My mouth stayed ajar as I surveyed the entire suite, appalled at the fact that it seemed to get worse and worse as I looked around.

"Uh shit, I'm sorry about this, Roscoe. How much do I need to pay to rectify all of this, man?" I turned to look at his distressed expression.

"We put in an insurance claim, so the cost came out to be $65,482.90."

Although I had enough money to never work again and still make my grandkids rich, 65 grand was still a lot of money to be spent on bullshit. I had to come up out of all of that money for fucking nothing. Almost $70,000 just gone from my pockets because my dad had played me for a fool again.

"No problem, Roscoe. I will have my club manager drop a money order off here around noon. Again, man, I'm so sorry about this. I thought that umm… yeah, I will have the money to you tomorrow."

"Great, and don't worry about it, Oden. Sometimes people just can't be helped. You're still one of my favorite patrons, and don't hesitate to ask me for another favor."

"Thanks," I forced a smile.

We left out of the room and when we got down to the lobby, he printed me up a copy of the official claim so I could see exactly what was damaged.

"Do you know where he is?" I questioned.

"No, we don't. He's been gone since this morning. He had the do not disturb sign on the door all day, and this evening one of the maids went in to clean and saw the room had been trashed. They had to wait until I got here so I could call you."

"I see."

I took the claim paper, and then left back out to my car. I sat there for a minute, staring at it, wondering how I let this nigga play me again.

A part of me wished that he was here and able to give me some sort of explanation as to why he'd done this, but he'd have to care to do that.

Once I got out of my feelings, I pulled off, headed home. When I got there, I immediately went to my bedroom to find Khyle asleep. I undressed down to my boxers, and got in the bed behind her. Wrapping my arms around her small frame, I pulled her into my chest and inhaled her scent. It was obvious she'd taken a shower while I was gone, because her favorite soap was potent. I kissed her shoulder blade, and ran my hand up and down her stomach. My baby was the only blood I was gonna be worried about from now on.

***

The next evening…

Real nigga, always been my main description. Always with some bad bitches like I'm in detention…

I was in my office trying to concentrate, but between the music blasting over the club, and thoughts of my father dogging me, it was very hard. Granted the music was fairly low, but at this point, I needed a prayer to concentrate, so anything, no matter how small, could distract me.

"Fuck," I grumbled, running my hand down my face. I needed to go on vacation or some shit, and soon.

KNOCK! KNOCK!

"Come in!" I hollered out.

"Mr. Bishop, a Naomi is here to see you. She's one of the club patrons but she claims to know you and wants to say hi," Cara peeked

274

her head in.

"Okay, go ahead and send her back here."

Cara nodded as she backed out and left. I ain't know what the fuck Naomi wanted to see me about, but I was hoping that she was on a totally different tip than the one she was on some months ago. We hadn't talked since, and frankly, I was perfectly fine with that shit. I didn't need anything in my life that would threaten my relationship.

"Hey boss," Naomi knocked lightly, coming in with a big smile. She closed the door behind herself as she admired my spacious and nicely decorated office.

"Sup, Naomi. How have you been?" I leaned back in my chair with my hands clasped behind my head. I was tired as hell and still had a lot of work to do.

"I've been okay. I've just been getting settled back into the Nevada life. I got a job with a new insurance company, so that was exciting."

"Yeah, that is. I'm happy for you," I spoke lowly as she neared my desk, sitting on the right edge of it.

"Thank you. So how are you? Still in love and trying to be faithful?"

"Yeah, I am. I'm doing great."

"Really? You don't sound like it. Usually you'd smile after saying such a thing, but you seem to be pretty down."

"Has nothing to do with my relationship though, so like I said, on that tip, I'm good, Naomi. But thanks for asking."

"No problem. No matter what, Oden, I will always care about

you," she stared down into my eyes, so I just nodded coolly. "I hope you feel the same."

"Of course I care about your well-being. I wish you nothing but the best in life, Naomi. I always have."

"You say that like I'm never gonna see you again."

"I mean, I'm just saying it like it is. I got love for you, and I'm always gonna care about you, but as a friend."

"I didn't need that friend part!" We laughed in unison. "I'm gonna be honest, Oden, I do regret my behavior from when we were together. We would probably be having our own baby by now had I not gone 'crazy'," she smiled, but it only lasted for a few short seconds.

"I don't know. I think the shit that happens in life is gonna happen no matter what. Khyle and I were supposed to be together, so even if you had have been the perfect girlfriend, I still would have ended up with her."

"I don't think so."

"That's what God wanted."

"How do you know what God wants?"

"Because look who I'm with… Khyle."

"So what, are you guys gonna get married and live the American Dream?"

I laughed.

"Probably the African American dream, but yeah, that's what I'm shooting for. I see life differently now and I just want to make my money and have a family, you know? I'm young but I have lived a lot more than people twice my age."

"Sounds pleasant." She brushed her fingers against my desk as if she were dusting something off. "Would you ever tell me if you weren't happy with her?"

"No, I would tell her so that we could fix it. I can't ever see that happening though."

"She's very luck to have you, Mr. Bishop."

"Thanks, baby girl. I'm luckier though."

Naomi just nodded with a smile, before changing the subject.

I was happy to see that she had pretty much given up that dream of us being back together… at least I hoped she did.

CHAPTER NINE

Santino

"The Rams are very interested, D'Stefano," my coach gripped my shoulder as a wide smile covered my face. "The 49ers too, so it's gonna be a bit of a bidding war."

Practice had just concluded, so he and I were sitting down just chatting it up. I knew this was my last year of school because God had blessed me. The longer you stayed in school, the less likely you were to be drafted. I wanted to go to the NFL freshman year, but I was told I needed to complete at least two years of college before getting drafted. And not only did one team want me, but two did. I'd dreamed of this damn day all my life.

"Damn, should I go for the most money or what? I don't want to go after the wrong thing and regret it. I wanna get on a team and stick it out you know?" I glanced at him.

"Understandable. Things happen though, and you may have to leave. But you're a phenomenal football player, so any team that you go to is gonna offer you big bucks and want to keep you."

"Yeah, God willing."

"You and Huelo are my best players. We lost him, and now I'm about to lose you. I pray we get some great freshman like we did for your year."

"I know. This year y'all scouted some whack ass niggas," I half joked.

It was true though. The niggas that came to the team this year were trash. I think it was because they were nervous during the games so they fucked up. College games were a little different than high school ones, so being nervous for the first few was acceptable. But by now, they should have their shit together.

"Yes. I still don't think Huelo would be getting drafted this year, but junior year for sure," he popped his gum.

Him mentioning Huelo reminded me of what I had planned to do tonight.

I saw my coach's assistant running up to us, and when he neared, he finally slowed up. My coach and I were already rising to our feet as he approached.

"Aye, Sanz, your girl is out there and she said she needs to talk to you. Said she's pregnant," my coach's assistant, Fred said, out of breath.

"You serious?" I frowned and he shook his head.

Grabbing my bag, I rushed across the field so I could see Bella. Her being pregnant was a surprise to me, even though I hadn't been protecting myself when fucking her. She was on birth control, so I didn't think we needed anything. Clearly that shit wasn't that effective.

The only reason I was low-key tripping out was because I knew she wouldn't be happy about it. I was perfectly fine with her having my baby, but Bella wanted to wait at least until she graduated from undergrad.

When I got out of the gate, I scanned the area looking for Bella. My brows dipped as I wondered if this was some kind of joke from my teammates and coach. I pulled my phone out, ready to dial, when a voice called my name from behind.

"Looking for your precious Bella?" Leena walked around to face me.

"Please tell me that you didn't tell my coach's assistant you were my pregnant girlfriend, Leena?"

"I knew it was the only way to get you out here. If I had have said it was me, you probably would have dodged me."

"Fuck do you want, man? Shit!" I turned my lip up. I couldn't be any more irritated than I was right fucking now. "Why the fuck are you even in Vegas! I'm so tired of seeing your damn face!"

"I want to give you a chance to talk to me!"

"About what? What the fuck is there left to talk about, Leena! We fucked around, I never made you my girl, and now I don't wanna fuck around no more. There ain't shit left to discuss! Stop bringing yo' ass up here to my fucking school on that stalker shit! I'm not with these damn games! At all!"

"You knew that every time you slept with me I was catching feelings for you!"

"Then why didn't you stop, huh? You could have said to me straight up that you were catching feelings and didn't want to fuck no more!"

"I ain't wanna deprive you of sex just because I was catching feelings!"

"Deprive?" I laughed, throwing my head back. "I had pussy thrown at me every damn where I went, Leena. Trust me, I would have been good."

"So you were fucking other girls while we were fucking?"

"Umm, yeah. We weren't exclusive, Leena. I fucked you and a couple of other chicks, and that was okay because we weren't in a relationship. And do you see them showing up to my school on some bull? Nah, because they knew what was up."

"Don't say I didn't try to give you a chance." She twisted her face up and shook her head at me.

"A chance to what?"

"To save yourself. You're gonna pay for the way you've been treating me, Santino D'Stefano, and you're gonna wish you never tried to play me."

"I didn't—" I saw some girls walking by staring at us so I lowered my voice. "I didn't try to play you. I told you the deal, aight? Fuck out of my face and out of my life with all that bullshit, Leena. Get a fucking clue and a life that doesn't involve me."

I walked past her and didn't look back. I was tired of her ass and couldn't wait until I got drafted so she couldn't find me.

***

Later that night…

It was around 9:27pm when I pulled into the dealership Oden and his friends owned. After practice, I'd gone to my dorm to shower, eat, study, and nap, so I hadn't been back out until now. I knew Oden would be here because I overheard Khyle tell Bella that he stayed at the dealership until 9:30pm every Wednesday.

I parked my car around back, leaving a space between my car and his fresh ass Porsche. This nigga always sported the nicest cars, and some days I looked forward to seeing what he had parked at the school on his class days.

Oden seemed to be a cool ass dude, but I was here to get at him about killing Huelo. I ain't know what I planned to say though, because I couldn't really be mad at him for defending his girl. Then again, Huelo was my homie and him being gone hurt a little.

I sat in my car until the clock read 9:35pm. Oden had finally emerged, and once I saw him pop his trunk, I got out. Before I closed my door good, he had his burner out, ready to pop me. *Damn, this nigga is fast as fuck.*

"Oh you, nigga, what the fuck are you doing out here this late?" he scowled, locking his gun back in his waist.

"I just wanted to talk to you really quickly. Is that cool?" I looked at him.

He didn't say anything, he just kept his brows furrowed as if he were waiting for me to continue.

From Oden's description, you would assume he was a pretty boy, but that nigga was nothing of the sort. I was a pretty boy, and he was far from being like me. The only thing 'pretty' about him was that big ass curly hair, and even that shit was low-key scary.

"See, I know you—"

POP! POP!

Before I could finish, Oden had shoved me to the side and let off two bullets into someone. When I turned around, I saw a figure dressed in all black and wearing a mask, bleeding out on the concrete. They were holding a handgun tightly in their dead hand.

"Fuck!" Oden shouted, as I stared at the body, horrified. "Yeah, where you at?" he spoke into a phone as he walked to the head of the body to take the ski mask off.

"What the hell?" I panted, seeing Leena's lifeless face.

"Aight, be quick. Like five minutes quick," Oden said before hanging up. "You recognize this bitch?"

"Uh…"

"Whomever she is, she was trying to kill yo' ass." He inspected her with his eyes. "She's cute," he grinned as if he hadn't just killed her.

I was still in disbelief that Leena was dead, and even more in disbelief that she had tried to kill me. All that shit she was saying earlier today made sense, talking about she tried to give me a chance. I always knew her ass was off, but I didn't think she was this crazy.

A big matte black van pulled up, and three men hopped out to pick up Leena's body and take it in, while the fourth man talked with Oden. As they continued to chat, two of the men came back and began washing the ground with chemicals, getting the blood out. In no time, the four men were back in the van, and the concrete looked as if nothing had ever been there. Oden was a real life criminal, like on some movie shit.

"Now what did you want to talk to me about my nigga? I have to get home before my girl starts getting suspicious."

"I just wanted to say that umm, when I'm gone away to California for long periods of time, I would appreciate it if you looked after Bella for me."

It wasn't what I had initially wanted to ask, but seeing how good he was at protecting people in his circle, I actually *did* want him to look out for my girl.

"Oh shit… of course. You ain't have to wait out here to ask me that my nigga."

"I didn't really know where else you would be so this was my last resort."

"Aight, well I got you. Even if you hadn't have asked, I would have looked out for her. Have a goodnight my nigga, and control yo' hoes!" he said before getting into the driver's side of his car.

I know I planned to come here and chat about Huelo, but after he basically saved my life, I didn't feel the urge to anymore. Plus, Bella was right, I had other shit that I needed to be worried about. And unfortunately, Huelo facing consequences over trying to rape Khyle wasn't one of them.

From now on, all I was gonna focus on was football and Bella. And now that Leena was no more, life was really gonna be the shit.

CHAPTER NINE

Jasmine

$\mathcal{I}$ stared down at my notes as I sat in the library, not taking in a damn thing. My mind was elsewhere, and it was so hard to pay attention to my work. All I wanted to do was make up with Anton, but I had to stay strong.

We'd been broken up for a nice little while now, and you'd think I'd be getting better with time, but I felt like my feelings were going the opposite way. I thought about him more than usual, and even found myself looking on his social media pages, knowing he hadn't posted in weeks. He'd texted and called me of course, and then that soon downgraded to simple likes on my pictures and comments about how beautiful I was. But now, I barely heard a peep out of him, and I guess that was best, right?

It would be easy for me to forgive him but I refused to. He'd lied to me about his child, and then tried to pretend like he withheld the information because it wasn't true. How could a DNA be false if he had it done himself?

I was hurt, and sort of turned off that he would act so immaturely about being a father. I mean, if he didn't want kids with these women, he shouldn't have been sleeping with them, and he definitely should have been more careful. As I thought about it all, I got a little bit angry.

"Fuck, I'm still stuck on this bullshit. It's like a foreign language to me," Reuben spoke up. He and I were studying together, even though neither of us were geniuses in the subject at hand.

"I know, I hate Geography with a passion," I blew out hot air. "I'm gonna fail this test coming up, and if you're anything like me, so are you."

"Don't say that, Tas. We just have to stay here until late."

"It's already 4pm," I whined, slouching in my chair. "I'm ready to go to my dorm and watch reality TV with Khyle and Bella."

"Yeah, because that's productive."

We laughed in unison.

"I know, but you're right. I need to put in the work, so it's looking like an all nighter for me."

"For us you mean," he nudged me lightly. "You know Tas, I enjoy spending time with you, and I think you enjoy spending time with me too." Reuben looked to his right at me, since we were sitting next to one another in the library.

"I do. I think you're pretty cool."

"I'll take pretty cool over nothing," he grinned. "So how about after we get through this test, we go out or something? Maybe like to the movies, dinner, or shit, just to get ice cream."

"Reuben, I don't know. I don't think I'm ready to go out with anyone else just yet. My last relationship was kind of… I don't know. I just don't feel like I'm ready."

"I'm nothing like Tony, Tasmine. He and I are two totally different guys, and will give you a totally different experience." Reuben touched my hand gently.

I liked Reuben, but not in the way he wanted me to. He was a nice-looking guy, could play basketball well, was smart, and even funny, but for some reason, I didn't see him like that. I felt like he was more of a brother or a best friend type. Just the thought of kissing or having sex with him made me want to vomit. Something just never clicked with us in the romance department, but I couldn't exactly say why.

"I know you're not like him, Reuben, it's just I don't think of you in that way." I frowned because I didn't want to tell him that, but it was the truth and the only explanation I had. "I'm sorry."

"Wow. I know I ain't the best looking nigga, but shit, you make me sound ugly as fuck," he chuckled.

"No, you're very handsome, but I just get a brotherly vibe from you. I don't see you like a boyfriend, more like a male best friend, or cousin. Just like a family memb—"

"Okay, please stop before you hurt my damn feelings," he taunted and we both laughed. "Honestly, I have never been told that before."

"I'm sure you haven't. You're a great catch, just not for me. But I like our friendship, and I think that's more valuable than being in a relationship."

"I agree," he nodded. "Did you have a friendship with your ex? Or was it just like fucking all day and shit?"

"Oh my gosh!" I hit him lightly as we laughed together. "No, we were friends too. We talked about everything. I loved him because he made me feel comfortable with things about myself that I've always been self conscious about."

"Like your body?"

"No, what are you trying to say?"

"Nothing. Your body is perfect, but girls are always complaining about physical flaws that don't exist, so I assumed. And half the shit y'all complain about, niggas don't even care about."

"So you don't mind dating a girl with cellulite, stretch marks, and a pudgy stomach?" I grinned.

"You don't have any of that."

"I know, but I'm asking since you said guys don't even care."

"Does she have a pussy between her thighs?" he raised a brow.

"Answer the question!"

"Answer mine first."

"Yes, she has a vagina, she's a woman."

"Then I don't give a fuck. As long as her face is pretty, she has good hygiene, and her pussy is good, her body can look like a fucking golf ball tiger mix, I will still fuck with it."

I burst into laughter at his response and shook my head.

"I've heard guys complain about stuff like that," I chuckled.

"Them niggas are probably gay. A real man is not gonna give a shit, he's going to smash and more than once if he can."

"I guess."

"So you loved Tony, huh?"

"I did."

"Well then, can I talk to you?" Anton's voice came from behind us, and when I looked back I saw him there, holding roses and a small gift box.

"Uh umm, I'm studying, Anton, I—"

"Take a break," he cut in.

"See you in class Monday, Tasmine." Reuben got up, grabbing his shit. He nodded his head up to Anton, who returned the gesture. He must have forgotten that he had to threaten Reuben with a gun inside of In-N-Out some time ago.

I waited as Anton sat down across from me. The library on this floor was completely empty, and the sole reason why Reuben and I chose to study up here. After Anton got situated, he fixated his eyes on me, just taking me in as if I were a work of art.

"Talk, Tony, I have a lot of material to look over and the night isn't young."

He pulled an envelope from his hoodie pocket, and then slid it across the table to me. Grabbing it, I looked it over as if the outside would give me an inkling as to what was enclosed. When I saw nothing giving the contents away, I rolled my eyes.

"What is this, Anton Nickerson?"

"Open it baby, please."

I fought back the smile that wanted to break through from hearing him call me baby in that sexy low voice, as I ripped the envelope open. I removed the paper from inside, and scanned the top to see it was a paternity test. Running my eyes down the paper, I saw that it said Anton wasn't the father.

"Is this regarding Violet's baby?" I frowned.

"Yeah, it is."

"How is this possible? Wasn't he tested already?"

"Yeah, but I had it done over. The nurse, Phoebe, that originally tested him was paid to change the results of the first test by Violet's sister."

"So Violet knew this whole time—"

"No, she didn't know. Her sister didn't like the way I was treating her, and she went out of her way to make sure that I came back as the father. She caught Phoebe as she was leaving the hospital the day Athen was born, and they made a deal. Violet apologized to me."

"Are you sure Violet didn't know?"

"Yeah, I am. Violet was never like Selinda and Kai. And I've dealt with a lot of people, Tasmine, so I can tell when someone is being genuine. That's why I'd been suspicious of Phoebe since she read them damn results."

"And where is Phoebe?"

"We're trying to find her. I guess she caught wind that I was on to her ass."

"What'd you do to Violet's sister?" my eyes bucked, making that sexy smile appear on his handsome chocolate face.

"Nothing. I thought about it but it's not worth it. She's bitter and loves her sister. And truthfully, I'm tired. All I care about right now is being with you."

"So we're gonna try this again?" I reached across the table to take his hands into mine. I loved the way our hands felt together.

"No, not try, we're gonna do this again. I promise to be honest with you, Tasmine. I should have been upfront with you from the beginning about what the results were and what I was feeling."

"Yeah."

"But I told Violet that I would still help her here and there with Athen. I got kind of attached to the little nigga. I hope you don't mind."

"Nope, that's actually admirable and makes you so much more attractive than you already are."

"Cool." He pushed the small gift across the table to me. "I got you something. It's almost like a thank you gift for making me stand up and be a man about shit in my life, namely getting these damn DNA tests," he explained as I opened the gift to see a beautiful necklace.

"Oh my gosh, Tony," I whimpered, feeling myself on the verge of tears as I stared down at the sparkly diamond.

"Let me put it on you." He stood up and came around, before removing the necklace from the velvet box, and fastening it around my neck. He then leaned down to kiss me deeply. It felt good kissing him again. "Perfect," he said once he walked back around the other side of the table to be across from me.

"Thanks, baby."

"Anything for you," he stared. "I missed you."

"I missed you too," I spoke lowly, keeping eye contact with him.

He looked over his shoulder, and then scanned the floor with his eyes. He then scooted his chair back and went under the table.

"Anton!" I shrieked, but lowly, feeling his strong hands go up my exposed thighs. "What are you doing, baby?" I asked as he placed my legs on his shoulders and moved my panties to the side.

Before I could ask another question, he was sucking on my pussy like it was a lollipop. Spreading my legs wider under the table, I pushed my center into his mouth more, letting him get all in there. My chest heaved up and down as he feasted on me, licking and sucking my clit while caressing my thighs.

"Oh shit," I mumbled. Only Anton would give me head in a quiet ass library. And boy was I happy I wore a skirt today.

His sucks became harder, and the flicks of his tongue became faster. I was damn near crawling up the wooden chair as he ate my pussy like I'd written him a check for it. I felt my orgasm all the way up in my chest as his full lips and tongue went to work on me. Wounding my hips against his mouth, I palmed the back of his head and closed my eyes.

"Oh fuck," I whimpered like a wounded animal. My voice was high pitched and breathy, as Anton attacked me. "Ah!" I called out over the whole damn library it seemed, as I came hard as hell. He licked me clean, and the whole time my body shivered and jerked from such a powerful explosion.

"Mmm," he moaned, as he cleaned me with his mouth.

I let my head fall back as I panted heavily, feeling him place the crotch of my underwear back in position. He crawled from under the table wearing a smile, but I was too beat to return the gesture.

"Wanna leave and finish this, or do you want to stay and study?" he asked.

He could barely finish the question before I was on my feet and shoving my books, notes, and notebook into my bookbag messily. Shit, fuck this test and this class!

296

CHAPTER NINE

Truman

One week later...

"What do you think of this one, baby?" Chiina stood by a wooden crib that had a pretty spiffy looking finish.

She and I were currently shopping for shit to put in the baby's room. She was still on that 'not wanting to live with me' tip, but I was hoping that if we had a nice baby room at my crib, she would change her mind. The baby would be here in a little less than six months, but I was praying Chiina and I would be 100% together by that time.

"I like it. I told you to get what you want. I'm just here to pay, baby."

"I know, but I want you to like the stuff too. It's not just my baby, Tru."

"Trust me, I know. I was there when we made him." I pulled her into me and kissed her soft, full lips.

Looking down into her eyes, a small smile crept across my face.

I remembered when I first met her, I planned to get some pussy and never see her again. However, she had roped me in, but slowly. First with her pussy because it was too good to hit just once, and then with her personality because I found it to be refreshing. Chiina was so full of life, and I loved that she had big dreams. She didn't think realistically when it came to her goals, and I admired that. "Thinking realistically keeps you in a box" she would say, and I fucked with that.

It was just crazy that we went from being fuck buddies to being in love and about to have a baby. Oden's grandpa would always say that men wanted a woman who wouldn't put up with their shit, and I assumed that was excluding me, until I met Chiina.

Pilar, I loved her with all of my heart, but she was weak. When I think back to the shit I'd done in the past year and how she was still willing to fuck with me, it made her seem so unattractive. I needed someone like Chiina, someone that would leave my ass and have me shook. I actually felt like I had a girlfriend for the first time in my life, and that I had someone I needed to do right by. It may sound weird considering the fact that I'd been with Pilar so long, but it was the truth.

"Stop giving me that look. I told you I want food after this," Chiina pecked my lips and backed away from me.

She'd just broken down and let me fuck two days ago. Surprisingly, I hadn't smashed any other girls while waiting on her, and that even had me floored. It took me changing my number, but it was worth it.

"I'm not looking at you like *that*, I'm looking at you because I love you."

"Awww, baby, I love you too." She reached up to caress the side of my face, and I kissed the palm of her hand.

We continued shopping, and by the time we checked out, I'd spent $3,000. That wasn't shit to me though, and it was money well spent.

After dropping everything off at my crib, we went to this Creole restaurant for dinner. It was a cool spot, and I liked that it was nice and quiet, due to it being the middle of the week. I noticed that the customer service was always better when it wasn't busy.

"Well hello," Pilar approached the table with some tall skinny nigga standing behind her. I guess I changed her type. "Theodore, you remember my ex-boyfriend Truman." I recognized him from somewhere.

"Nice to meet you." Theodore pushed up his glasses and stuck his hand out to me nervously.

Oh yeah, I clocked him at TAO.

I shook it and then said, "This is my girlfriend Chiina." He nodded to her, shaking her hand in the process.

"Well, it was nice to see you guys." Pilar pranced off and sat at her table.

"I think she still loves you," Chiina whispered and smiled once Pilar was out of earshot.

Chiina was so beautiful.

"I hope not. But even if she did, it wouldn't matter to me."

"You don't love her even a little bit? I mean, you guys were together for years so it wouldn't be too odd you know."

"I know what you're trying to do, and no, I'm not in love with her.

I care because we have history, but I don't want to be with her like that."

I wasn't falling into that damn trap.

"Good answer," she laughed.

The waitress came over to take our orders, and then I excused myself so I could go to the restroom. As I was washing my hands, Pilar came into the men's bathroom smiling.

"Still going strong with little Lolita, huh?"

"And I see you got a good thing with Urkel."

"Yep. I'm surprised you didn't punch him again. That would have been a bad look in front of your baby mama."

"I didn't punch him because I don't care. I see y'all never lost touch though."

"No… we didn't. I was actually fucking him the whole time you and I were together that last go 'round. That business trip to New York was just something I made up so I could go see him and fuck his brains out while you laid up in the hospital half dead."

I laughed to myself as I dried my hands.

"I'm sorry, Pilar."

"For what, nigga? I'm good."

"Are you? I mean you followed me into the bathroom to tell me how you were playing me, and I don't really see why you'd do that if you were happy."

"I am."

"You're not, and that's why I'm apologizing. I hurt you and I turned a great woman into what I see before me. All I ask is that you forgive me, and don't ruin what you may have with him because of what I did to you. There isn't a thing wrong with you, you just weren't right for me."

"I don't need you to tell me that! I know ain't shit wrong with me! I was never the problem, you were!"

"You're right. And again, P, that's why I'm apologizing. I just don't want you to become one of those damaged girls that can't keep a man because of their past. I don't want you to be ruined because of me."

"Well I'm not ruined. I'm in top notch condition." She checked herself out in the mirror before looking back at me.

"You are. Enjoy your dinner." I walked around her and used the paper towel to open the door.

"Thank you, Truman," she muttered as I was passing the threshold.

I gave her a half smile and then went back to sit down with my lady.

"You okay?" Chiina asked.

"I'm perfect." I kissed the corner of her mouth, making a warm smile light up her beautiful face.

∗∗∗

That night…

"Ah, baby," Chiina whimpered in her soft voice as she spilled her juices into my mouth. I lapped it up, before kissing from her stomach to her lips.

Positioning the head of my dick at her snug opening, I began sucking on her lips as I pushed myself inside. I groaned into her mouth at the feeling her wet walls gripping my dick. Her pussy was so wet, so wet that I barely wanted to moan just so I could hear myself dipping in it.

"Mmm, fuck," I growled, pinning her hands behind her head.

Her legs were locked around my waist, allowing me to go as deeply as I wanted… and I did. Flicking my tongue over her perfect brown nipples, I let my tongue circle one of them before sucking it roughly. Slamming into her, but pulling out slowly, I continued to switch back and forth between her nipples.

"I'm gonna cum," she whined just as I felt a wave of her nectar coat my rod.

"Marry me, baby," I said before slipping my tongue between her full lips. "Say yes."

"Yes, Truman," she let out just before I kissed her harder, beating her tight pussy up.

If I had to only be with one woman for the rest of my life, I was gonna leave the game with the best they had, which was Chiina.

CHAPTER TEN

Bella

*P*utting the last mini banana nut muffin into my mouth, I then grabbed my fuzzy socks and slipped them on. Khyle and Tasmine were coming to my dorm so we could just chill until Santino, Oden, Anton, and Truman got back from some place. They didn't tell any of us where they were going, but we all knew they'd be together tonight.

As I was drinking my water, Perry came into the room. She was wearing some little ass shorts, a tube top, and her hair was longer so I knew she had tracks in her head. Lately, she hadn't been spending the night in the room with me. I didn't complain because Santino and I could fuck all night and as loudly as we wanted to. But seeing her dressed like… like… well like me, had me interested to know what she was up to.

I was mad at her for telling Raquel about Khyle's abortion, but that didn't mean I couldn't get some tea. And as anxious as she was to be cool with us again, I knew she'd dish her social security number if I asked.

"Where have you been sleeping lately?" I inquired, twisting the cap back onto my water.

"With a friend." She tried to hide the smile on her face before slipping her small hands into her jean short pockets.

"A friend? What kind of friend?"

"A regular one."

"Does he have a penis or a vagina like you?" I folded my arms, walking over to her side of the room.

"He does have—"

"*He?*" I grinned. "Bitch, let me find out you're getting fucked finally! Maybe that's what your weird ass needed. Now that you've gotten some dick, maybe you can be cool with us again."

"Really?" her face lit up like a Christmas tree.

"Yeah… well, I don't know. I forgive you for being a little skank and trying to date my boyfriend, but that's only because I knew you were taken advantage off. As for Khyle, that may not be so easy."

"I know."

KNOCK! KNOCK!

"That's her and Tasmine now. So maybe you should try and say something to her. She's been in a great mood lately so…" I whispered before pulling the door open.

Khyle and Tasmine walked in, both wearing tights and tube tops. I didn't know when Khyle's stomach would expand though. She was already four months and her stomach could still pass for flat if she stood at a certain angle. If I hadn't witnessed her throwing up and eating like a hog, I wouldn't even think she was pregnant. I prayed that

I carried like her.

"This bitch," Khyle mumbled referring to Perry as she strutted to my side of the room.

"Khyle, Perry has something to say. She's gotten a new outlook on life now that she's been getting dicked down."

Even though Khyle was mad at Perry, the look she gave her upon hearing she'd been getting some dick showed she wanted more information. Tasmine's eyes were wide as well, and her jaw was damn near on the floor.

"Okay, talk," Khyle said as Tasmine took a seat next to her on my bed.

"Khyle, I'm sorry for betraying you and telling Raquel about the abortion. I was upset with you because I felt like you weren't trying as hard to be friends with me like you were doing with Bella and Tasmine. I mistook my wanting to fit in and admiration of you for love. For some reason, I thought if Oden left you, you would maybe be with me, but also I wanted to hurt you for hurting me. I know it's stupid but I'm sorry."

"Why me though, Perry? Tasmine and I treated you the same."

"I'm not sure. I guess I was more drawn to you. I wanted you to accept me and want to hang out with me like you did them. But I swear I've grown some, and gotten some more confidence."

"Through dick?" Tasmine giggled, texting on her phone.

"Austin is more than that, he's very smart," Perry smirked.

"Austiiiiinnnn," the three of us sang in unison.

"What does he do? He goes to UNLV?" I questioned.

"No, he's an umm, pharmacist?"

"Like for Walgreens or like he sells dope?" Khyle frowned, eating some snack she'd put into a Ziploc bag.

"The second one," Perry replied shyly, and we all burst into laughter at how she didn't want to come out and say it.

"Wait… Perry and a dope boy? What the fuck has the world come to?" Tasmine covered her face and shook her head.

"Well Khyle, do you forgive me?" Perry looked to Khyle with sad puppy dog eyes.

I tell you, it was hard to stay mad at Perry. She was like that little poodle in your house that did bad shit, but you were too soft to reprimand it. I was surprised Khyle didn't fully whoop her ass. Then again, Perry's face was pretty fucked when I saw her two days after Khyle decked her.

"Only because he and I got back together, but Perry, if you ever do something like that to me again, I will fight your ass for real and never talk to you again."

"Deal!" Perry smiled.

"But there is one thing I need you to do for me, and then I will fully forgive you." Khyle rose to her feet. "I need you to drive us to that frat party tonight, and then get Raquel and Siena to come outside so Bella, Tasmine, and I can throw eggs at them bitches."

Tasmine and I started cracking up at Khyle's ass.

"Why eggs? Just fuck her up," I said.

"No, I can't with my baby in here. Trust me, I looked it up to see if I could fight them bitches, but it said the baby could suffer if they get me one time."

"Let us beat her ass," Tasmine suggested.

"No, if I can't do it, I have to find the next best thing, and that's egging them bitches with cold hard eggs."

"That shit will hurt," Tasmine commented, grinning.

Laughing, I asked, "So now we have to get some eggs?"

"No, I bought them this morning so they would be good and cold by tonight. I planned to drive, but I had no way of getting them hoes out of the house. Now I do." Khyle stared deeply into Perry's eyes.

"Well let's go," Perry agreed, surprising the fuck out of me. Then again, her ass wasn't as innocent as she led us to believe.

An hour later…

"That bitch had better not played us," Khyle spat, referring to Perry.

We were currently standing off to the side of the house the party was being thrown in, each holding a carton of a dozen eggs. I was sure we all planned to use each and every single one of these damn eggs on these hoes. They'd been starting shit since we got here damn near, and since I already whooped both of their asses, throwing cold hard eggs was good enough for now.

"Oh shit, I hear Perry's voice!" Tasmine shouted but in a whisper.

The three of us giggled lowly as we watched Perry walk out with

Raquel and Siena. We opened our cartons as Perry spoke to them about something, and slowly began easing out from the side of the house.

"Perry you said that— Ah!" Siena screamed after the first egg Khyle chucked hit her in the collarbone.

"Ah! Oh my gosh!" Raquel hollered as all three of us began to throw egg after egg at these bitches. Perry had darted to the side.

They started to run down the row of houses, but the three of us were right on their heels throwing eggs like we were one of those fucking baseball machines. Every egg landed on them, hitting their hair, backs, legs, and everything. Tasmine sped up and rushed around them to start throwing eggs at the front of their bodies, and when they backed away, they realized they were surrounded.

"Stupid bitches!" Raquel yowled as we continued to egg her and her weak ass homegirl.

By the time the neighboring houses' porch lights started to come on from the girls' screams, we were out of eggs, so we booked it back to where Perry's car had been parked. Suddenly, we heard a loud horn, and when we looked, we saw Perry had driven down to us. Laughing excitedly, we rushed and got into her car.

"Keep fucking with us, bitches, and see what happens next!" Perry yelled out the window, sending Tasmine, Khyle, and I into shock.

"That was so much fucking fun. Something that fucked up, should not be that fun," Tasmine laughed once we'd gotten a few blocks away.

"I know. I thought the idea was stupid as fuck at first, but that shit was kind of better than beating their asses," I agreed.

"See, I always have good ideas," Khyle chuckled and so did we. "Good job, Perry. You're officially back on the winning team."

We stopped to get food since Khyle's ass was hungry like always, and then went back to the dorm. When we got out the car, some black truck came swerving through the parking lot bumping loud ass music. When it pulled up next to us on some *Too Fast, Too Furious* shit, we all tensed up.

"Look what I got baby," some cute brown-skinned guy smiled after rolling down the window. He was very cute actually, but we had no idea who he was talking to.

"Nice," Perry replied, prompting Tasmine, Khyle, and I to look at one another, astonished.

"You gon' come take a ride with me?" he licked his lips.

"Hell yeah. Oh guys, this is Austin. Austin, meet Bella, Tasmine, and Khyle."

"Nice to meet you ladies."

"Nice to meet you," we all kind of rambled, somewhat simultaneously.

Perry hopped into the passenger seat of his car, and he sped out of the parking lot on two wheels.

"Okay, I don't know if I'm more surprised by the fact that Perry is dating a drug dealer, the fact that he was cute as fuck, or that Perry cursed twice tonight," Khyle said, sending us all into a fit of laughter.

We entered the dorm building still chuckling at Khyle's ass, when I noticed Santino sitting in the lobby area looking at me. He was wearing a warm smile, as he waved for me to come over to him.

"See you guys in the morning," I waved.

"Ugh!" they sang together. "Hi Santino!"

"Sup," he nodded his head up, biting his sexy bottom lip as he watched me walk over to him. The lust in his eyes had me feeling myself.

Sliding into his lap I asked, "What are you doing here?"

"I came to ask you something. And I live in this building too."

"I mean in the lobby, what are you doing in the lobby looking like you were waiting for me?" I giggled because his seriousness had caught me off guard. "And what did you want to ask me?"

"If you would be my wife someday?" He popped open a red velveteen box, and inside was the prettiest diamond I'd ever seen.

"Of course, baby, but not—"

"Until you graduate. I know, but I wanna be engaged to you."

"I wanna be engaged to you too," I whispered as he slid the ring onto my finger. "How did you afford such a nice ring?"

"Oden hooked me up with his jeweler. That's where I was today, looking at rings. I got a good price for it, and umm, the guy was willing to let me take it and pay him later once I get drafted in some months."

"For real?"

"Yeah, he and Oden are cool, and since Oden vouched for me," he shrugged.

"Well, I love it, baby. I can't wait to graduate so we can get married."

"Same. I love you, Bella D'Stefano."

"I love you more, baby."

When I first saw Santino that night at Blueberry Hill, I didn't think I'd be able to make it through college. And when he approached me, wanting me back, I didn't want to give him a chance. But I'm so happy that I followed my heart instead of my brain in this case, because I was back with the love of my life.

Life was great for me. I finally had best friends, good grades, and a man who loved me. What more could I ask for?

CHAPTER TEN

Anton

"You're dumb as hell for coming here," Oden said, snatching Phoebe up.

The bitch had been ducked off in that little house we used when we needed to be hospitalized. If she were smart, she would have skipped town. Then again, the bitch was dumb for thinking she could get over on me and live on, so I don't know why I expected her to be smart about this.

"Please, I— ow!" she screeched when Oden tossed her down the steps of the basement.

"Damn, nigga," I chuckled at his crazy ass.

"She slipped from my grasp," he lied, going down the stairs with me following him.

Phoebe was standing to her feet slowly by the time we'd gotten down there, groaning in pain like she was so hurt. She didn't even hit them damn stairs that hard so I didn't know what the fuck she was bitching about.

"Please," she swallowed hard. "I will do anything… just let me go."

"Why did you do it? I mean, don't we pay you enough?" I frowned, folding my arms across my chest.

"Yes, but she offered me a large lump sum, and- and I thought what could it really hurt? I mean you're rich, what's one little baby?"

"I should slap the shit out of you, but I won't."

POP! POP!

I sent two bullets through her dome and she slumped to the floor. I didn't want to talk anymore. It was exhausting enough hunting her ass down just to find out she'd been in our damn spot the whole time like a fool.

Oden called clean up, and once they'd made everything look normal, he and I left out to get into my car.

"How are you doing, man?" Oden inquired as I let the windows of my car down.

"I'm straight."

My mother died two days ago from a drug overdose. I knew her ass was on that shit, no matter how many times she tried to act like she wasn't. It was like she didn't care about herself. She already had HIV, yet somehow she thought it was a good idea to get back on drugs. I wanted to help her, but I knew it was no point. My mother was who she was, and her life was bound to end just the way it had.

"She had her cool times though," Oden said.

"Yeah, she did. When she was clean, she was the greatest mom ever, hands down. But she loved drugs more than she loved anything else, and a person like that can't be saved."

"Who are you telling?"

"Still ain't found your dad, huh?"

"Nope, and I been stopped looking. That was the last time I help his ass… with anything. I'm more mad at myself for falling for that shit."

"Don't blame yourself, man. He had everybody fooled. I ain't never seen him be clean for that damn long. Shit, I thought he was being real this time too."

"All I know is he will never fool me again."

"I hear you."

I dropped Oden off at his spot, and then drove around the complex to get to mine. When I got inside, I smelled something good, but I didn't know exactly what it was. When I walked into my kitchen, I saw Tasmine moving around it like she was a certified chef or some shit. I had to give it to her though; her food was bomb as hell.

"What are you making?" I asked.

"Stuffed chicken breast, mashed potatoes, and a salad."

"Stuffed chicken? I ain't never had no fancy shit like that. But it sounds bomb as hell." I looked through the window of the oven, before standing back up and planting a kiss on her lips.

"You're gonna love it. It's almost ready so do whatever you need to do so we can eat," she shooed me.

I went to the back to shower fairly quickly, and change into something more comfortable—just boxers. When I returned, she was just setting down our plates in the dining area, so I joined her so we could eat.

"I swear you're gonna make me marry you based off just your cooking skills, baby," I munched on the baked chicken which was filled with cheese and bell peppers somehow.

"I could deal with that," she flashed her beautiful smile.

"I love you, Tasmine, everything about you. And it seems like the more time we spend together, the more things I find out about you that I love."

"Baby," she touched the side of my face before leaning in to kiss me. I pulled her over to me, and made her straddle my lap. "Tony, the food!" she giggled when I ripped her underwear.

Pushing her nightshirt up and off, I latched my mouth onto her nipple while bringing her down onto my dick. She was so fucking tight, and had me ready to nut al-fucking-ready.

"Mmm," she moaned softly, gripping my shoulders as she bounced up and down slowly.

I never thought in a million years that I'd find a woman who could make me be better while still being fun time. And I surely never thought I'd meet one that was beautiful, could cook, suck dick, and had good pussy… but I had. And boy was I thankful… Blessed.

Chapter Ten: Perry

"Ahh! Ahh!" I called out at the top of my lungs as Austin humped me from behind. This was what they called doggy-style, and even though I was hesitant to try it, it was now my favorite position.

"Shit, P," he grumbled, hugging my back against his chest and kissing my neck. A few pumps later, he was shooting his load into the condom.

We sat there, panting and hugging until we had enough strength to get up and shower. We listened to rap music as we cleaned up, and that was something else I'd learned to like as well. When my friends used to play it, I hated it, but for some reason, Austin had me loving it. I think because it was sexy the way he rapped the words to me sometimes. No matter how disrespectful the lyrics were, it was still romantic of him.

"Hungry?" he asked as we got dressed.

Austin had taken me shopping earlier so I could get some new clothes. I complained about my old stuff being too frumpy, so he was more than happy to take me shopping. I got all kinds of things that I'd seen Khyle, Bella, and Tasmine wear. It had me feeling much more confident in myself, not to mention I had a male companion that complimented me regularly.

"Yes, I am."

"Let's eat fancy tonight. There's this bomb ass steakhouse inside of the Palazzo hotel. I think you'll love that shit."

"Sounds good."

Once I was dressed in a black skirt with the matching strapless top and some black stilettos, Austin and I were out the door. He opened the passenger side of his truck for me, and then jogged around to his side before speeding out of his spacious complex.

He dipped through the streets with his music loud and his windows down, allowing the cool Las Vegas air to blow through my expensive extensions. I loved having long hair.

After parking his car out front with valet, we went inside of the Palazzo hotel, and crossed through the casino floor until we arrived at this place named Carnevino. It was really nice, nicer than the places my parents took me to, which said a lot. I had lived in Vegas all of my life, but I realized I hadn't actually lived until I met Bella, Tasmine, Khyle, and Austin.

"You were right, this is fancy," I said once Austin and I were seated.

"Told you. Only the best for my shorty."

I realized him calling me shorty and ma was a term of endearment. I didn't hear that term too much out here, but I guess it was popular where he was from.

"Am I your girlfriend?" I quizzed.

I'd been wanting to ask that for a while, but every time I got in his presence I would forget. He was so much fun, and I really had a blast when I was with him. It was like I became a better version of myself. Life really felt like it was worth living with Austin. He was so carefree, and usually always in a good mood.

"Hell yeah. You've been my girl since you told me I was the first to hit that pussy."

I still had to get used to him saying that word. It was a slight turn on in the bed, but not so much when we were in public or just talking.

"Good."

I turned my attention back to the menu, and by the time the waitress came over, Austin and I both were ready to order. Like always, he ordered two alcoholic drinks for himself, and let me sip some of one of them on the sly.

I just loved how he went against the grain all the time, always living on the edge. It was so opposite from the way I used to live my boring ass life. I will say that my friends spruced it up a bit by forcing me to go to parties with them, but it was nothing like what Austin had been showing me.

The food came pretty quickly and after scarfing that down, along with dessert, Austin paid the bill and we were on our way.

Pussy niggas love sneak dissing 'til I pull up on 'em, slap 'em out with the fire. Wet your mama's house, wet your grandma's house, keep shootin' until somebody die…

The guy playing on Austin's radio rapped as he and I passed the blunt back and forth. I moved my body a little to the music as I got high, letting the wind blow through my hair and the weed take me higher.

Suddenly, Austin turned the music down, just as I was taking a pull on the blunt. I looked to him after I blew out the smoke to see him grinning sexily.

"You look good as fuck, smoking that blunt like that," he said. I just giggled in response. "Wanna go to Los Angeles for the weekend?"

"Uh sure, why not?" I smirked.

He leaned over some and we met in the middle to kiss. He swerved out of his lane a little, and I shrieked with laughter. As he pulled onto the I-15 freeway, headed towards California, I leaned back against the headrest and just enjoyed the scenery.

Somehow, I had found me a real one.

CHAPTER TEN

Shayne

I was lying down in the bed, watching some TV and waiting on my love to get back. He went out to get us some food, because I was starving and didn't feel like cooking this morning. I had already showered and brushed my teeth, and since I was off today, I just planned to chill with my baby and fuck.

I stood up to go to the bathroom, and when I did, I got light headed. My mouth started getting this salty taste in it, so I knew I was about to throw up. Rushing out of my bedroom into the restroom, I pushed the toilet top up and let everything out.

This was the second morning in a row that I'd thrown up and I was not feeling this shit. Khyle convinced me to buy a pregnancy test when we were out yesterday, but I hadn't planned on using it, until now.

I bolted to my bedroom, and grabbed the test from my vanity drawer. I then went back into the bathroom, and shut and locked the door, before peeing on the stick. I washed my hands before setting a timer on my phone, and then brushed my teeth while I waited impatiently for the timer to let me know it was finished. When it was done, I walked slowly to the counter to look, and almost fainted when it said I was pregnant. I wanted to be angry, bothered, and afraid, but I felt happy. I actually found myself smiling at the fact that I was pregnant by the man I loved.

Sitting down on the closed toilet top, I dialed my sister because I wanted her to be the first and only person to know outside of Lloyd. When she first found out she was pregnant, she told me before her friends, so I wanted to do the same.

"Good morning," she answered happily.

"Guess what?"

"What?"

"I'm gonna have a baby."

"Oh my gosh! I told you! You swore up and down that you weren't pregnant and now look at you."

"I know. I think I just didn't want to be pregnant, but come to think of it, I'm actually happy about the baby you know."

"Me too. I think you're gonna make a great mommy."

"You too, even though you still have school to finish and stuff. You'll be able to pull it off. You've always been the type to succeed."

"And you've always been the type to hustle. I always admired that about you, Shayne. You do what you want no matter what others think, and you never let a situation keep you down for long. And most importantly, you are never without."

"I do my best," I chuckled.

It felt good to hear someone like Khyle say that she looked up to me. My little sister was near perfect sometimes, so to know that she saw things in me that she wished she possessed, boosted my ego just a little bit.

"What did Lloyd say?"

"He's out getting us food, so I haven't told him yet. You think he will be happy?"

"Yeah, I do. Between you and me, Oden said Lloyd is obsessed with you. He probably got you pregnant on purpose."

We laughed together.

"I wouldn't be mad though. Now if it were Pierce or something then yes, I would be highly perturbed."

"Pierce," she sucked her teeth. "Is he still with Alanna?"

"Oh yes, didn't you hear? They're engaged, and he gave her my old ring."

Before I finished, she was laughing heartily, which in turn made me laugh.

I couldn't care less about Pierce being with Alanna anymore. To me, they were both some fucking suckers and deserved each other. For her to accept a ring that he'd proposed to another woman with was just low, but that was Alanna and Pierce for you. He was a man who always took the easiest way out, and she was a woman who would accept the bare minimum instead of demanding a nigga step it up.

"That nigga has been weak since day one though," Khyle finally came back from her laughter. "But Alanna is just sad."

"Tell me about it."

I chuckled lowly as I thought about how Marisol and I were pretty much best friends at this point. It was crazy considering we couldn't stand one another at first. She was cool though, and I think it was because she was a lot like me. I thought I would hate to be around someone like that, but actually, it was fabulous. I didn't have to worry about her judging me because of shit I said or felt. She understood exactly where I came from and how I loved that bourgeois but hood lifestyle.

Khyle and I talked until I heard the front door open and close.

I quickly came out of the bathroom and saw Lloyd holding some Styrofoam containers with our food. In his other hand he had a drink tray, carrying our orange juices.

"Hey beautiful," he smiled, walking into the kitchen.

"Hi."

I followed behind him, waiting until he set the food down so that I could tell him the good news. Well, it was good news to me, so I hoped he found it to be good news as well.

"Okay, I got you waffles like you wanted. Them niggas tried to tell me the combo only came with one waffle, but I made their asses add another one."

Laughing I said, "Thanks, babe. I have to tell you something."

"What? What's wrong?"

"So you know how you mentioned that I've been eating a lot? Well, I threw up too and…" I stopped when I saw his eyes widen a little.

"What?"

"Nothing, finish."

"I'm pregnant, Lloyd— ah!" I chuckled when he picked me up as if I weighed nothing, and wrapped my legs around his waist.

"I knew it, baby. Fuck, I was hoping for that shit." He looked up at me as he held me.

"You were?" I cupped his face and kissed his full chocolate lips.

"Yeah, I was." His voice was soft.

We kissed again but more deeply.

"I'm so happy I found you, Lloyd."

"Me too, shawty. I never thought I'd be with a girl like you, but you're a perfect fit for me." He licked his lips. "You love me?"

"I do."

"I love you, too."

CHAPTER ELEVEN

Two months later…

Oden and I were in Los Angeles right now because I was on Thanksgiving break, and we were gonna have a big family dinner with my parents. Lloyd and Shayne were even gonna be there, and I was so excited.

My belly was growing like crazy now too, which I admit had me feeling anxious to meet my baby. I was worried for a little bit because I didn't see many changes in my stomach, but my doctor told me that every woman just carries differently. My belly was still small, but it was there and I loved it. I couldn't wait to see it get even bigger.

"I need brown sugar, Oden," I whined, not wanting to move around this big ass grocery store. I tell you, it paid to have a strong man with you because he could lift things and get shit that you didn't feel like going to get. I was small but I still felt tired and hungry all the time.

"Aight, stay right here." He kissed me before jogging down the aisle.

I stayed planted at the front, sipping my herbal iced tea that I'd gotten from Starbucks. I tried to stay away from caffeinated shit while being pregnant, which meant no lattes or black/green teas. I was dying at first, but now I was used to living like that.

As I sipped my drink and texted Bella and Tasmine here and there, I spotted a very familiar face. She was pregnant as well but much further along, and she appeared to be looking for something. I couldn't turn away because I hadn't seen her in a while, and I was kind of interested to know how she'd been all this time.

It seemed like one day Emery and I were best friends, and the next we were strangers. I didn't really miss her I guess, because she was a pretty bad friend, but knowing how our friendship ended still bothered me.

"Hey!" I called out to her, seeing she was about to go down an aisle without speaking.

She looked to me, and then smiled when she recognized my face. As she walked over, her eyes darted to my midsection. I had on a tight tube dress, so it was obvious I was carrying a baby. I smiled, seeing her eyes feast on my little munchkin because I was so excited to meet him. Yes, it was a boy, and I was ecstatic about it.

"New baby?" Emery chuckled, rubbing her huge belly.

"No same one. How far along are you?"

"I'm just hitting eight months. What about you?"

"I just made it to six."

"Wow, you look so small though. That's why I asked if it was a new baby and not the one you told me about. Are you sure?"

What kind of question is that?

"Trust me, I'm sure. I've been keeping track like crazy. I thought it was odd too, but my doctor said it wasn't and that I was perfectly fine. And its been about six months since I told you I was pregnant, Emery."

"I know, you just don't look six months pregnant is all I'm saying. Seeing you with a belly for the first time is so weird, Khyle." She stared at my stomach a little longer before saying, "I mean in person because I saw the post you made with Oden on Instagram."

"Oh yeah," I smiled, thinking about it.

Oden and I took a picture, where he was hugging me from behind with his hand on my small exposed belly. I had on a two-piece bikini, so my bump was very noticeable. I had to stand to the side though so that people could really see. I laughed as I thought about the comments I read when Oden posted it on *his* Instagram as well.

"I'm happy for you, Khyle. I didn't think you two would make it this far but you really did. Y'all had something real, even though it didn't seem that way in the beginning."

"Yeah, we did. He's great." I cleared my throat. "Do I know the father of your baby? I mean, you don't have to tell me if you don't want I guess."

I looked to see Oden headed over, but he got distracted by the display of cookies, making me chuckle lowly before turning back to Emery.

"Yeah you know him. It's umm, Brian."

"Brian? Brian my ex-boyfriend? Please tell me you're talking about someone from high school that I don't remember, and *not* my ex."

"No, your Brian. The soon to be doctor."

This bitch must have an obsession with niggas I've dealt with.

"Emery, how? Why? I mean, when?"

This meant that the day she told me to confront my parents about my pregnancy alone, she was pregnant by Brian *then*. Snake ass bitch.

"Well, we started messing around a little bit before you went to UNLV and—"

"Wow, are you serious?" I was a little mad, but honestly, my life was too good to even sweat this messy ass situation.

"Yeah, I am. We stopped though for a long while, and then started back up and now I'm pregnant."

"And let me guess, now he's your man and you're in love?"

"I'm gonna get in line, baby." Oden kissed the side of my face and took the basket from me. I just nodded fairly quickly.

"No, he's with Jacqueline still. He kind of told me that the baby wasn't his, and that he never wanted to see me again. He was cool the first three months though."

"I umm, I don't feel bad for you, Emery. You're such a selfish person, you know? But I hope that your baby will change that about you."

"Khyle—"

I walked off, not interested in hearing whatever the fuck she had to say. Brian wasn't shit, and neither was she, but I hoped that baby was nothing like its parents.

"Why didn't you speak to Emery?" I hugged Oden's torso once I reached him in the line.

"Why, so you can get mad and not let me fuck tonight? Nah."

We laughed together before he kissed me deeply.

"You know me so well, baby."

I could honestly say I was at peace with my life, and therefore nothing could disturb me at this moment; especially shady nonsense like what Brian and Emery had going on. Neither of them were my concern, and I preferred it that way.

CHAPTER ELEVEN

Oden

*P*OP! *POP! POP! POP!*

Anton, Truman, and I stood outside of Cecil's warehouse, listening as our team lit his ass up with bullets.

See, I was gonna let the nigga live since he put me on to that Italian cat with car connections, but he tried to cross me. Giovanni agreed to have separate deals with us, but Cecil tried to make him believe that I was attempting get over on him by selling the cars for higher than he and I had agreed. So, by saying that, Cecil had to die. I already put Giovanni up on game, and he didn't care. Cecil wasn't making him any money like that anyways. That was to be expected though, which is why he refused to make the deal with just Cecil in the first place.

"All clear, boss." Our clean-up crew walked out and hopped in the van with a long black bag.

"Come on," I told Anton and Truman.

They were excited as fuck about the deal I'd gotten months ago with Giovanni. We'd been making way more money than one human being needed, by getting cars straight from the source. Not to mention, we didn't have to go around stealing whips, which was getting harder and harder with the improvement of vehicle technology. The only downside was that we had less of a variety of cars. However, most of the niggas we sold to overseas didn't give a fuck what we had in stock, they just wanted a luxury car to ride around in.

"Damn, this nigga had a damn dealership in here," Truman smiled, rubbing his hands together.

"Told y'all, and we're about to clean up with this shit too," I assured them.

"Just thinking about the money has my dick hard," Anton stared the cars down, looking like he was about to salivate.

"Aye nigga, don't nobody wanna hear about yo' dick," Truman shot back. I laughed because I knew he was gonna say something.

"Nigga, all these *bitches* wanna hear about it," Anton replied.

"You better shut the fuck up before Tasmine hears you," I chuckled.

"If y'all break up one more got damn time. I ain't never seen two muthafuckas who just can't get it together," Truman sucked his teeth.

"Nigga, we ain't broke up in a minute, and it's gonna stay that way. I think I got her pregnant, so you know she ain't going nowhere," Anton smiled.

"You don' resorted to trapping, Tony?" I grinned.

"Nah, not like that."

"This nigga. Ain't you don' had enough baby mama drama? Fuck you out here trapping for my nigga?" Truman backed me up as he and I roared with laughter.

"Shit, I'm starting to think you tried to trap Selinda, Kai, and Violet!" I taunted.

"Oh, I know the nigga did now," Truman added on.

"Fuck y'all. Hating ass niggas."

We continued ragging on Anton for a little bit, before discussing business. We agreed to meet in the morning to go over distributing these cars with the team. I was excited. Any time I knew I was gonna be getting money, I got giddy as fuck almost.

I made it home about an hour later, and found Khyle watching TV on the couch. She had on a thin nightshirt that clung to her small stomach lightly. The living room was dark, but the TV beamed on her, showing all of the beauty that she possessed.

"What you watching?" I asked, about to make my way over to her.

"*Facts of Life,*" she responded, with the last word trailing off at the sound of the door.

Someone had knocked, so I stopped and turned around to look through the peephole. I saw my father standing there looking like he'd been locked away, smoking nonstop. When Khyle was about to speak, I put my hand up to stop her. I watched my dad through the peephole, resisting the urge to snatch the door open and whoop his ass for how he'd done me as a kid all the way up until now. But I didn't because I needed to let that part of my life go.

He knocked three more times before he finally gave up and walked away. I kept my eyes on him through the door until he disappeared into the dark. When I couldn't see him anymore, I went to the back to change clothes, and then joined Khyle on the couch to watch TV with her.

"Who was that, Oden?"

"Nobody, trust me."

She looked at me for a little while, and then cupped my face to kiss my lips a few times. She then draped her arms around my neck, so I hugged her body as tightly as I could with my eyes closed.

"I love you, Oden, and I will always be here for you," she whispered as we sat there, embracing.

I quickly wiped the lone tear that was waiting to fall from my eyes before saying, "I know, baby, and I love you too. You and my son."

It was crazy that she knew exactly who was on the other side of that door.

"Are you hungry? I can make you something to eat?" she pulled away.

"This late?"

"I can be fast. You love pasta and it doesn't take me that long to make," she giggled, getting up from the couch. "I got it," she looked at me when I tried to help her.

As I sat there scrolling through my lineup of text messages in my iPhone, I heard another knock at the door. Knowing it was that deadbeat ass nigga again, I shot up off the couch ready to tear into his ass. He had me fucked up. I tried to let him go, but since he obviously wanted this tongue lashing and possible fade, I was gonna give it to him.

I darted to the door, but when I snatched it open I saw two policemen standing there. Confused, I said nothing for a little bit as we all stared at one another.

"Can I help you officers?"

I glanced over to my left to see Khyle watching me from the kitchen with a worried expression on her face.

"You Oden Bishop?" one asked.

"Yeah."

"Mr. Bishop you're under arrest for the murder of Huelo Kaiwi," he replied, going on to read me my Miranda rights as the other one snatched me out of the door and slammed me up against the wall.

Who the fuck snitched on me?

TO BE CONTINUED

Join our mailing list to get a notification when Shvonne Latrice has another release! Text **SHVONNE** to **66866** to join!

To submit a manuscript for publishing consideration, email us at
fcpublishinggroup@gmail.com

www.ingramcontent.com/pod-product-compliance
Lightning Source LLC
Chambersburg PA
CBHW061338310726
48974CB00001B/99